Fête

by Sharon Bill

Fête Fatale

by Sharon Bill

To my dear Billy,
    the ultimate Drew in oh, so many ways x

Chapter One

Beth Williams sat at the dining room table looking out onto the garden idly stirring her porridge and sipping her tea. This process could take quite some time as she always ate her breakfast oats lukewarm and stodgy. Andrew, her husband, was carrying a bag of layers pellets down to the hen enclosure and she gave him a little wave. She smiled to herself as she laughed at her long-standing joke. When they first met in the art department refectory she had nick-named him 'Drew' in reference to his field of study and now his occupation. She thought the nickname hilarious then and still laughed at it now, thirty years later, even though nobody else did and usually responded with an obligatory rolling of the eyes. They both worked from home, Beth as a piano teacher and Drew as a free-lance architectural illustrator combining his flair for artistic expression with his skill in technical drawing. On occasion he also worked at the Whitworth Art Gallery, Manchester in the conservation and restoration of art there. They had laid the foundation of their relationship well in those early years by the refectory coffee machine and these days shared tea breaks were still plentiful. Looking up she saw Drew blow her a kiss across the lawn and returning the gesture she roused herself and thought of the day ahead.

She'd arranged to spend the morning with Phoebe de-stoning a cart load of damsons and acting as general dogs-body in a marathon jam making session for the forthcoming Women's Institute Summer Fête. It wasn't her ideal way to spend a morning and she was reluctant to make a move. Through the window she wiggled her cup at Drew to ask if he wanted to join her and a thumbs up spurred her to go and put the kettle on. Surely the world wouldn't end if they didn't churn out forty jars of damson jam that morning. However, checking that thought Beth considered that it just might. Phoebe's jam was earth-shatteringly delicious and Beth had been trying to get a recipe out of her for years. Phoebe's culinary skills were more art than science. She didn't own a set of measuring scales and cooked by intuition and "the rack of the eye". The only way to try and pin it down was to see her in action. That in itself was worth pitting hundreds of damsons. This morning even more was at stake than just discovering confectionery secrets as the jam was to be judged for the annual Women's Institute award and this was a serious matter. Although the damson jam was bound to be a podium winner the coveted first prize was by no means secure as Jean's rhubarb and rose petal jam was also a hot favourite. It was a close contest and things could get sticky!

Drew came in from the garden and planted a kiss on Beth's lips. 'What are your plans for today?'

'I'm at Phoebe Simmonds', remember? We're filling the world with damson jam today. We need to get it done before that load of fruit gets past it - unlike you or me.'

'Speak for yourself. It sounds like you need some added sugar or you'll stop the jam from setting with that attitude. I'll get my own lunch then and I'll see you for a quick brew before your pupils start to arrive.' He looked over to the sofa and spoke to the dog. 'It's just you and me today, Noodle. Some guy time at last buddy.' The aged Bichon, Poodle cross exposed a fluffy tummy to express his appreciation of the prospect.

Phoebe was already elbow deep in purple goo and a deep, fruity smell enveloped Beth as she stepped inside. Carefully controlled chaos was evidently in progress. The kitchen was a small square of ancient pine. Honeyed pine cupboards, gone orange with age, lined the walls and a small pine table with three chairs sat tucked away in the corner next to a pantry recessed into the wall. The table was covered with jam jars, each with a dose of water inside, waiting to go into the hot oven to sterilise. Bags and bags of sugar waited ad-hoc on the work surface and the jam kettle sat waiting on the hob. Beth wondered at the title 'jam kettle.' It was a wholly inappropriate name for what amounted to nothing more than a huge boiling pan. For years she had imagined a gigantic, copper coloured kettle with a vast, curvaceous spout and a tin lid which rattled ominously as the jam simmered beneath. She still hadn't outlived her disappointment at such a misconception and she looked at the slightly battered mini cauldron with regret. This was going to be jam making via the old school - no need for measuring scales, specialist jam sugar or sachets of pectin. All that would be required would be the basic ingredients and a certain amount of sweat and tears if Beth was left unsupervised for too long.

The morning passed pleasantly and there was plenty to chat about over the thankfully regular tea breaks. Phoebe asked about Beth's family. Emma Graham, Beth's daughter, was married to Nathaniel and lived at the edge of the village in "Lilac Cottage" with their four year old daughter Primrose and Walter the Labradoodle, who caused more fuss and mayhem than Primrose ever could. Jonti, Emma's elder brother, lived in Manchester and was a trombonist with the BBC Philharmonic Orchestra. Matt, the youngest, had not long since left home and now lived in a small apartment in the nearby market town Aldersfield. As Beth was stirring the bubbling mass she asked,

'How is Mike getting on with his hens? Will he be ready for the poultry competition at the Fête?'

'He's out there all the time!' Phoebe complained about her husband. 'The hen house is cleaner than this kitchen. He doesn't like them getting their feet dirty and if they get a bit of mud on them he's created a special foot spa so that he can soak their claws. I wouldn't be surprised if he gave them a manicure next.'

'It sounds quite luxurious. Do you think he'd let me have a go? I don't mind sitting next to some hens so that I can have a foot massage. He's taking the poultry competition very seriously. Do you know who's judging it this year?'

'It's John Barlow, and Mike's not happy at all.'

'I'd heard that old Davidson was passing on the baton. Nobody is going to be able to follow in his footsteps very easily. I'm sure that John will be as fair as he knows how.'

'I do know that he's taking the responsibility very seriously and he's doing a lot of reading up. I suppose that's all he can do. Nobody else seems very keen to take on the job.'

'There will be quite a few contestants and they won't want to miss out on competing by acting as judge instead. I'm sure that Mike wouldn't want to give up the chance to take part. He's pretty keen on his subject, but he'd rather compete, wouldn't he? He'd be just the man for the job.'

'Every time somebody shows just a polite interest I can guarantee what he'll say next. He'll launch into his favourite speech and say "You know, hens and racehorses are very similar." He thinks this is funny, it's not - it's sad!'

'I can't wait to hear how.' said Beth.

'His punch line is that if a race horse breaks its leg it has to be killed, and so does a hen. He doesn't quite see that a prize race horse is almost priceless whereas a hen can be replaced for a few quid. Did you know that he uses a soft baby brush to smooth down their feathers? It's worrying I tell you!'

'He probably brushes their feathers more often than I brush my hair ... Ouch!' The spluttering lava of sugary liquid spattered over Beth's arms putting a stop to any further conversation and gave Phoebe the signal to take over. She openly scorned the mention of a jam thermometer. All she needed was a saucer in the fridge and an expert digit on her right hand. As they were pouring the molten liquid through the funnel and into the warm, dry jars Beth said 'You know, I think Emma's microwave method might have some distinct advantages. At least she doesn't get blisters on her arms.'

'You've got something there, and her lemon curd is really tasty. But, if you make it her way you only get two or three jars at a time.'

'It's not normal to want about 40 jars at once though, is it? We don't need to preserve our summer produce these days and, no matter how tasty your jam is, if you had to eat all of this yourself you'd rather starve than see another damson by the end of the year.' said Beth. 'I hope you've made the winning brand!'.

'I'll kill Jean Barlow if she wins again this year. We could try bribing the judge - if we knew who it was. Perhaps it's as well we don't! We'll trust to luck instead.'

On that same morning the rival preserve was in preparation. Jean Barlow took lone command in her kitchen. It was a large, modern room of light beech wood and black marble. Every surface glistened. A large pan stood on the hob of the stainless steel double oven which housed racks of warming jam jars. Alongside the precise rows of rhubarb cubes lay heaps of pink and yellow rose petals. Unlike Phoebe, Jean adopted the scientific approach and a jam thermometer, sachets of pectin and specific jam sugar stood at the ready. She'd explained to Beth once that specialist preserving sugar is made up of larger crystals which allows the sugar to dissolve more slowly and reduces the risk of burning. At that moment Jean was carefully weighing piles of rose petals on a set of sensitive digital scales - first prize was at stake and she was leaving nothing to chance. Her husband, John, had gone out for the morning.

Since the onset of diabetes jam was considered off the menu for him and it was all a bit too unfair to have to smell it all morning and not get a taste. Secretly Jean had laid aside a small jar as a special treat. Surely one little jar of jam eaten in small rations over a few days couldn't do any harm?

The next morning Emma and Primrose were walking towards the Post Office when they saw Henrietta taking Toby to school. The High Street boasted only a handful of shops but it was still the main thoroughfare through the village. Henrietta was new to the area and she was something of a mystery. Nevertheless, by degrees, her reserve was thawing and she and Emma were tentatively striking up a friendship. Her air of mystery was heightened because, although she wore a wedding ring, only she and her son were ever seen in the village and the absent husband was something of an enigma. Toby was only a year older than Primrose and he was dark haired and olive skinned, like Henrietta.

'Hi!' shouted Emma. 'I'm glad I spotted you. I've been wanting to ask you if you wanted to join in helping out at the Summer Fête? Could help me in hosting the cake stall? If you could help me with some baking then that'd be even better - if you wouldn't mind too much.'

'Oh, hello Emma. I'd love to join in and help. I'm more than happy to lend a hand, but I'm not sure my skills in the cake department are up to much. I'll do what I can though.'

'Good! I'm glad you'll join in. Don't worry too much about baking genius - it's only the WI annual first prize I'm after, that's all!'

'Fancy telling me that now. I think I'd better keep out of the way if there's a competition involved.'

'I'm only kidding. Well almost - there is a competition involved and some take it very seriously. It's just generally helping out in dealing with the quantity that I need. I can easily show you what to do, it's not rocket science. Perhaps I could pop around one evening and we can sort out a time to get stuck in? I'm not the only person baking and we only need to do a couple of stints, so it shouldn't take too long.'

'I'd like that. Any time to suit you will be fine. I'd better get marching now though, otherwise this little Toby-Terror will be late for school.'

'Lovely, I'll see you soon.' Turning to Primrose Emma asked if she wanted to go and visit Grandma to see if she'd recovered from a heavy session at the jam kettle with Phoebe.

Beth was shuffling around in her pyjamas and dressing gown when the girls arrived. Drew was already in his studio in the converted garage just off the kitchen but a quick call from Emma soon brought him into the lounge and it wasn't long before he was lying full stretch on the lounge carpet with a selection of colouring pencils alongside Primrose. Emma apologised for breaking into his work time but Beth quickly dispelled her apology saying 'He's only doing the same thing as when he's officially working - so you see, you've not disturbed him at all.' A deftly aimed cushion to Beth's head illustrated Drew's opinion of the comment.

'How are things going for the Fête? I saw Henrietta just now. She's going to help me with the baking and on the stall too.' said Emma.

'That's good. It'll be a good way for her to get to know folks. Phoebe and I got our quota of jam done yesterday and I know that Jean Barlow will be making a batch of her famous rhubarb and rose petal jam. I think Phoebe has decided that your microwave method is quite civilised, but maybe a bit long winded for a large batch.' said Beth.

'I suppose it is, but I can't face spending a whole evening making a ton of lemon curd in one go. It works for me and it does the job. Who else is pitching in?'

'As far as I know Nicola is organising a flower stall and will donate what she can from her Florist shop. Mike Simmonds has also given over his greenhouse to the cultivation of prize Chrysanthemums for the past few months and he's donating some of them to the Fête. I'm not sure whether I should put my origami flowers on the flower stall or on the craft stall. I presume that we'll still be making the sets of doll's cot bedding from that roll-end of quilting I found?'

'Oh, yes. I've already made a start on them. Nathaniel was up early for the dairy the other day and I couldn't get back to sleep so I made a start until Primrose woke up.'

Checking off on her fingers Beth worked through the list of exhibits for sale and continued.

'Kirsty will be selling tickets for her garden tours - providing that the weather stays fine on the day and the horsey crowd from the stables will be offering led horse rides across the length of the field, like donkey rides on Blackpool beach.'

'I think they will prove to be very popular but I do wish that Jim's cows were still in that field instead of segregated horse paddocks. I think that cows are calmer somehow.'

'I don't think Primrose would enjoy a cow ride quite so much as a horsey ride.' said Drew. 'So you can all get off your own high horses and be more gracious.' Mother and daughter groaned at the dreadful pun and, shaking their heads, swapped pained expressions.

'Kirsty is home today. She's taken the day off to get some gardening done to make sure everything stays ship-shape for the day of the Fête. I'm going to visit her as soon as I'm changed. You can come with me and we can take Primrose too. We'll leave your dad to do some grown-up colouring in for a bit.' said Beth.

'OK, I'd like that. I haven't seen Kirsty for ages.' said Emma.

Predictably Kirsty Pepper was to be found outside, in her back garden. Those who knew her well knew better than to knock on any door but march through the gate straight to the garden. If her husband, Carlton, was home he'd probably be in the computer room upstairs and it was circuitous to have him trek all the way to the front door to simply be redirected to the garden. Beth led the way through the gate and along the path until they found Kirsty in the rose garden. Straightening her back and relaxing her grip on the secateurs she stood up to greet them. Primrose flung her arms around Kirsty's knees and then led her away by the hand to the garden bench situated next to the natural garden patch.

'Be careful here 'Rose, there are nettles here that will sting you.' Kirsty warned.

'Have you decided on what to include in your guided tour?' asked Emma.

'Yes, I think so. I've decided on what I'll talk about in each of the sections and I've typed it onto an information sheet just in case we're inundated with visitors and need to divide into separate parties. If somebody else needs to take a party they can just read off the sheet if they're stuck. I've bought some magnifying glasses just in case any children come along on the day, then they can go exploring for bugs and wildlife if the subject of plants gets a bit too tedious for them. Carlton has designed and printed off some tickets for admission. Perhaps Nicola could sell them on her flower stall?'

'Has anybody volunteered to give you a hand here?' asked Beth.

'Jean has offered to spend most of the day here to collect tickets, but I think other volunteers will be found when we discuss arrangements at the WI meeting.'

'How is Jean?' asked Beth. 'I didn't see her at the last meeting and Henrietta told Emma that John hasn't been well at all recently.'

'How does Henrietta know that?' asked Kirsty.

'She's started a little cleaning job at Jean's, just a couple of mornings a week.' said Emma.

'I wish I could have a cleaner come in twice a week, though I hardly think that would be often enough!' said Kirsty.

'Jean's really lucky she can afford it. If I had a cleaner I'd have to tidy up before she came!' said Emma. 'I know John's getting to grips with his diabetes - he's learning a new healthy eating lifestyle. Knowing John he'll be super strict about it. Henrietta says he's been ill recently. I think that stress is making him feel ill and they're having to cut back a bit - not that we'd notice a difference in their budget. The strain must be telling though as John went to see Dr Wainwright last week.'

'Goodness, it must be bad!' said Beth. 'Dr Wainwright is such a dishy bloke that most of the women won't go to him because they blush as soon as they look at him and the men won't go because of the way the women go on about him. The end result is pretty useful though, at least people only go when they really need to make an appointment. That way nobody's time gets wasted and if you're really ill you can be pretty certain of seeing the doctor when you need to.' Kirsty was handing a magnifying glass to Primrose and setting her off on a search in the herb garden as Beth said, 'What a shame. Poor John. I hope they can still keep that lovely holiday home they own in the South of France. The locals there think it's really funny that in French John is spelt as "Jean," which means that they both have the same name. I like John, and Jean isn't so bad once you get past her icy reserve. I often wonder if she isn't just a bit shy and feels out of it all. She doesn't help herself, I know, but she's all right really, if you give her a chance. She says that she'll definitely be at the next meeting. Will you both be going?'

'Yes, I'll be going.' said Emma.

'We'll all need to be there as it's the last meeting before the big day. I expect it'll go on a bit later than usual - we'll get less time in the pub before we wind our way home.' said Beth.

'Yes, I'll be there. I'll see you both at the meeting, if I don't see you before then.' Kirsty said. The others stood up to leave but any further farewells were interrupted by Primrose tripping over and landing in a Lavender bush. This didn't seem to bother her in the least and, not letting go of the magnifying glass, she stoically decided that this was a good opportunity to have a closer look at the herb in question. Emma hauled her out of the herb patch and with Beth they began to walk home.

Chapter Two

The Mossleigh Women's Institute met on the last Friday night of each calendar month and while the women met together the men congregated in The Badger's Den, the local pub. So on the last Friday night of July Beth, Emma and Kirsty walked along the the High Street to the village hall. Friendly greetings and a hot brew welcomed them into the hall and Phoebe and Natalie strolled over to greet them. 'Hullo you!' barked Natalie in her usual stentorian tones. Natalie Lewis was a woman of indeterminate age. Everyone guessed that she must have been well along the way to meet her 70s, but her attitude and appearance resolutely clung to a much earlier stage in the journey. Her short, spiky hair gave no helpful clues either. In this particular instance it was a determined purple hue, but the tint changed with alarming regularity and showed a total disregard for subtlety, in fact the technique was positively brazen. Her vigourous outlook also belied her age and nothing seemed to quench her. Both she and her husband, Terry, had always been indomitable. In the past it wouldn't have been unusual to find them both lugging hods of reclaimed bricks down to the bottom of their garden because they fancied an outdoor pizza oven or a brick supported bench in a particular spot of sunshine. They'd even laid their own driveway cobble by cobble with their own bent backs and fair hands. Out of the blue Terry had suffered a stroke which had curtailed his home improvement ambitions, but even this hadn't halted them completely. The stroke had affected his left side but he could still wield a drill single-handedly with his right hand, though tasks took longer to complete now. His one concession to the blow was that he needed a wheelchair for prolonged walking. None of this appeared to have altered Natalie's breezy outlook on life at all. Her only recognition of the misfortune was for her to shrug her shoulders a little and say, "Well, you've got to just get on with it."

Trailing behind Natalie, owing to an absorbed interest in the obligatory slice of Victoria Sponge, was Nicola Farrington. Nicola was the youngest member of Mossleigh Women's Institute. At only twenty two she had it all to come, whatever, "it" was. It was likely that she'd be more inclined to follow Natalie's example. At such a young age she had surprised everybody by taking over an empty premises on the High Street. After moving away to study for a degree in Floristry at Risehead Agricultural College she had then come right back to the village with a devoted young man in tow and had launched her own Floristry business. She had then caused further shock by taking private lodgings in the flat above the shop with her live-in partner, Gareth Foster. The fact that Gareth was a genuinely nice guy settled the matter and he was soon embraced by the clientele of The Badger. Gareth was an accountant and was finishing his training at Sheppards & Moss in Alder Leigh. His firm but gentle oversight of the business would keep Nicola safely on track.

There was no opportunity for anything more than cursory hellos before the meeting was called to order and everybody found a seat. Natalie was known to slosh a healthy measure of Single Malt into her tea and she was resolutely clinging to her cup as she took her place. The President, Mae Holland, opened the meeting and Beth provided a rousing accompaniment to the usual rendition of "Jerusalem" before Mae quickly got through the business of signing off the minutes from the last month and noting apologies of absence for this month. Only a couple were absent from this important pre-Fête meeting. When it was announced that Betty Barnsford sent her apologies there was an audible sigh of relief from the rows of chairs before the President's table. Betty, at 86 years old, was the longest serving member of the Mossleigh WI and matters were becoming very awkward. There was no doubt about it, but the fact that her mind was wandering made for considerable consternation. Whilst on a personal level everybody genuinely liked Betty, it made organised activities very difficult. It was the same at rehearsals with the Templeton Singers. She'd been a member of the choir since it first began. No doubt Betty had sung "Messiah" more times than most had eaten hot dinners but her enthusiasm was no longer matched by her ability and she regularly launched into top 'A's (or close enough to A) a good beat or two before was strictly necessary. She was completely unabashed by these solo performances and enjoyed an embracing sense of abandon regardless of repeated exposure. Everybody was earnestly hoping that she would voluntarily step down from the public eye as nobody wanted to hurt her feelings by having to ask her to leave in the end. Physically speaking it was all getting too much as she surely couldn't be expected to stand and sing for almost an hour before the interval at a performance, and she could no longer manage to climb the steps onto the stage. To be asked to resign would leave a bitter taste in everybody's mouth. The mystery was what could have kept her away tonight? Nevertheless, the atmosphere tangibly relaxed from that point on.

'This month's meeting will not follow our usual procedure.' said Mae. Some mild heckling from the back created a hiatus in the presentation. With a smile and a nod to the renegades (Beth and Kirsty) Mae continued. 'We won't be entertaining a guest speaker or holding any demonstration activities. Instead, tonight will be given over wholly to the final preparations for our annual Summer Fête which will be held in three weeks time. As in previous years we have opened out the event and invited other individuals and small groups to host a stall or attraction in exchange for a tithe of their takings on the day and we also ask them to make a donation to our chosen charity. In order for everything to be properly organised I suggest that we discuss each stall or activity in order and each member responsible will come to the front to explain the protocol and answer any questions. We'll take a short break once we are about halfway through the agenda.'

Matters were dealt with efficiently and the Fête was organised with military precision. The Templeton Singers were to showcase a few of their choral items and, as Mae was deputy conductor of the choir, she could act as spokesperson here. She suggested that they sing Mozart's "Ave Verum" and Parry's "I Was Glad". It was also decided that the Fête would close with a performance of the Parry anthem "Jerusalem" with which the WI was associated. All of this could successfully be carried out with relatively few singers and were all generally well known to the public. Mae's husband was the official accompanist for the choir and had consented to swallow his artistic pride, and for the sake of ease and economy would accompany the singers on a portable keyboard. Times at convenient points in the day were quickly decided on and Mae agreed to take a list of volunteers at the end of the next choir rehearsal, making sure that those involved knew when and where to congregate.

Nicola was the next to take the floor. She had volunteered to hold a flower stall and rumour had it that Betty had generously undertaken to cover the costs of stocking the stall so that Nicola's fledgeling business wouldn't suffer. Nicola suggested that she would spend the days running up to the Fête making arrangements to sell on the day and would man the stall herself as the Saturday girl and Gareth could manage at the shop - it probably wouldn't be too busy if all of her potential customers were at the Fête. Even so, she said, any offers of help in making arrangements and manning the stall would gratefully received. A few suitably skilled ladies offered to lend a hand during the week before the Fête and Nicola was reassured that she wouldn't be forgotten on the day.

The next item on the agenda was Kirsty's long awaited garden tour. The ladies noticeably sat up at the prospect of hearing what she had planned for the day and all eyes were attentively on her as she took her place.

'I've photocopied some information sheets.' Kirsty began. 'I'm hoping that there'll be plenty of interest and we can divide into separate parties. I know that most of you have seen my garden and are generally aware of the information here, but perhaps some may want me to quickly run through the main points?' At this point she cast an enquiring glance about the room. Her gaze was met by unanimous nods of approval. Even those who knew Kirsty's garden well were always eager to hear more about it. She nodded assent and continued. 'The garden tour is divided into four main areas. If we split into separate groupings no more than four can be escorted at any one time so that we can rotate easily between sections without overlapping. There is a cultivated flower garden planted with various popular annuals. I've sketched out a basic diagram and labelled the flower areas, though I'm sure that you can easily spot Begonias, Fuschias, Busy Lizzies and Snapdragons for yourselves.

'Just around the corner is the herb garden and again I've listed the names of the herbs and their typical uses. It's helpful if you don't rush visitors here so that they can have a chat and a browse. Herb lore is really interesting and, although I've listed some uses of the herbs, you'll probably find that there are plenty of old tales surrounding each plant. Some applications are medicinal and some are cosmetic but often the categories overlap. For example, Camomile tea is a well known soporific but it can also be used as a rinse for fair hair or an infusion with wheat oats for a relaxing bath soak. Feverfew is mostly used to alleviate headaches, but folklore also has it as an alternative to moth balls. Thanks to recent TV dramas some of these herbs have more sinister connotations, so linger around the poppies if you need to encourage some lively conversation.' This raised a murmur of interested approval. Kirsty continued a verbal tour of her garden moving on to the next section of garden.

'The rose garden is exactly what it says on the tin, but I have introduced another note into the equation, if you'll pardon the pun - all the rose bush names have a musical element. The full list is on the sheet and I'll attach a name tag to each rose bush. Varieties include names like "Golden Mozart," "Traviata" and "A capella" which should generate some chit-chat. At the risk of being condescending I've outlined some background information on each of these names. For example "A capella" literally means "in the church style" but nowadays more generally means merely "sung without accompaniment."

'The last section is the natural garden and it's most obviously recognised by its more scruffy appearance. As the title suggests, I don't interfere too much here but merely hold things at bay. Plant stalks, leaves and moss are largely left to provide shelter for small animals and nesting material for birds. I've planted a variety of purple plants to encourage bees to visit the garden. Foxgloves are left to prosper mainly because their prolonged flowering season gives the bees the longest harvest possible. Tradition has it that foxglove flowers are home to the fairies. So as to create equal opportunities for the gnomes I've allowed a few fly agaric mushrooms to flourish naturally beneath the Silver Birch tree - because we all know that's where gnomes live!' This brought a ripple of laughter from the enthralled listeners. 'Be careful not to allow people to touch these, although if they do they can just go and wash their hands. There's no real harm but it's better to be on the safe side. Also, advise visitors to steer clear of the nettle patch so that nobody gets stung. I keep a healthy clump of nettles handy because I regularly harvest them and then allow them to rot down in a pail of water as a natural plant food. They also make a decent tea and excellent wine, but I don't keep them in the herb garden as they're not so pretty.

'Carlton has designed and printed some admission tickets to be sold on Nicola's stall and visitors will need to hand these in at the garden gate for admission. Jean has kindly agreed to take in tickets and organise groupings, but if others could take a turn at the duty then Jean can have a break and visit the Fête. I'll be conducting tours for as long as necessary, so if there are any queries I'll be on hand for you to just come and ask.'

As Kirsty resumed her seat she was given a resounding round of applause. Mae took up her position at the head of the table again and thanked Kirsty for her efforts. 'It seems that I was wrong at the start of this meeting. We did have a guest speaker after all - and a very interesting one too! I'm sure that everyone will thoroughly enjoy your garden tours. I just hope that the weather is fine to do them justice.'   Looking around the hall Mae asked,   'Have the flyers been posted in some prominent positions?'

A general nod of assent showed that the Fête was being well advertised and several shouted locations from where they sat. 'I've posted one up in The Raven, in Harrisfield. As soon as it was up I heard some guests staying there saying that they really must go. Surely that bodes well.' said Natalie.

'That's very encouraging. Thank you.'   said Mae. ' I think that this is a good time to take a break and make the most of the delicious cakes that Natalie has made for us.'   At this point everybody moved away to replenish their cups and plates. Beth fell into easy conversation with Mae as they met at the refreshments hatch. She quickly got down to the heart of the matter and asked what had so unusually kept Betty at home. It transpired that a plot had been hatched once it was known that Betty had a slight cold. Eileen had encouraged Betty to stay home so as to be fighting fit for the day of the Fête and had agreed to stay back from the meeting to keep her company. She had done this for the general good and smooth running of the meeting, but it was with the strict proviso that somebody would visit them both the next day to tell them everything that had been discussed in minute detail.   This then also accounted   for   the   second   absence.   In acknowledgement of the generous sacrifice made by Eileen and genuine good wishes for Betty, Mae explained that she would be meeting them both at Betty's house tomorrow lunchtime. It has also been preordained that Eileen could take her pick of duties and that a suitable responsibility be given to Betty - it was important that she felt valued and useful but wouldn't be exhausted beyond her measure.

'Of course, the tricky bit now is to decide what exactly Betty could manage to help with which won't tire her out.' observed Beth.

'I'm sure that something will reveal itself.' said Mae. 'Come on, we'd better get back to it. There's a fair amount still to deal with and if we don't hurry we'll never get to the pub.' She returned to the top table and called everybody back to their seats.

The rest of the agenda was worked through with relative ease. John Barlow would judge this year's poultry competition, which was a brave endeavour as it was a difficult act to follow when bearing in mind the expertise of the previous judge. Mae asked Jean to pass on the group's thanks for his willingness to take the role on. Beth and Emma were officially allocated to organise and supervise the cakes and preserves stall and they asked for donations to be submitted. 'Of course, cakes need to be delivered either on the day or the day before, so as to be fresh. If you can get your preserves done earlier then that will help us to be better organised. We can either store them here at the hall or you can bring them to my house. Please clearly mark any submissions that are to be considered for the competition.' said Beth.

'I've bought my jam with me tonight.' said Jean. 'Poor John isn't supposed to be eating jam and it seems really cruel to have him smell it as I make it and then have to stare at it for weeks without being able to eat any. I've put a small jar to one side for him as a surprise later but at least I've got the rest of the batch away from under his nose and out of temptation's way. Of course, I'll be entering a jar for the competition if you can keep one back from sale on the stall.' This was met with murmurs and predictions of winning first prize hands down.

Natalie projected a stage whisper and hissed quite audibly, 'I think that what we have here ladies is a bad case of premature adjudication!' At this point the meeting collapsed into hoots of raucous laughter and it was some minutes before Mae could gather either herself or the meeting back to attention.

The planning of the Women's Institute of Mossleigh Annual Summer Fête progressed with minimum fuss. Empty stalls were filled, volunteers were allocated and the ladies swiftly manoeuvred into their accustomed places. A pooling of donations of crafts, edibles and raffle items was promised over the ensuing weeks. The meeting closed with the first verse of the National Anthem and then the ladies either made their way home or to The Badger. Over the next days and weeks the village of Mossleigh became a hive of industry as bumper batches of jams, curds and chutneys bubbled in vats. Knitting needles clicked, sewing machines whirred and the backs of cupboards were scoured for bric-a-brac and raffle items. Day by day the date of the Fête drew nearer and the residents gradually began to get to bed on time again.

Chapter Three

Although the Fête didn't officially open until 10.30 that morning, and owing to the military precision of the last couple of weeks there wa no particular need for Beth to rush. Nevertheless, Beth found herself waking early that morning. After pottering around downstairs and clattering dishes into the dishwasher she emerged into the bedroom bearing a tray laden with tea and toast. Drew sat up in bed and, munching his toast, began leafing through the next in the series of novels he had recently discovered. Beth gulped the last of her tea and stood up. Walking over to the bed she kissed Drew's forehead. '"Once more unto the breach" dear boy, let's get this show on the road.' Walking into the bathroom and looking back over her shoulder she shouted, 'You shouldn't eat toast in bed. You know the crumbs supernaturally migrate to the bottom of the sheets!'

At the same time that Beth and Drew were munching on their breakfast John Barlow was sitting in his study making a last attempt at researching points to look for when judging varieties of poultry. Even if everything else was falling around him in ruins he was going to make sure that he did a good job today. He'd had to sit Jean down and explain to her the failing nature of his foreign business interests and what that would mean in their daily life for the time being. He was surprised that the tête-a-tête had gone as well as it had, but in many ways that made it even harder for him to bear. Jean had been disappointed but understanding. Her natural reserve didn't allow her to express too much sympathy but he could see that she'd understood his worries. He knew that it was going to be difficult for her to adjust to a little economy but she'd said that she was willing to tow the line and for that he was grateful. Her only point of refusal was that she insisted that she wasn't willing to slave over a hot cooker every meal time - she was too busy for that. John could acknowledge that for years his wife had been a prominent member on the WI committee and also sat on the choir's general committee and music sub-committee. She was also a regular helper at the residential home in Alder Leigh and the charity shop linked to it. He could understand that she wasn't willing to give up these activities and they'd have to continue to eat out as a rule. If he was honest he wasn't sure that this would be possible, but he'd cross that bridge later. At least for now Jean had willingly agreed to spend less generally on non essentials and would ask Henrietta to come in and clean only once a week for now. Nevertheless, he felt ashamed at having to broach such a topic and his sense of failure was strong. He resumed his reading of the library books on showing poultry that he'd hired - he'd at least make sure that he made a success of the competition today.

The weather that morning was typically British in its ambiguity, leaving plenty of opportunity for debate on how to arrange the Fête. As Beth and Drew pulled up onto the car park discussions were heating up as to whether to host the stalls inside the hall as much as possible or if the tables and gazebos might be erected outside. Nathaniel and Emma, with Primrose belted in between them, pulled the truck into the quickly filling car park. They carried an assortment of canvas, steel tubes and pegs which would soon transform into gazebos and tents to host the stalls. The question of the weather was raised and Nathaniel cast an expert glance into the cloudscape and predicted clear, dry skies for the day. 'Farmer Jim said that the cows would have dry pasture into next week, before rotating the grazing - and he's never wrong.' The expertise of Nathaniel and farmer Jim settled the matter and galvanised the work force into action. Much pacing of plots and laying out of poles swiftly followed over the next hour. The exhibits for each of the stalls had been placed in groups inside the village hall and it would be swift work to relocate the stock for each stall once the tents were up.

This was the best part of the day, as far as Beth and Emma were concerned. They imagined that they were like Amy March from 'Little Women' as she was setting out her art display. In the classic tale small acts of jealousy robbed Amy of her wonderful stall and she was demoted to a wilting flower stand. Thankfully, at this Fête any discrepancies were unlikely to result in open rivalry and Beth and Emma reveled in creating an artistic display of cakes, jam, curds and chutneys. Beth had also hit upon how to solve the dilemma of how to best occupy Betty and had created a traditional Bran-tub. This wouldn't be too tiring as Betty could sit at the stall to sell tickets for each person to delve into the tub and then once all the tickets were sold and the prizes retrieved she could bask in the satisfaction of a job well done and then wander at will. Beth also had a strange ulterior motive for introducing the Bran-tub into the Fête. As a piano teacher she was always trying to find new ways to encourage pupils to practice their scales. She'd been given what she thought was an excellent tip: If each scale was written on a separate slip of paper which was then folded up and placed in a tub she'd suggested that students could make a scales Bran-tub and they could pick out scales at random to test themselves. The idea would have been perfect were it not for the fact that the younger students had no idea of what a Bran-tub was. Here was the perfect opportunity to remedy this gap in their education.

It was not only the ladies who were subject to last minute bursts of inspiration. Drew and Nathaniel had mysteriously disappeared once the framework of tents were up. They reappeared about half an hour later on their motorbikes and then vanished again, only to quickly reappear in one of farmer Jim's tractors and behind them came Matt in an E-Type Jaguar sports car loaned from an enthusiast's club he belonged to. It seems that they had run off to get the go-ahead from Mae and had then created an impromptu motor vehicle display in an empty corner of the field. Standing side by side were Nathaniel's Triumph Tiger and Drew's Triumph Bonneville motorbikes. They'd even crossed a pair of Union Jack flags at the back end of each bike. Drew had called Matt to contact his friend to include the Jaguar for the day. The car was loaned on the proviso that promotional material for the club could be on display and the promise that the car wouldn't be left unsupervised. The tractor was the final burst of inspiration and Nathaniel expected to be kept busy lifting eager boys and girls in and out of the driver's cab. Primrose was prettily modelling the Bonneville as Drew explained,

'I thought that this would redress the testosterone balance a little. When the chaps are fed up of jam and cake they can come and hang out in the man-zone for a bit.'

'That's a fantastic display! Well done guys. I think it's a great idea to have some attractions that don't need to be paid for.' said Beth.

'I've spoken to Terry and he's happy to keep an eye on things if we need to help elsewhere.' said Drew. 'It's impossible for him with the wheelchair on the grass and I think he'll be quite content to sit in an E-type for most of the day if we don't abandon him entirely and keep him supplied with tea and cake - not consumed in the car, of course.'

'I don't think he'll be short of company, in fact I think he'll be at the centre of attention here where the men and children are concerned.' said Beth.

The Fête was soon due to officially open and there was a converging of members to the village hall as the sense of expectancy rose. Mae took hold of the opportunity and banged a set of teaspoons on a trestle table to attract everybody's attention and make an address.

'Firstly, let me say a huge thank you to everybody who has worked so hard to get today's Fête up and running. I won't begin to try and name everybody - I know that all of you have worked exceptionally hard over the last few weeks and I know that the work is far from over. I hope that you have enjoyed the buzz of preparation and I hope that you will enjoy seeing the fruit of your labours as the crowds arrive and enjoy the day.' she began. 'In a few moments the Fête will officially open and Darcy will be taking up her position at the pathway to take admission fees shortly. I hope that you all have lots of interest in your stalls. All that I ask is that you look out to help one another and that you have a good time chatting to our visitors. Remember, each one of you is representing the Mossleigh Women's Institute and our aim isn't simply to raise money but to raise the profile of our group. Enjoy the day!'

A thundering round of applause seemed the best response. Nobody really knew quite what they were applauding. Most probably they were recognising the effort that they had all put into the Fête and it was also an outbreak of celebration recognising a high point in the social calendar of the village. Mae was wise enough to know that they weren't applauding her rousing speech and so she stepped away from the central focus and joined in the applause. That seemed to cover it and the sound gradually faded as people headed off to their posts. Darcy picked up her cash box along with a flower stamp and ink pad ready to steer the tide of visitors through the entrance stile that had been concocted. For the price of a pound you purchased an impermanent tattoo of a buttercup and subsequent entry into the field with all its delights. Some years ago Darcy had emigrated from Mt. Rainer, Washington to England and now resided in the village of Mossleigh. She had followed her husband around the globe as his career had dictated. Once his corporate days had finished it was expected that they would jet back to the USA but neither of them seemed in a hurry to return and it was now presumed that they were in Mossleigh to stay. Darcy had occupied the position of treasurer for the Mossleigh WI for two years now and, so long as she was happy to continue, nobody desired to jockey for her position. Her no-nonsense American manner and shrewd sense of business were excellent qualifications for the role. The magical extra ingredient to her success was that she was also genuinely kind and was utterly committed to Mossleigh village life. She was firm but fair, with compassion where needed. Everybody liked Darcy, even if they were a little afraid of her.

For all of the previous day and well into the night Emma and Henrietta had been busy baking, filling and decorating cupcakes. They had decided upon cupcakes as they guessed that other submissions for the competition would be the more traditional sandwich sponge cakes or fruit cakes. They also thought that these would be more successful for sales on the stall as people would be more willing to spend a few pence for a cupcake to eat there and then or a couple of pounds to take some home in a cake box. They had made chocolate sponges with white and dark chocolate marbled butter cream rosettes on top, miniature Victoria sponge cupcakes and fairy cakes with Emma's home made lemon curd as filling with iced latticework piped on the back of the sponge "wings". As they'd baked Toby had been tucked up on a mattress in Primrose's room and he had been wrapped up in a blanket and pushed home in his buggy just before midnight. It had been a good opportunity for the two ladies to get to know each other better. Being relatively new to the village Henrietta didn't really know many of the residents and the two young mums were keen for a chance to get to know each other. The shared task of baking cakes filled any otherwise awkward silences and provided a neutral platform to begin a stronger friendship. The subject of the mysterious wedding ring and the secrecy of the absent husband was a source of gossip in the village but Emma wisely steered clear of what was obviously not a matter for general conversation. The topics of mutual likes and dislikes and the common ground of young children provided enough subject matter for the present. It was good to see them standing side by side on the cake stall obviously enjoying the strength of their new-found friendship and being visibly at ease in each other's company.

It was not by chance that the cake stall was situated next to the preserves. Although the two stalls complemented each other and were natural neighbours they shared the same gazebo canopy because they were both to be judged for the annual WI prize. Neither was it a matter of coincidence that Beth and Emma had chosen to oversee both of these stalls as this meant that they could legitimately spend the day together. Natalie had also volunteered to "preside over the preserves" and, as she had supplied a substantial volume of produce on the cake stall, it was only right that she should enjoy the compliment of selling them.

'Goodness girls! It seems that you were very busy indeed yesterday. What super cakes you've made - and so many.' said Natalie.

'I've never made a cake before.' said Henrietta 'It's a bit scary that my first attempts are to be judged for a prize. I've learned a lot from Emma. I didn't think I'd be able to make one cake, never mind so many - although Emma did all the hard work.'

'If you mean switching on the food mixer, then yes - you're right. I never get my hands messy when baking, this is the Twenty-first Century after all.' said Emma.

'Oh, yes. I've heard all about your slovenly ways.' said Natalie. 'And I know your treachery in making jam in the microwave. Don't let her lead you astray, Henrietta, my dear. You know it'll end in tears. In my day we had to make do with a wooden spoon!'

'Natalie, we know full well that your kitchen has every "mod-con" available in it, so don't think you can pull the domestic martyr card on us.' said Beth. 'Henrietta, you may as well know now that the art of being recognised as a successful baker is to be able to tell barefaced lies. I'm afraid that you've made a bad start, both of you, by admitting that you took the easy way out.'

'Well, the proof will be in the pudding, or more accurately, the cake. We'll see if telling the truth wins us the prize, won't we Hetty?' said Emma.

'I'm afraid that it would end in tears if I thought I would have to make all of those cakes with nothing but a bowl and a wooden spoon. I don't care how many "mod-cons" you've got in your kitchen now Natalie - you deserve them. You must have had arm muscles of steel!' Henrietta then turned to Emma and said, 'If you think you'll be OK on the stall for a bit, I think that I'd better go and rescue Nathaniel. He'll be worn out from lifting Toby in and out of that tractor cab.' She waved good bye and walked off into the increasingly busy field in search of her son.

Between bouts of conversation and commerce Mae nipped into the cake tent and congratulated Emma and Henrietta on their depleting stocks and asked if anybody needed anything.

'No, thank you.' said Emma. 'We're managing fine between ourselves. We've been very busy though, we've even had some American Tourists buy our cakes. They were really thrilled to be doing the authentic English thing. You'd think we were a Delicatessen in Covent Garden for how thrilled they were browsing around our stall.'

'Yes, they did seem to be doing the whole "English Fête" thing to the limit. They were talking to John earlier and asking when the Poultry competition was to be held. They were very excited. We've taken it in turns to wander around the Fête to join in the fun and Drew or Nathaniel are making sure we get regular drinks and nibbles - we don't much fancy cake at the moment.' said Henrietta.

'And as you can see, we've got our extra little helpers.' said Natalie as she steered Toby and Primrose away from sampling more of the cakes.

'How's everyone doing?'said Beth. 'Where are you off to now? Perhaps I can walk with you?'

'Everything seems to be going smoothly and everybody looks like they're having a good time. I'm going to the craft stall to check on them there and then I was going to walk over to Kirsty's to see how her tours are doing before I need to come back for the prize giving in the cakes and preserves competition. It'd be nice if you could come with me. Can they spare you for that long?' said Mae.

'We've nearly sold out, so I'm sure that I can come. I want to visit the craft stall as I've loaned them my Celtic embroideries. I made sure to tell them to mark my sewing as 'Not For Sale' but I can't quite rest until I've seen for myself. I've been having premonitions of them selling years worth of stitching for two pounds fifty!'

'We'd better hurry then. I'm sure I heard someone trying to buy one not long ago.'

Beth didn't believe her and caught the mocking tone in Mae's voice but she nevertheless made a bee-line for the craft stall as they began walking. As they turned the corner the stand came into view and Beth visibly sagged with relief as she saw her precious stitching clearly marked as not available for purchase. Fastened to the roof supports Beth's embroideries hung in pride of place. They were intricate Celtic designs taken from "The Book of Kells". Drew had painstakingly transferred the complicated designs onto natural linen of an oatmeal hue and Beth had carefully followed his lines in a neat, curving stem stitch with the addition of some French knots, blanket stitch and simple back stitch for the very small, complex areas. Each design was worked in a monotone, sepia coloured thread and the finished pieces were mounted onto stretched canvas. Each one was a labour of love. Once she knew that her precious pieces were in safe hands she could relax and enjoy browsing around the rest of the exhibits.

Beth was thinking that she was glad that the days of crocheted doylies with starch stiffened swans swimming around the perimeter were now over. No doubt the techniques were skillful, but they certainly were ugly! This year there was a surprising renaissance of interest in tea cosies and the stall holders were evidently doing a brisk trade in both knitted and quilted varieties of all designs. The market share for such wares was surprisingly diverse too. Trendy young girls weren't ashamed to be seen buying such items but instead held them out proudly to their friends for approval. Emma and Beth had made doll's cot bedding using a remnant roll of qulting and off-cuts of ribbon and lace. As an afterthought they had also filled a wicker basket with home-made fabric hair scrunchies in the colours of the local school uniforms along with some more vibrant fabrics they had to hand.

Alongside these were the usual cross stitch designs and amateur watercolours. In pride of place were packs of notelets which were reproductions of pen and ink sketches that Terry had drawn. After his stroke Terry had inevitably struggled to occupy his time and talents - he couldn't be expected to instantly bounce back to single handed drilling. In the intervening period of convalescence Drew had got alongside Terry and encouraged him to pursue a more sedentary occupation. They had tried oil painting, watercolours and pastels before Terry had found an affinity with a draughtsman-like pen and ink technique. Although his confidence with the drill had returned his stamina wouldn't allow for continuous physical labour and so his interest in art had continued. The benefits of this computer age meant that he could easily reproduce his artistic endeavours and they were evidently selling like hot cakes - or just as well as the cold cakes on Emma's stall further up the field.

Mae and Beth continued their path through the stalls and out of the field to Kirsty's house a few streets away. They met Jean sitting at a table across the open gateway to the garden and, near at hand in a box, sat of heap of admission tickets - the tours had evidently proved as popular as expected and it looked like they'd had a busy day so far. Jean explained that earlier in the day three and, at times, four groups had been conducted simultaneously and Kirsty's information sheets had been a goldmine of information for the extra volunteer tour guides. Things had eased off this last hour and the extra helpers had left to join in the fun in the field and to browse around the stalls. As Mae and Beth walked along the garden path they could hear Kirsty talking to the group she was leading. No doubt this was the umpteenth time that she had delivered her talk as she walked through the garden but she presented it to this current group as if it was the first time. Her enthusiasm was as fresh as her garden. 'Although

Parsley, by classification, should be situated in the Herb Garden I have them planted here in the Rose Garden as they are a natural deterrent to aphids. We can't really have Golden Mozart covered in bugs now, can we?' Kirsty said.

Mae walked back to the gate to speak to Jean. 'Do you want to have a walk and go and browse around the Fête? They'll be announcing the prize winners soon and John will be judging the poultry competition.'

'Thank you for asking, but I'm quite happy where I am. If I win the jam competition I'm sure that somebody will tell me and I rather think that John would prefer to make his judging debut without me breathing down his neck. I'm going to put the kettle on in a moment to make Kirsty a drink.' said Jean. 'I think that she has given a cut-off time to Nicola on the flower stall, so we'll probably come and join you soon anyway. '

'Thanks for all your help, Jean. I know that Kirsty really appreciates you staying here with her. Hopefully we'll see you back at the village hall later.' Mae then made her way back to join Beth who had tagged along with the garden tour and was currently standing next to the herb garden listening to Kirsty enthuse about her plants.

'Mint is a vigorously growing herb which most of us associate with lamb or as a garnish on desserts. It has far more uses than we give it credit for. A cold mint tea can be helpful in controlling embarrassing flatulence - should you privately wish to know.' Kirsty said, which gave rise to some embarrassed giggles. 'Sage produces lovely purple flowers which attract bees to your garden and we all know that it makes a lovely stuffing with dried bread crumbs and onion. It's perhaps less well known for its application to dentistry.' Kirsty explained. This produced enquiring glances which she answered by saying, 'Yes, it's true. Sage leaves rubbed against your teeth act as an efficient, natural tooth whitener. More interestingly, Sage tea can help to overcome menopausal sweating, which must surely be a milder approach then pharmaceutical HRT.' As the group wandered around the herb garden touching and smelling leaves, Kirsty continued her discourse. 'Once again the classification boundaries overlap here. I could include the nettle patch in my herb garden as the young nettle leaves can be eaten as salad leaves - the young leaves don't sting. Also it makes good beer and infused it has a mixture of uses. As a tea nettles are an effective natural laxative. Mind you, if you make a blended nettle and mint tea I don't think I can be held responsible for the digestive consequences!' Less inhibited laughter punctuated this little gem of wisdom.

'Perhaps now might be a good time to wander over to the natural garden.' Kirsty suggested and the group followed her to a point at the bottom of the garden. As the group was walking to the end of the garden Mae snatched a little of Kirsty's attention to seek reassurance that all was well. They arranged to meet in the village hall, where refreshments were being served, later in the day. As Mae and Beth turned to leave they heard Kirsty continue her enlightening tour saying, 'I keep the patch of nettles here as they can look a bit scruffy and I don't want to risk getting stung each time I want to pick a few herbs. In the 1500s the Elizabethan herbalist, Gerard, wrote that nettles could be found "oftentimes in gardens ill husbanded." This section of the garden is the least work because if I interfere too much it wouldn't be very natural, would it? My job here is to let things be and just make sure no one plant gets too out of hand. Some things I have actively planted but some of the vegetation has just made itself at home. I try and let that steer my designs here as much as possible.'

Mae and Beth made their way back to the house and joined Carlton and Jean in the kitchen where they were making a drink for when Kirsty had finished the tour. They thought that this was to be the last party for the day. Carlton asked how the Fête was going and was invited to join them in their walk back. 'Come and see for yourself.' said Beth. They walked to the cakes and preserves tent and Darcy had just finished judging the prestigious competition entries. She handed the results to Mae who then displayed the winning jars and cakes on the two separate podiums. For the cakes the highest central plinth showing first prize held Natalie's Coffee and Walnut Cake. On its left, a little lower down, in second place was Emma and Henrietta's miniature Victoria sponge cup cake and in third place sat Betty's Lemon Drizzle cake. Emma and Henrietta hugged Natalie and agreed that obviously wooden spoons were best - even if they were electrically operated. Henrietta was thrilled that her initial efforts had won second place and everybody warmly congratulated Betty on gaining a prize. Mae then placed the preserve jars onto the podium in reverse order. Onto the lowest plinth, the Bronze award was given to a chili salsa, which was unconventional and perhaps suggested that the WI was catching up with modern times. Emma's lemon curd was positioned on the middle plinth as fitting for Silver, again showing that the modern-day microwave method was gaining recognition. A vacuum was created in the tent as everybody took a deep breath to see who would crown the top plinth. A shock wave went around as two jars were placed side by side on the top plinth. It seemed that the judge simply couldn't choose between Phoebe's Damson jam and Jean's Rhubarb and Rose Petal jam and for the first time in Mowesly WI history first place was shared. Darcy had shown true American grit in recognising the shared quality of the jams and regardless of precedent had stuck to her guns.

There was hardly time for adulation as a pestering crowd urgently called for Mae's attention and demanded that she walk over to the poultry area. As they walked into the general hubbub it seemed that feathers were getting a little ruffled in more ways than one and the entrees for the poultry competition were getting flustered as John hadn't yet made his way to the allocated area. Nervous and irate poultry fanciers were bad enough but nervous and irate poultry was a very sticky situation in all senses of the word. The hen-husbands had kept their birds scrupulously clean and had left them at home until the last possible moment so as not to sully their appearance but they'd been kept cooped up in small carrying cases and were showing no regard for the standards of hygiene that their owners strove to maintain. The situation needed to be dealt with quickly and as it became apparent that John simply wasn't to be found it was evident that a solution had to be sought quickly. The only options were to either cancel the competition, which was no solution at all, or to quickly find a substitute judge. An alternative judge needed to be found, and quickly, in order to placate the irate fowl fanciers. Mae quickly took hold of the situation and Carlton was quickly dispatched to ask Dr Wainwright to please step into the breach. He'd shown a polite interest in John's background reading into the topic, in fact he'd positively encouraged him in his research as he wanted to promote his positive pursuits to alleviate his stress. He was a highly regarded figure in the community and could command respect, and he was also walking towards them at that moment. Mae quickly secured his services without giving him time to consider his options and so he tried to mentally adjust to his new found position as the poultry entrants were lined up ready for inspection. 'He doesn't know a Bantam from a Barn Owl!' grumbled Mike. However, when it was explained to him that the only alternative was for him to withdraw his own candidate and act as judge himself he quietly took his place in the line-up.

They were deprived of the opportunity to test the mettle of Dr Wainwright's poultry judging ability by the arrival of a most breathless Betty. She was so agitated and flustered that it was difficult at first to grasp what she was saying. Mae steeled herself for the onslaught - this really wasn't the time for a "Betty episode". She took a deep breath and, as patiently as she could manage, she asked,

'What is it Betty? What's the matter?'

'I've found him. I've found him - he's dead!

Mae barely managed to conceal a sigh of irritability and asked again. 'What are you on about? Are you talking about John? Is he ill?'

At this point Dr Wainwright intervened and, feeling himself to be in a situation that he was far more able to cope with, he took control. 'Where is John, Betty? Perhaps you'd better take me to him.' Turning to Mae he said 'It's best that everybody stays here. John won't want a crowd about him if he's not well. His sugar levels have been unpredictable recently so perhaps he's had a relapse.' Turning to Carlton he continued. 'Could you please come with me, and would you arrange for Jean to be brought over here? She may be needed.' Then, turning his attention back to Betty he said, 'Thank you for finding John. Please take me to him.'

'He's on a chair by the dustbins at the back of the village hall, where people sit if they want to smoke.' said Betty. 'But John doesn't smoke, does he? He's dead I tell you. I can see that for myself.' Betty marched off at a surprising pace, heading towards the village hall. Carlton and Dr Wainwright followed closely behind her. They didn't speak as they walked but exchanged a questioning glance. They could only guess at what they'd find. The question that was uppermost in both their minds was

"Why was John sitting next to the dustbins in the first place?" As they turned the corner to the rear of the village hall they were struck by the sight of John Barlow gazing unseeing into the glaring sunshine. He was leaning back in the plastic patio chair, his arms hanging limply down by his sides. Dr Wainwright moved towards him to test for a pulse, but it didn't need a doctor to make a correct medical diagnosis. Betty was right. John Barlow was dead.

Chapter Four

In an impromptu gesture of kindness, not to mention an inclination to join in the fun, Jonti had brought a few friends along to the Fête and had set up an ad-hoc swing band next to the village hall - conveniently close to the refreshments area. He had always possessed the knack of getting on the good side of old ladies in possession of tea and cake. Jonti said that coming back to play for the Fête was good for him and made him remember the good old days of playing in the middle of a field with clothes pegs fastening his music to the music stand. Today they may well have begun with some sheet music but not much evidence of following the notes was apparent judging by the prolonged passages of "Chattanooga Choo Choo" which became quite unrecognisable. The only form of any sort of organisation was that someone had to walk over and tell them to shut up in time for the Templeton Singers to do their bit. They were in the middle of a seriously extemporised version of "Fly me to the Moon" when the pale, drawn features of Dr Wainwright walked past. Following behind the doctor came Mae wearing a similar expression. With hardly a nod Jonti quickly brought their number to a perfect cadence and walked over to Mae to find out what was going on.

'He really is dead.' she said. 'I can't believe it, Betty was right. He really is dead.'

'Goodness, Mae - what are you on about? Who's dead?'

'John Barlow. We just thought he was ill and his diabetes was playing up a bit, that's all. I guess his diabetes really was playing up - and now he's dead! I knew he was a bit stressed lately and wasn't feeling well, but I had no idea it could have led to this. Poor Jean, she doesn't know anything about it yet.' Jonti laid a hand on Mae's arm as the enormity of the situation hit her. Mae looked up and her attention snapped into focus as she saw Betty scurrying excitedly about the field heralding the news abroad with gusto. 'Oh, no! Betty's telling everybody. I can't let Jean find out this way. I'll have to go and stop her.' Mae practically ran across the field making a bee-line for the voluble old lady. Jonti ambled over to the ensemble to explain the situation and a unanimous decision was made to retire to The Badger. Of course, their main aim was to be helpful in getting out of the way. Saying nothing to the landlord of recent events they set about restoring the viscosity of their embouchure as only brass players now how.

Inside the village hall a confused debate had arisen. As there was already a doctor present nobody seemed to know what the correct procedure now was. Dr Wainwright had easily certified John as dead. He was found sitting in a plastic garden chair set amongst the trade refuse bins and surrounded by discarded drinks bottles and spent ashtrays. His arms were hanging limply parallel to the chair legs and his head had fallen backwards leaving him gazing, eyes open and unseeing into the now bright sunshine. The fact that Dr Wainwright had walked up to John and felt for a pulse was perfunctory - he was obviously dead. He'd have to speak to Jean to find out if they'd made any pre-paid arrangements but there was only one funeral director in Mossleigh, so he knew who he'd be calling. He also said that he'd need to contact the local police.

'That's a bit drastic, isn't it?' said Carlton. 'It's not as if there's been an accident and nothing can be done for the poor chap now.'

'It's just a matter of form.' said Wainwright. 'An unexpected death, and with no apparent witness will need a few conventional questions answered. I suppose that as his GP I'll be the one answering most of those questions, so that's all right.'

'I'll go and see if anybody has found Jean yet. When you've finished your calls come into the kitchen and we'll prepare for the onslaught.' said Carlton as he walked into the adjoining kitchen. It was a large, high ceilinged room which was bare except for an old gas cooker, a sink unit, a large table and a wall cupboard. It was currently occupied with several ladies of the WI walking busily to and fro across the parquet floor feeding the refreshment hatch, which in turn fed the visiting throng. In the far corner of the kitchen he found Beth administering the tried and tested British remedy of sweet tea to Jean. Natalie had caught the look in Beth's eye as she and Jean were passing by the cake stall and, leaving the younger ladies in charge, wordlessly joined in escorting Jean back to the village hall. Gradually the situation had unfolded and Natalie, like a magician, produced the ever present hip flask and sloshed a healthy measure of single malt into the teacup which was being offered to Jean. The fact that Jean never took sugar in her tea and never drank whisky wasn't relevant in this instance and although she grimaced a little at her first sip the cup nevertheless soon emptied. Jean's glassy, uncomprehending stare gradually began to clear as the reality of the situation began to dawn upon her.

'I know he's been a bit off-side lately, but I didn't think he was really ill.' she said. 'I'd have been more patient, if only I'd realised.' At this point the flood-gates of her emotion burst in a tide of words and tears. 'It's all my fault.' said Jean. 'I shouldn't have given him that jar of jam. I thought I was being kind and I really didn't think it'd make that much difference.'

'Nonsense.' said Natalie, ever to the point. 'No diabetic I ever knew stuck to their diet like John did. The wonder was that John was so disciplined. A few days of jam on toast is a drop in the ocean. Don't even go there, Jean. Nobody expects to die and I'm sorry that it's happened, but these things just can't be helped.'

Dr Wainwright walked into the kitchen to find Carlton and the ladies. Carlton had kept apart from the trio thinking that this moment was best left to the women. He looked up as the doctor joined him. 'I've telephoned the police station.' said Wainwright. 'Sergeant Maddox is on his way. I've given him a brief outline of events and it doesn't seem necessary for anybody else to come. We should be able to deal with the procedures between the two of us. I just need a few details from Jean and then I'm going to wait in the office here until Maddox arrives. I just want to check that Jean is all right.' Walking over to the corner of the kitchen he pulled up a chair so as not to loom over the huddled figure and said, 'I'm so sorry that this has happened and I know that it's a huge shock but I do need to sort a few formalities. Do you think you can help me?' Jean looked up at him and smiled a crooked smile in acknowledgement. 'Do you have any funeral plans organised? I don't need too many details, but is there a particular funeral director I can contact for you to sort things out?'

'We both organised pre-planned funerals last year.' Jean replied. 'The advertising worked! You never really think you need to, do you? It's Brough's from the village. Ring Fred Brough, he'll know what to do.'

'That's great, Jean.' Dr Wainwright gave Jean a beaming smile which would have usually had his patients fainting and hoping for resuscitation. Then his expression became more serious as he said, 'I'm afraid that's not quite all, Jean. The police are on their way and they will need to have a word with you. It's nothing to worry about, it's just a formality because it's an unexpected death - not that any of us ever expect to die. I'll speak to Maddox first as John's GP but he'll want to speak to you, and maybe some others too. Before we begin to organise matters though, do you want to go and see John, or would you rather not?'

Jean nodded her head and got up to follow him, but them stopped and didn't seem sure. He gently guided her from the kitchen and, looking over his shoulder, gave Carlton a beckoning glance. Understanding the indication Carlton got up from his seat and followed behind as they walked to the back of the hall. John was still as they had left him and was guarded from view by a couple of sentries that Dr Wainwright had posted at the corner of the building. As Jean approached the burdened chair her pace slowed and she stretched out her arm and placed it mechanically on John's shoulder. She then straightened her back, squared her shoulders and turned to walk back to the kitchen. Once Jean was again in the capable ministrations of the ladies Dr Wainwright and Carlton walked to the side of the village hall and into the office building which communicated with the main building. The doctor doubted that Jean would accept their attentions for much longer. She'd shaken off the mantle of grieving widow as soon as she laid a hand on her dead husband's shoulder.

'Thank you for coming with me just then Carlton.' he said. 'You can never guess how someone will react. If she was going to faint I didn't fancy catching her by myself. Mind you, it seems like she's steeled herself to the situation and has adopted the stiff upper lip mechanism. Everybody copes in different ways.'

'I know that you say it's a coping mechanism, but it does seem mighty heartless. It looks like she just doesn't care - but what do I know about such things? I presume that you'll want to speak to Maddox in private. I'll go and find Kirsty, she's probably about here somewhere by now - I suppose the news will have got around.'

The office to the village hall was a small, squat structure literally stuck onto the side of the main building. A nod towards matching the bricks to the hall had been made but that was as far as aesthetics had gone. It had a flat, pitch roof and inside was best described as functional. Linoleum was rolled out over the floor and the only furniture was a brown metal filing cabinet and an old teacher's desk which was rescued from the school's skip during a clear out years ago. Sitting behind the desk and reaching into his jacket pocket Dr Wainwright hit the number for Brough's funeral directors. In his line of work he had cause to call them regularly, particularly as visiting GP to a residential retirement home nearby. He knew Fred Brough well and after introductory chit-chat he gave directions to remove the body once Maddox had given clearance. A minute or two later his thoughts were interrupted by the entrance of Maddox and one of the ladies from the refreshments battalion bearing a tray carrying a black coffee for the doctor, an extremely sweet tea for the sergeant - who was well known for is sweet tooth - and a selection of sandwiches. Up until that very second Dr Wainwright hadn't thought about food but he now realised that he was ravenous. Giving a hearty grin, which made the tray bearer's knees tremble and sent a wave of bright red blood cells to her cheeks,' he attacked the sandwiches and thanked her with a mouth full of salmon and cucumber. Turning his attention to Maddox he proffered the plate of sandwiches and allocated him his sweet tea. Nursing his coffee cup he set an amicable tenor to the meeting and asked about Maddox's health and family.

Maddox was in his late twenties, painfully single and living with his widowed mum. The introduction of Henrietta into Mossleigh village had obviously knocked him sideways but he had so far run into a brick wall in that arena. Continuing to munch on the sandwiches Dr Wainwright brought the conversation around to the matter in hand.

'You know, I will always remember my old medical tutor at college telling me that the most important piece of advice he could give to any doctor was, "Always be prepared to be surprised." Yet I have to admit that I am surprised by the death of John Barlow. We were always told that every human being reacted differently and held the potential to not follow expected results, but I am very surprised by this death.'

Maddox cast a searching glance at the doctor and asked, 'Do I need to read something into that? Do you think that there's more behind this than an old man dying unexpectedly?'

'That's quite a strong suggestion, isn't it?' said Wainwright. 'I can't say that I would positively say so, but I certainly didn't expect John to die. I'm sure you know that he suffered with diabetes - which always places matters on a knife edge, but his condition was mild. He had only a gentle onset of Type II, which means that it wasn't too invasive into his life. He didn't need to inject but just needed to regulate his diet as his condition dictated. I don't think that he'd ever had either a hyper or hypoglycemic episode at all as far as I'm aware. He was unusually adherent to my advice about diet too. I only wish that my other patients were so conscientious. It's true that he'd had some business worries recently and he'd had to embrace a bit more responsibility, which was causing him further worry and distress, when he thought he'd practically retired. I don't know the details here, you'd have to speak to his wife. I know that stress can do strange things to a man's constitution - but all the same, death is a bit drastic! I guess it just goes to show that you never know when your time's up. But I honestly don't know what I can put on the death certificate as the underlying cause of death.' Looking at Maddox he said, 'In our lines of business we should both be used to unexpected death, but you never get used to it, do you?'

'Well, I'm not used to it at all.' said Maddox. 'But that's because I've never had to deal with it before. I've dealt with a few nasty car crashes and the odd pub brawl which have shown me some grim injuries but I've never personally dealt with a fatality. It seems a straightforward case of natural death from the information you've given me, but I've no previous experience to refer to to help me know how to deal with this. I'll have to be guided by you and then report back to see what the Super says.' Getting down to practical matters Maddox asked, 'Have Brough's taken the body away yet?'

'No, but they're on stand-by for when you give the go-ahead. I thought you might want to view the scene before we tidy things away.'

'Fair enough. I suppose I'd better.'

They walked together to the back of the village hall and standing at a respectable distance were Brough's men, ready to restore John Barlow to a more dignified pose. Maddox walked over to the chair that John was still sitting on. He looked desperately uncomfortable with his head so awkwardly thrust back, though such things as earthly comfort were beyond him now. Maddox took his notebook out and made a scribbled account of the scene that lay before him. He noted the red complexion of the deceased's face, the abstract litter that lay about - half empty drinks cups and food wrappings, and he asked if John smoked, noting down the negative answer that was given. A cursory glance revealed no blemishes to the skin and after taking some photographs with his mobile phone there really was nothing more to do but give a nod to the waiting men to tidy the body away.

'Just take him and leave him as much as possible for now, please. Don't tidy him up, just yet.' he said as an apparent afterthought. Turning to Dr Wainwright he explained, 'I'd better make sure things are left alone as much as possible until I've spoken to the boss.' He then stepped aside to let the funeral directors get on with their work.

'Do you need to speak to Jean now?' asked Dr Wainwright.

'I'll need to speak to her soon but I don't think I need to right away. She's got enough to be dealing with just now and there's no reason to make matters worse. I'll go to her house and speak to her there later on this evening. Had you better come with me if she's in a state?'

'I can come along if you'd like me to, but I get the impression that I really won't be needed. She's quite a trooper and she seems to have got a hold on herself pretty quickly. It won't be until much later that it hits her, if it does at all. Give me a call if you think you need me - as my professor said, "Be prepared to be surprised." '

The two men then said good bye and went their separate ways. Maddox walked back to the small village police station and, seeing that the ladies were no longer in the kitchen, Dr Wainwright walked out into the field.

The general atmosphere of the continuing Fête was untouched by the death of John Barlow and as Dr Wainwright walked into the crowd the atmosphere of an ongoing holiday was refreshing. There was an unofficial gathering at the Cakes and Preserves stalls and the hot topic of a joint first prize had been superseded by news of the death. General milling around and subdued chatter rippled under the external noise of the Fête. A separate bubble had formed a nucleus within the festivities as people quietly discussed the tragedy and what bearing that might have on the day. Nobody was certain what they ought to do next. As they were discussing matters Fred Brough's men carried John's body away. It was a discordant sight, the dark jackets and striped trousers of the funeral garb in the midst of the holiday apparel of the Fête. The festivities were due to end soon and the Templeton Singers had planned to round off the day by singing "Jerusalem" with the Mossleigh WI joining with them. There didn't seem to be any reason why this shouldn't go ahead as planned and so the singers began to make their way to the area where Richard was waiting at the keyboard. Jonti and his chums had torn themselves away from The Badger and, after glancing approval from Mae, looked over the music on the keyboard stand to check which key to play in before they took up their positions to join in. Everyone was surprised to see Jean take her place in the alto section, but her neighbours quickly shuffled aside to make room for her. With a gentle squeeze on her shoulder they then joined the rest of the choir to watch Mae's baton for the down-beat to start singing.

Music ever was a restorative to the soul and in the light of recent events there was more than one dewy eye in both the choir and the audience. Nathaniel, Matt, Drew and Terry had joined the crowd on hearing the news and the music united them all in their sorrow. It uplifted and encouraged them too. It seemed a fitting tribute to both the close of the Fête and also a suitable impromptu memorial service to John Barlow, who had been liked by all. The only member who looked resolutely unmoved was Jean. In her newly acquired widow status she appeared frostier than ever. It would affect her more deeply, no doubt, and who could tell how grief could affect those it touched most? If anything this made her plight all the more sorrowful and caused her to look more fragile than any demonstrative outpouring of grief ever could. As the last instrumental strains of the Coda faded away Jean's friends led her kindly back to the village hall. There didn't seem much more that they could do. Brass band music had always deeply affected Beth. The piercing tones of the trombone touched her to the core. She always thought that the trombone had a plaintive timbre and she was now crying openly. Drew came alongside her and embraced her, letting her tears naturally ebb away. After a moment's pause the spell broke and people began to drift away. The Fête was nearly over and Eileen and Betty volunteered to escort Jean home thinking it not right that she face an empty house alone just now. The rest of the WI stayed behind to begin the Herculean task of tidying up once the final visitors had left.

Darcy moved to take up her position at the entrance-cum-exit of the Fête with her cash box at the ready to take in the tithes and donations from external stall holders. She sat in her capacity as Treasurer rather like an Abbot balancing his ledger at the close of St Peter's Fayre. It was advisable for Darcy to display a certain amount of trust in such a venture. To insist that each stall holder count out every penny of their earnings and for her to cross-check their tally so as to be able to accurately calculate the percentage due would have been far too time consuming and would have been damaging to customer relations. Nevertheless, she'd kept a shrewd eye on business throughout the day and if an apparently busy stall holder professed minimal takings she wouldn't be hoodwinked. Soon the representatives of the official WI stalls would also begin to drift in with their day's takings. The costs of hiring the hall and the field, and the purchase of refreshments to sell on, along with any other valid expenses accompanied by a receipt would need to be deducted from the sum total of the day. Even so the day promised to prove financially successful. The first to submit their takings were Emma and Henrietta. Their stall had sold out some time ago and they needed to get their tired children home. Nathaniel, Drew and Beth would stay behind to help clear up. Matt had left to return the car as the choir was singing "Jerusalem" and the tractor and bikes could be removed once the tidying up was organised. Bereft of his sports car Terry made his way to the refreshments hall and rolled up his sleeves to get stuck into the washing up.

After the joviality of the day it was usual during this last part of the proceedings for volunteers to sag. Once well stocked and artistically displayed stalls were now bound to look dilapidated and the stalls looked astired and dishevelled as the vendors themselves felt. It was natural for a lull to occur before helpers could once again launch into action to get the clutter cleared away and the gazebos dismantled. A certain amount of brushing oneself down and finding of a second wind was needed before labour could resume. The sadness and shock of John's death seemed to rob everyone of that second wind and it took Mae a good deal of chivvying before activity recommenced. The only real sense of motivation was the fact that many of the volunteers had got late evening bookings in the restaurant of The Badger. The landlord's son was chef in residence and was making quite a name for both himself and the pub. He was well on the way to Michelin stardom. No matter what the day had brought it wouldn't do to keep the chef waiting - and they were all getting hungry. A final push achieved the required result and when the lights in the village hall were finally switched off the would-be diners were grateful to press their way through into the restaurant of The Badger where there was no shortage of appetite or conversation.

Chapter Five

Police Sergeant Robert Maddox was good at his job. As a village policeman he had unending patience to sit with a cup of tea listening to the petty grievances of lonely old women. He could break up a local pub brawl whilst exuding friendliness to all parties and would probably end up with a complimentary pint as he sat chatting with the combatants at the end of the evening. He was more than happy to give up an hour of his time for Jean on the evening of the Fête. He wouldn't rush the conversation and would drink as many cups of tea as were necessary to put the lady at her ease so that he could gather the information that he needed by gleaning it from the tide of irrelevant chatter. His only concern was that Jean wasn't the gossipy type and would merely answer his questions formally which was likely to result in incomplete information. He knew that if she offered to put the kettle on things were likely to go well. The ringing doorbell was answered by Betty who seemed thrilled to see him. 'Hello Bobby, how nice to see you.'

'Hello Mrs Barnsford. I didn't expect to see you here, I'm glad that you're looking after Mrs Barlow.'

'You'd better come on in. Jean's been expecting you since she got in. We've made sure that she's had a rest and a bite to eat but she won't settle until she's seen you. I suppose that she just wants to get all this unpleasant business out of the way.'

Maddox was led through a grand hallway, which was sparsely furnished except for a large abstract painting on the wall next to the staircase, into the vast kitchen. At a low marble topped breakfast bar sat Jean and Eileen. Eileen was fussing over a teapot and a plate of scones while Jean sat staring vacantly at the TV which was recessed into the small, grey slate wall tiles. Looking around he could see that the room was aggressively immaculate. The stainless steel double oven looked as if it had never cooked a meal. He simply couldn't imagine roast beef residing in the oven and besmirching the pristine glass or the gleaming shelves. Nor could he picture a saucepan of gravy spitting its contents up the metal back plate which gleamed and twinkled reflections from the angled LED ceiling lights. Henrietta must have her work cut out for her continually polishing all of these glossy surfaces. His attention was drawn away from thoughts of Henrietta by Eileen who was pouring him a cup of tea and talking to him. 'I imagine that you'll want to talk quietly together, so we'll get out of your way. Be sure to call me, Jean, if you want anything at all. I'm only a few minutes away at any time of the day or night, so promise to ring if you're not feeling up to managing yet.' said Eileen. Jean drew her eyes, if not her attention, away from the TV and nodded to Eileen and Betty as they were leaving.

Although Maddox was now holding the prerequisite cup of tea it had not been offered by Jean herself and he was unsure of his welcome. He had a feeling that this was going to be uphill work. Taking a deep breath he made a start. 'Shall we go and sit somewhere we can be a bit more comfortable?' he asked. He was silently led into a creme carpeted lounge and was directed to sit on a pale oatmeal coloured armchair. The only vibrant splashes of colour were the Royal Doulton Flambé ornaments positioned at intervals about the room. He now heartily wished that he wasn't carrying the inadvisably hoped for tea and fully intended to empty his cup down his throat as quickly as possible before he spilled anything on the immaculate carpet or furnishings. He secretly wondered if anybody ever sat and relaxed in this room, or was it reserved for visitors? At least it was away from the active TV and he should be able to hold her attention better in here. 'I'm so sorry for your loss, Mrs Barlow. I know that you must have an awful lot on your mind. If you could just spare me a little time to gather a few details - you can imagine the paperwork I've got to deal with, I'm sure.' Jean smiled at his light hearted manner, but she was distant and it didn't seem like he was getting through. Nevertheless, he ploughed on. 'I understand that John had been diagnosed with diabetes not too long ago and that he had been unwell recently. I've spoken with Dr Wainwright but, if I'm not mistaken, I don't expect he went to see him very often.' Jean gave a distant smile and agreed that this was the case. 'I'm hoping that you can give me some more detailed information so that we can find an explanation for what may have caused John's death. Dr Wainwright wasn't of the opinion that John's medical condition was serious and so we're wondering what other factors might have exacerbated his symptoms. Can you tell me about some of the things that had been worrying John?'

'John was very careful about his diet, more than anybody I knew. I used to complain about his fussiness and said he was like a hypochondriac. I didn't think it mattered as much as he made out. Just this week I gave him some of his favourite jam. I didn't think it'd matter, and now he's dead.'

'Dr Wainwright is convinced that such a small deviation in diet couldn't have proved fatal. You mustn't even consider such a thing. I can't blame John for eating a little bit at breakfast, it won first prize at the Fête I gather.'

It won joint first prize. It's just like Darcy to not make up her mind, not that it matters now.'

Jean shook her head sorrowfully, but no tears followed and Maddox thought it safe to continue. 'Can you give me any idea of what was troubling John? I know that he'd had some worries, can you give me some details of what they might have been? I understand that he'd recently had to come out of retirement to deal with certain business matters. Is that right?'

'Yes, it was so tiresome his being shut up in the office so much. I never really paid much attention to his business. He tried telling me but I didn't understand what he was saying so I'm afraid that I wasn't really listening. He was on the telephone to Greece quite a lot recently, I know. One time I was trying to call Kirsty to ask if I could have some rose petals as I hadn't enough that weren't going brown at the edges. Every time I picked up the receiver he was still on the line. They were speaking English so I could tell what they were saying, but I hung up each time until the line was free.'

'Have you any idea of what was going on, even if it's just the smallest guess - something which could explain the sudden collapse in John's health?'

'I know that he's had problems with some property he owns over there. I think I heard something about tax, but more than that I really can't say. I'm sorry, I left all of that sort of thing to John.'

'It's getting late now and I'm sure that you've had more than enough for one day. Would you mind if I came back again tomorrow and had a look through the paperwork in his office before I write up my report?' Jean nodded her consent but her attention was dwindling. 'Is there anybody you'd like me to contact for you? Do you want some company tonight?'

Jean shook her head and said that she'd like to be quietly on her own. 'I don't think I could stand another cup of tea. I'd just like a hot bath and then get into bed, I'm so tired. I can telephone Eileen later if I change my mind, don't you worry about me.'

Walking to the door Maddox said, 'If you're sure. Once again, I am very sorry. If you need me or think of anything you want to talk about before tomorrow just ring me at home - you know my mum doesn't mind.'

Jean smiled and thanked him and then closed the door the instant he stepped outside.

Thinking that the interview had been less than successful Maddox walked the few streets home. He entered him mother's kitchen through the back door with a renewed sense of gratitude. Although their house was positively lowly in comparison with the house he'd just been to the sense of homeliness was tangible. The smell of the cottage pie he'd eaten before he'd left to visit Jean still hung in the atmosphere and the bits and bobs of clutter gave the place an everyday welcome. You just knew that anybody could pop in for a chat and be at ease. Towering over his diminutive mother he gave her a close impression of a bear hug before he walked into the living room to pull off his boots. Mrs Maddox beamed at the unexpected gesture, but was wise enough not to question it.

'How did you get along? Not a nice job for you tonight, huh?' she said.

Kicking his boots to one side Robert stretched his long legs out towards the empty hearth in an accustomed gesture, even if it wasn't lit on this warm evening. 'I didn't get along at all, that's how! Jean couldn't tell me much and she wasn't in the mood for talking. I'll have to go back and try again tomorrow. Hopefully she'll have had chance to gather herself a bit by then. I don't like pestering her, but it's got to be done.'

'Poor Jean, sitting there all alone. What can have finished John so unexpectedly do you think? I don't suppose any of us can expect a written warning though, can we? Not that I'd want one, thank you. I think John's way was the best - no warning at all. One minute you're here, one minute you're not. It's for the best I say.'

'You're probably right, but I can't put that on my paperwork and neither can Dr Wainwright. He can't positively say he expected it and so I'll have to rummage through John's business dealings while

Wainwright rummages through his medical notes and hope we can come up with some reasonable explanation between us. I'm going back to Jean's tomorrow and then I'm having a meeting with Wainwright. Hopefully we can wrap it all up. If not we'll have to suggest he topped himself.'

'Shame on you! Don't let me hear you spouting such nonsense again. It's very unprofessional for a start, not to mention unkind. Now have your supper and get yourself off to bed. Then you can get up and start tomorrow like a sensible human being!'

Robert stood up and kissed his mother on the top of her head and for once was happy to do as he was told. He plodded up the stairs, taking his buttered toast with him, wondering if Wainwright had come up with any inspiration or if he would find some himself tomorrow morning in John's office.

In the restaurant of The Badger most of the diners were leaning back in their chairs and a good number of them were loosening waistbands as far as the design of various articles of clothing would allow to accommodate their increased girth. As The Badger's Michelin star's trajectory rose a correlation occurred in the diminished availability of tables at which to dine. Fortunately the main party of workers from the Fête had booked tables well in advance, but latecomers like Jonti and his friends had had to make do with a bar meal. No doubt this was more suited to their liking as they could sit and eat more closely situated to the beer taps. The more civilised diners began to limber up and make their way from the restaurant to join the throng and sit in the bar area but Beth and Drew stayed standing so as to say their farewells and organise sleeping arrangements with Jonti for his friends.

'I need to get home.' explained Beth. 'Uncle Benji said he'd call me tonight to see how the Fête has gone. I'll leave the back door open for you and a selection of pillows and duvets. You'll probably have to draw straws for the beds upstairs and those left will have to make shift on the chairs and sofa. If you want to spill over into Emma's you'd better give her a call as she won't want to be waiting up too late.'

'Say "Hi" to Uncle Benji from me and ask him how his quaint police band is doing.' said Jonti.

'I'll do no such thing.' said Beth. 'You can ask him yourself, if you've the nerve, next time you see him. I'll see you in the morning - be quiet when you do finally decide to come home.'

Benedict James was Beth's twin brother and had carried on a family tradition of showing a flair for unravelling problems and mystery by climbing the ranks of the Cheshire police force and was now a Detective Chief Inspector at Winsford HQ. He was also first clarinetist in the police band and subject to much harmless derision from his nephew. Some years ago Beth and Benji had joined forces in conducting research into their family history to confirm a long held rumour that their Grandmother, Agnes Healey, had been a member of the code-breaking team at Bletchely Park during the war. Between them they had uncovered evidence to confirm the rumour and had discovered that her reputation as an invincible crossword solver and setter had brought her to the authority's attention. After the war not much more could be found out about her as it wasn't something she ever talked about - small wonder after living most of your life bound by the Official Secrets Act. Their mother, Martha James, had often told Benji that he took after his Gran but nothing was mentioned of the details of her role in intelligence during the war. It seems that after the war Agnes settled into domestic life. She married Henry James and had Martha. Agnes had always encouraged Martha to think things through in a logical manner and was continually setting her crosswords and maths problems. From an early age Martha said that she could remember solving simple puzzles and sitting chatting over her evening malted milk drink having conversations on reasoning and logic with her mother. Martha James had continued this mode of impromptu education in the raising of her twins, Benedict and Beth, only giving hints at the heritage their Gran had left them. It was no surprise to his mother when Benedict began to rise through the ranks of what seemed the natural profession for him.

Beth had just changed into her pyjamas, to ease her happily constrained waistline, and was standing in the kitchen looking dejectedly at the pile of dishes still crowding the sink since breakfast time. She was saved from having to actually tackle them just then by the ringing of the telephone. Carrying the handset through to the lounge she settled into the armchair and, tucking her legs under her she clicked the green icon and said, 'Hi Benji. How are you?'

After the regulation exchange of pleasantries and enquiry after family members they finally got down to the subject of the moment.

'How did the long awaited Fête go? Did everything go to plan? I bet Emma sold out of her famous Lemon Curd pretty quickly!' said Benedict.

'She came second in both the cakes and the preserves competitions. We were really pleased. The first prize was a bit contentious, though. Darcy gave joint first prize in the preserves to Phoebe and Jean. I can understand why she did, both are really delicious. But it didn't go down too well, as you can imagine.'

'You have all the intrigue in village life. Did plenty of visitors turn up and forego the luxury of a pound for all the delights of the fair?'

'We did a brisk trade and I'm sure the day was a success. We were thrown off course a bit this afternoon though. John Barlow was found dead behind the village hall.'

'I think I remember John. Didn't he live in that big house at the end of the village?'

'Yes, that's him. He should have been judging the poultry competition but he didn't show up. Folks were searching for him everywhere until Betty found him sitting between the bins. I don't know how long he'd been there. It's horrible to think, really.'

'Crikey, what was he doing back there?'

'I can't imagine, Benji. Perhaps he just wanted to find a quiet spot for a while, but it's not very pleasant there. Robert Maddox and Dr Wainwright are sorting out all the paperwork tomorrow I think.'

'I don't think Maddox has had to deal with a fatality before. I'm sure that Wainwright will sort him out. I was ringing to say that I'm home alone tomorrow as Lexi has booked a train ticket to Manchester and is spending the day shopping with her sister. I was hoping that, as it's the summer holidays and you're not teaching, I could invite myself to dinner tomorrow. I could get to you by mid-morning, would that be OK?'

'It'd be lovely to see you Benji. Matt's gone back home, but you might be lucky and catch Jonti before he heads back to the city. I warn you though, he's been rehearsing some disrespectful insults about your police band. I'm sure Emma and Nathaniel will join in and bring Primrose over. Perhaps we might strike lucky and entice Matt back for the evening?'

'It'll be quite a family gathering. We'll see if Jonti is man enough to practise those insults to my face, hey? I'll see you as soon as I can tomorrow morning.'

After pleasant "good byes" until tomorrow Beth returned to the kitchen with renewed vigour. An impromptu dinner for seven used to be something that she could concoct without batting an eyelid not so long ago. These days it was mostly just herself and Drew, or maybe a guest or two and so Beth decided to take the easy way out and rustle up something in the slow cooker. That way she wouldn't miss any precious family time later in the day either. She pulled a couple of packs of mince out of the freezer that she'd bagged up from her bulk buy from the abattoir next to the farm and as a last minute extravagance she put the oven on a low 150° and whisked up half a dozen egg whites with sugar to make two meringue bases. They could be cooking for an hour as she set about clearing the dishes which would otherwise have waited until the morning. Once the dishes were done and the hour was up she could cut the thermostat on the oven and go to bed, leaving the meringues to cool slowly overnight. It was "even odds" whether they would stay intact and be served tomorrow as Strawberry Pavlova or if they would crumble as she removed the baking parchment and become separate servings of Eton Mess. Either way they wouldn't last long at the dinner table. Upstairs Drew finally drifted into sleep listening to the same noises that had awoken him earlier that same day - Beth clattering around the kitchen without panache.

Chapter Six

At 9am Sergeant Maddox rang Jean Barlow's doorbell once again. She answered the door looking much brighter and more alert than the previous evening. It was to be supposed that a night's rest had done her some good. 'Hello Robert - I'm sorry, Sergeant Maddox. Come inside. I must apologise for being less than helpful last night. I really wasn't my usual self.' said Jean.

'Oh, no need to apologise Mrs Barlow. You'd had a bad shock yesterday and you mustn't know whether you're coming or going even now.' said Maddox as he followed Jean into the hall.

'Well, of course it was a shock, but I think what I needed was some time to myself to sit and be quiet. I'm sure that Eileen and Betty meant well but they were driving me crazy. I don't think that I ever want to see a cup of sweet tea again! Once I was left to myself I had a glass of sherry and a hot bath. After that and night's sleep I feel much better and ready to face things.'

'It's very brave of you Mrs Barlow.'

'Even so, I'm not sure that I can be any more help to you than I was last night because I really didn't have much to do with John's business and can't tell you what his concerns were. I'm surprised that you have to look into it all so much as you do. I'm very sorry to put you to all this extra work, not that I can help that of course. I'll do what I can, that's all I can offer.'

'If you could just put your thinking cap on please, Mrs Barlow. Can you suggest any small indication of what might have been such a stress to your husband? We're trying to finalise the paperwork and need to dot the "I"s and cross the "T"s. Because we presume that John was alone when he died Dr Wainwright needs to be able to suggest an underlying cause of death as John's medical history wasn't acute and so his death is unexplained at the moment. If I can just have a browse through his business paperwork and if I think I need to take something away with me I'll give you a receipt and get it back to you as soon as I can.'

'Take whatever you need, and there's no need to bring anything quickly back. It's not as if I'll know what to do with it all. I suppose I'll have to get Gareth Foster to help me sort things out as soon as I think I can face it.'

'I don't think there's any rush for that sort of thing. Just take your time and I'm sure everybody will help you when you need it.'

'Here is John's study. Give me a shout if you need me. It's Henrietta's morning here and instead of cleaning I've asked her to help me upstairs. We're going through John's things. I know it's ridiculously hard on the heels with John only dying yesterday, but I feel better getting on and dealing with it instead of trying to ignore matters.'

Maddox blushed a little at the mention of Henrietta being in the house and he quickly stepped into the study to hide his embarrassment. As he sat in the leather swivel chair he could hear the ladies upstairs. He listened to Henrietta's voice as they discussed where would be best to donate certain items and he thought that she would be more helpful to Jean than the fussing old ladies last night. Realising that he was sitting staring idly into space he sat up and focussed upon his own task in hand. As he had expected John's office was meticulously tidy. The only items which sat on the desk were a lap-top computer and desk calendar which still displayed the date that John had died and suggested that John must have been in his office even on that busy day. The desk was made of light beech wood and curved to follow the corner of the room. The office chair faced the corner of the wall and nestled into the curve of the desk. On a shelf to the right of the chair sat a printer which was well stocked with paper and on the wall, at the end of the left hand side of the desk, stood a filing cabinet which proved to be locked. Maddox lifted the lid of the lap-top and as he was waiting for the screen to load he wondered if John was the sort to make much use of a computer. The loaded printer suggested that it was in use. Maybe he was a "silver surfer"? As the screen awoke a password encryption page loaded and confirmed that John made proper use of his computer. He'd have to take this away and one of the boffins at the station would have to find a way into the hard drive. Quitting off and closing the screen he shifted his attention to the desk drawers.

Beginning methodically with the top desk drawer Maddox removed all of the contents and placed them onto the surface of the desk. After carefully inspecting each item he either replaced irrelevant items back into the drawer they came from or he placed objects of interest into a plastic zip-lock bag to take away and study more carefully.

Anything that went into the bag was itemised on a receipt pad. So far the plastic bags contained the laptop, some business letters, a couple of outstanding invoices and some brochures featuring a holiday home. In his hand he held a week-to-view desk diary and he was flicking through the pages of this when Henrietta knocked on the study door and came into the room carrying a tray holding a mug of tea (with three sugars, according to his taste) and a plate of digestives. Overcoming his shyness he asked Henrietta to ask Jean if she knew where John kept the keys to the filing cabinet. She nodded her head in acknowledgement as she left the study and Maddox gradually managed to turn his attention back to the diary and continued to flip ahead to the date of the Fête. He disregarded the earlier entries as too out of date to be of interest. On the week of the Fête, amongst reminders to make optician's appointments, scheduled social engagements and notes about the poultry competition a name caught his attention. It was scribbled in the margin of the page that held the date of the Fête and so there was no way of knowing if it was intended to be attributed to any of those particular days at all. It may have just been jotted down there as it was the only piece of paper to hand - there were certainly no notepads or scraps of paper anywhere on the desk now, nor did it seem likely that there ever were. It was a name that Maddox was sure he'd heard before. It rang a bell in his head, but he couldn't put his finger on who it was or where he'd heard the name before. The fact that it was written on the page of the Fête could be just that - maybe it was something to do with the arrangements of the Fête.   The fact that John had died at that particular stage in the diary raised the pitch of the bell that was ringing.   All that he could do was to place the diary in the zip-lock case and think about it later.

As he was writing the entry of the diary onto the receipt of items to be taken Jean came into the room with several bunches of keys. 'Have you found anything of interest?' she asked.

'Just the usual run-of-the mill stuff, really. Invoices, letters and so on.   Do you know who C. Jefferson is?' said Maddox.

Jean wrinkled her brow in an effort of concentration but ended by shaking her head in the negative. 'Is it a man or a woman?' she asked.

'I was rather hoping that you could tell me.' said Maddox.

'Well, if it was a woman you can be sure that it was strictly business.' said Jean. 'John really wasn't the philandering type.   He was much too typically respectable - boring, you might say. Certainly not the sort to have a secret of that sort.'

Maddox looked startled and quickly said, 'Oh, no! I wasn't meaning anything like that Mrs Barlow.' and he was ashamed to admit to himself that the thought really hadn't entered his head.   And yet, why not? Old people had love affairs, didn't they? He still couldn't comprehend it and yet he realised that he was being naive. As a policeman he should consider all possibilities and it was foolish of him to not reckon on the seedier side of life.

'I really can't think who it is. I'm sure I've not heard the name before. I'm sorry that I can't be more helpful. These are all the keys that I can find. I presume that the ones you are looking for will be amongst them.' Jean placed a selection of keys on the desk and turned away to carry on bagging up John's personal effects.

Maddox reflected that this prompt business-like way of bagging up someone's life so quickly after their death - someone so close, was really quite sad. To have to bottle up grief so soon and get on with business highlighted the fragility of Jean's situation. He thought of his own mum when his dad had died suddenly. He was only fifteen at the time and it had hit both him and his mum hard. He'd rallied quite quickly - youthful exuberance wasn't easy to quench, and he'd got his friends to rally round him too. He remembered anew how fragile his mum had seemed at the time but she had in fact been really tough. Of course his mum had her friends to help her too, but it was bound to hit her hardest. He realised now that having to look after a son must have been the mainstay for his mum. Jean and John hadn't had any children and so what else was there for Jean to do but clear away and move on? Such forthright practicality was more pitiable to him now than the stereotypical helplessness and a wave of sympathy for Jean swept over him as he realised how he'd misjudged her.

Shaking off his melancholy he turned his attention to the pile of keys. The shape he was searching for was easily recognisable and he quickly ignored the ubiquitous shed keys that had probably not fitted into any shed lock for a very long time. Garage keys and defunct door keys could also be quickly laid aside. The few likely candidates remaining were carried over to the filing cabinet to be tried. His first attempts were unsuccessful and he realised that these were more likely to be UPVC window keys. The penultimate key proved successful and he treated the contents of the filing cabinet to the same methodic treatment which had served him at the desk. This time however he worked from bottom to top, judging the lower drawers to be the most out of date as it was unlikely that John would want to be stooping down to low files on a regular basis. This proved correct and the lower drawers held nothing of interest. The topmost drawer appeared to be given over to the last six months of business and so Maddox concentrated on this. If John had needed to surface from retirement recently as a result of business worries then the secret would probably be in this drawer. Maybe he would find something here to account for a sudden medical relapse. He might find a hefty fine from the authorities, an exceeded overdraft or a court summons. From what he had heard and from the paperwork he had found it seemed that John's property interests were focussed mainly in Greece and Spain with just a splash of speculation in France. Maddox was surprised to learn that, not only did John own and lease out residential properties, he also owned a beach bar in Spain. He was sure that Jean would be equally surprised about these interests too. He bagged up some outstanding invoices and some letters from the Greek tax authority and then began to tidy up and prepared to leave. He met Henrietta in the hallway. She was lugging heavy duty black bin liners full of shirts and pullovers ready to be taken to the church hall to be given to various charitable causes. 'You're not going to manage all of those! Can't you get a lift with all these bags?' he said.

'Oh, I shan't take them all at once. I'll just take a bag at a time. I'm leaving in a moment so I thought I'd make a start with one or two.' said Henrietta.

'Just give me a moment to ask Jean to sign these receipts and then I'll come with you and carry a couple as we go. That'll be two less at least.'

Maddox thanked Jean for her help and got her signature for the items he was taking away and then joined Henrietta in the hallway. Adding a couple of overflowing bin bags to his loaded zip-lock cases he made his way with her into the street. 'I'm glad that you're helping Jean out. I don't think I've properly understood her and I put her down as something of a dragon.'

'Jean's all right. She's a bit strict, but she pitches in like the rest of us. She's not too easy to get to know, that's all.'

'Folks could say that about you.' said Maddox.

'I don't know how you dare!' said Henrietta, but she laughed as she said it. 'It's not easy moving into a little village where everybody really does know everybody else. How can I be expected to jump straight in and get chatting to everybody. I can't just butt in, can I? I'm settling in gradually, thank you for asking.'

'I'm sorry, that didn't come across too well at all did it? I'm glad that you're getting to know Emma. Did you enjoy the Fête?'

'Yes, I did. It really helped me and Toby feel a part of things, finally. I learned how to bake a million cupcakes too! It's such a shame that John died at the Fête. I don't know why but it seems worse for him to have died there and on that day. But that's nonsense, isn't it? There's no good time or place really, is there? '

'No, but I know what you mean. It's not very private, that's for sure.'

'Why are you having to go poking around his stuff? Can't Dr Wainwright just say "He died." and have done with it? People do just die.'

'I'm afraid it's never so simple. On the death certificate he has to give a reason for the death and because John had no acute medical history he has to give a tangible reason for the death. He can't just base it on hearsay, we have to give evidence to support any reasoning. It's more complicated too because nobody was with him when he died, or at least nobody has come forward to say that they were there. I'm meeting Dr Wainwright this lunchtime so I'm hoping we can tie it all up today. I'll have to be guided by him.'

'I hope you get it tidied up soon. Jean is a quite a tough cookie, but I do wonder what's going on beneath the surface. She must need closure before she can properly think about looking ahead.'

They'd reached the church hall at this point in the conversation. Bobby deposited the bags of clothing in the entrance to the church hall and made his way back to the police station with an extra jauntiness in his step.

Detective Chief Inspector Benedict James of Winsford Police HQ, Cheshire was sitting at Beth's kitchen table cradling a steaming mug of hot coffee in his cupped hands. His whole demeanour brought to mind solid oak. It wasn't merely the fact that he wore a brown checked shirt with brown corduroy trousers. His entire stature was one of solidity. He was tall and broad with thickset limbs. His brown hair, which was becoming peppered with a distinguished grey, and his gentle brown eyes confirmed the impression but it was more to do with an aura of rock-solid dependability. There was a penetrating shrewdness in his gaze but the wrinkles around the edges of his eyes hinted at a kindness and a willingness to smile, given half a chance. Beth was positively diminutive when standing next to her twin. In childhood it was common in mixed sex twins for the girl to be born the biggest. This had been the case with Beth and Benedict, but as soon soon as Benedict's years hit double figures he made up for lost time and soon towered over his sister and very little of their early physical similarities remained. However, the mutual bond of understanding had not diminished. Very few words needed to be spoken and subtleties in conversation between them were quickly comprehended. They were now discussing the untimely demise of John Barlow.

'Drew met Dr Wainwright on his way to begin his morning surgery and was told that he was meeting with Bobby Maddox this lunchtime. They're hoping to pin down a suitable cause of death. As there was no serious medical history and nobody witnessed the death it isn't plain sailing. I think they're hoping to thrash it out today so that they can give Fred Brough the go-ahead to begin funeral preparations.' said Beth.

'Do you think they'd mind if I stepped along and stuck my nose in for a while?' asked Benedict.

'I'm sure they'd be glad of your advice, but I don't think there's much to attract your curiosity.'

'You know me, I can't resist meddling. If I see a couple of loose strands I can't help but give them a pull. Do you mind if I abandon you for a while? I won't be long and I'll keep you up to date with the gossip - as far as professional etiquette allows, of course.' Benedict gave his sister a wry smile which suggested that he was prepared to significantly stretch the boundaries of professional etiquette. Nevertheless, he knew from past experience that Beth could keep a secret.

'Of course, you go off to play. I'll get my head around what to do with these meringue bases until you get back. Come back for some lunch if you can.'

Inspector James walked into the waiting room of the Doctor's surgery and explained to the receptionist that he knew that the Doctor was in a meeting with Sergeant Maddox but would she please interrupt the meeting and say that DCI James of Winsford HQ would like to join them. He was sure that it would be OK and they wouldn't mind her interrupting them. He knew that if he hadn't added the full weight of his title she would never have considered breaking protocol. The mention of police HQ did the job and he was soon escorted into the consulting room. Surrounded by blood pressure cuffs, plastic models of the heart and the digestive system and other medical paraphernalia sat Sergeant Maddox endeavouring to spread out relevant examples of the paperwork he'd found earlier that day. He and Dr Wainwright happily greeted Inspector James and drew up a chair at the already cramped desk so that he could join them.

'Hello James, how good of you to join us. Surely you can't be here in an official capacity? said Dr Wainwright, glancing over James' decidedly unofficial attire.

'Goodness me, no.' said James 'Beth has been telling me all about it and because I was "on the spot," so to speak I couldn't resist sticking my nose in. How are you getting along?'

'I've looked into John's appearance when we found him dead. Maddox has the photographs here if you want to see. I can say, quite certainly, that he died of a heart attack. That's the easy bit - you can see he face is the classic cherry red. My problem is that I can't suggest what caused the heart attack. The death certificate stipulates the need to state an underlying cause, as you know. In other cases I could put "Myocardial infarction owing to diabetes mellitus (Type II)," but in this instance I really don't think that will do. John had absolutely no history of heart disease and had only the mild onset of Type II diabetes which was well regulated. He'd had no sort of diabetic episode at all. Our only other line of explanation would be that of undue stress. There's no doubt that extreme stress can do strange things to a man and so that's what we're searching for evidence of now.' said Wainwright.

'You're absolutely right not to jump to conclusions. For all we know he might have swallowed two bottles of paracetamol that morning in an attempt to get out of judging the poultry competition'. said James.

'I know that you're joking but I'd made the same joke last night. I suppose it isn't a joking matter but it raises new possibilities, doesn't it?' said Maddox.

'Don't you worry about joking, young man. In our job it's the only way to cope. There's no disrespect in it. Nevertheless, sometimes it brings to light avenues you might otherwise have missed. There's always a surprise around the corner.' said James.

'It's strange that you should say that. When John died I remembered my medical tutor telling me "Always be ready to be surprised." That's the problem with John's death, I am surprised. I certainly didn't expect him to die and I can't think why he did. I have no alternative explanation for his death, but I can't honestly sign the death certificate as things stand now. I don't know what to think.' said Wainwright. 'From what I knew of him I don't honestly think that John Barlow was the type to commit suicide but as I have no reasonable explanation I'm sorry to say that I think I'll have to refer the case to the coroner. I'm sorry for Jean, but it's my neck on the line if I submit shoddy paperwork. What's your advice, James?'

'I suppose that you'll get referred to Winsford in the end, which is my patch, so I might as well jump in straight away as I'm here. I'll give the office a call now and speak to the coroner to get things moving right away. If you'll just excuse me for a moment I'll step into the corridor and make some calls.'

As DCI James naturally assumed command Sergeant Maddox sagged with relief. 'I'm so glad that Inspector James is here. I don't like to think of facing Jean Barlow with the news without some stiff hierarchy behind me. She won't dare argue with him though.' he said.

'It may not amount to much. Just because the case has been referred to the coroner it doesn't necessarily mean that any further investigation will be required. Nevertheless, I quite agree with you. I'm glad to have Detective Chief Inspector James at my back.' agreed Wainwright.

Some ten minutes later James walked back into the room and gave a nod in answer to their enquiring glances. 'I've spoken to the coroner and after outlining the basics of the situation he's given me the go-ahead to begin a few preliminary enquiries. We both agree that our first port of call is to get a full toxicology report. That should end matters once and for all, or it will give us a clue as to what we do next.

I'll give some of the chaps at HQ a call and they can whizz over with their various syringes but it'll take weeks of bending over petri dishes before they come through with any results - if there are any to be found.'

'It all seems a bit drastic, don't you think?' said Maddox.

'That depends upon what you think is drastic. We certainly can't make up the death certificate for a quiet life and we'll just have to do a bit of digging in the mean time. Now don't think that I've come along to take over. I'm just here to lend a hand and give a bit of weight where I can to speed things along. I've spoken to your boss, Maddox, and she's happy for you to be my wing man for the present. She just asks that you report back to her regularly and keep her informed, so don't you go getting me into trouble by ignoring her or putting her nose out of joint.'

The doctor and police sergeant made it quite obvious that they were more than happy for Detective Chief Inspector Benedict James to take over. He continued to plan their strategy and suggested that while they waited for his team to arrive they continue browsing through the material from John's office. 'Why don't we get back to my sister's house? We can continue there. I don't know about you but I'm ravenous and there isn't room to swing a cat in here.' said James.

Maddox stood up and began to gather the strewn paperwork but Dr Wainwright said that he needed to prepare for his afternoon's consulting session. 'Now that I can hand over the follow-up to you, James, and Maddox isn't on his own with this I need to get back to my own work. This is your show now, but I'd be grateful if you'd keep me in the loop. Now that I've set this ball rolling I'd like to keep an eye on it and see where it ends. If you need any medical information you know you've only got to ask.' said Wainwright.

Assuring him that they'd stay in regular contact James and Maddox left the doctor and walked back to Beth's. As they walked Maddox gave an overview of what he'd noted in the business documents so far. 'Overall I'd say that business was a bit tricky for John just recently. I'd no idea he'd got his finger in so many pies. Generally speaking it appears that income was drying up as overheads were mounting up. The same old story really, but on a grand scale. Tenants were getting pretty thin on the ground in Greece as the Greek Government was continually increasing property tax, which must have been reflected in the rental fees. This isn't a surprise really when you think of the Euro crash from a few years ago. I'm guessing it was a similar situation in Spain. Business in his bars must be suffering since the decline in tourism there. That's the general drift I got from the paperwork. I've got some outstanding bills, letters from the Greek Tax authorities and so on but I've no idea of the severity of the situation - you'd need an accountant to comment on that. Maybe it's desperate or maybe its just a blip. I'd be terrified at dealing with those kinds of figures but maybe it's all just in a day's work.'

'No doubt we'll be getting to know his accountant and solicitor quite well over the next few weeks. Was there anything else of interest?'

'I've got John's lap-top here with me, but it's password encrypted so I don't know if there's anything there. I didn't have John down as the cyber-secret type. There is one thing that did spark my interest, but I can't put my finger on why. In John's diary, on the margin of the page that was the date of the Fête alongside a note to book an optician's appointment, there was a name scribbled. I'm sure that I've heard the name before but I can't place who it is or where I've heard the name. Does C. Jefferson mean anything to you? I asked Jean and she has no idea who it is.' said Maddox.

James whistled through his teeth and said, 'I'm quite sure she didn't know the name. Well now. My oh my, it seems that our Mr Barlow might be a bit grubbier around the edges than we all thought.'

Chapter Seven

Jonti had finally surfaced from his old bedroom and the various members of the band had cleared themselves and their bedding away, de-littering ad hoc sofa beds and chairs, and were now awaiting a train back to Manchester. On hearing that his Uncle was visiting for the day Jonti had rearranged his plans so as to join in the family dinner. He was just leaving the house to round up and evict any hangers-on that had commandeered his sister's lounge for the night as he met his Uncle in the doorway. A hearty hand shake and the mandatory banter surrounding Benedict's involvement in the police band ensued. Sergeant Maddox deposited his cargo onto the kitchen table and Inspector James asked about the prospect of lunch.

'I'm making some cheese on toast for me and Drew, will that do?' said Beth. Recognising their hungry nods as agreement she turned the grill on and set to preparing lunch. Beth began slicing the white, crumbly Cheshire cheese - which was the only acceptable form of cheese to adorn toast in that area. Sliced tomatoes and brown sauce provided the perfect accompaniment to the mild flavour and saltiness of the cheese from that district. Once one side of the wholemeal bread was toasted she loaded the slices with the cheese and set it under the grill. It quickly bubbled to satisfaction and after topping the slices with the sauce and tomatoes she set it before the policemen with hot drinks before ringing the bell to summons Drew to come and eat his lunch. The silver service bell was something of a standing joke in the village. Beth had introduced the institution when the children were small, saying that she was weary of yelling across the house, or down the garden to alert the family that a meal was ready. The fact that the neighbours often also knew that a meal was ready to be served was of secondary importance. These days she rang the bell out of habit and her only concession to the limited radius of appeal meant that she sounded the toll with less gusto and less repeatedly than in previous years. It evidently still performed its duty as Drew ambled into the kitchen like Pavlov's dog expecting to be fed.

Between mouthfuls of creamy cheese on toast they all chatted about the recent turn of events. It wasn't necessary to procure promises of silence or mention the concept of breach of confidentiality - it was already understood. Having a Detective Chief Inspector in the family made this a matter of course and Benedict would never have divulged anything of an overly sensitive nature. He was quite happy to set up a temporary centre of operations in his sister's kitchen. The tongue-and-groove panelled walls had been privy to many mysteries in the past and many a misdemeanour had been solved over the large pine breakfast table. The hospitality and canteen arrangements were far more conducive to thought than a stark office. After explaining that matters might not be as straightforward as they at first hoped the two policemen began to talk amongst themselves, referring at intervals to invoices and letters. Drew returned to his art studio and Beth continued with the washing up and preparing for the evening meal in-between topping up the mugs of the engrossed policemen.

'You say that you know who this C. Jefferson is then.' said Maddox. The inflection of his voice lifted at the end of the sentence turning his statement into a question.

'I know who it could be and I doubt there could be two of such a name cropping up in an enquiry like this one. The only Jefferson that I know of around here is Conrad Jefferson, a potentially respectable businessman and also an executive fraudster. He did a stint inside not too long ago and came out early on the grounds of it being his first offence and on good behaviour. It may well have been his first conviction but we're all quite sure that his list of offences would be as long as your arm if he wasn't clever enough not to get caught before. The only surprise is that he got caught this time.'

'I knew I'd heard the name. It was quite the topic of conversation when I came to HQ last year on a training course. I'd heard that he'd finally been sentenced but I've no idea who he is or what he looks like.'

'He's a personable chap, quite likeable really - just too clever for his own good.' said James. He picked up his iPad and, after passing through a variety of security screens pulled up a photograph of Jefferson.

Without thinking Beth looked over her brother's shoulder to look at the image and said, 'I saw him yesterday! He was at the Fête. He came to our stall with a lady, I presumed it was his wife. He looked thoroughly bored, though he didn't complain.

I think he was trying to be interested and offered to buy her anything she wanted. They bought quite a lot off us in the end.'

'Now that is interesting.' said James. 'It's a bit too much of coincidence for my liking - though I can't imagine what it is that I'm inferring. Even so, I think that we shall have to pay him a visit. He lives in Harrisfield. His story is that, after succumbing to the temptation to embezzle away company funds - just the once, mind you, he says that he's learned his lesson and is staying on the straight and narrow for sure now. What can he be doing turning up in this chain of events? I think that he can wait his turn for now, though. I'd better get along to Brough's to meet the Forensic boys and girls, Do you want to come along, Maddox?'

'I don't think that I'm overly keen to see anyone shove hypodermics into a body that's been dead a day already, thank you. I'll report back to the station and then head off home, if you don't mind of course.'

'Fair enough, though you'll have to overcome such squeamishness sooner or later. Leave this paperwork with me for the time being, I'll look after it - don't you worry. I'll be getting back to the office in the morning to see how they want to play things and I'll give you a call some time tomorrow to tell you how the land lies.'

As Maddox closed the back door James sat back down at the kitchen table. 'I'll have another coffee before I make my way to Brough's if you don't mind. I've got a bit of time if Maddox isn't keen to be initiated in the wonders of Forensic retrieval. There's no point me hanging around and watching them. I want to have another look over some of these papers so I've got a good grasp on things before I speak to the Super' tomorrow. The toxicology report will be a month or so before we get any results back and we'll have to do the best we can until then. There's no point in guessing what he might have done and I need to establish some facts.'

He reached out and opened up the lap-top and then sighed with exasperation at his futile attempts to get past the password screen. 'I'll have to hand this over to the lads at HQ. Once they get their hands on it they'll get into it in no time at all, but no doubt I'll have to join a very long queue to get it to them. I'll be waiting for weeks to probably discover there was nothing worth bothering about in the first place. I'd like to have a good look at Mr Barlow's dealings now that I know his name is tenuously linked with Jefferson. There's nothing for it but to sit and wait my turn. It's so annoying doing nothing just because you're in a queue. I hate having to sit around.'

Beth looked thoughtfully at her brother and made the staged gesture of a polite cough. 'If you don't mind bending a few rules I might just be able to help you out there.' she said.

'How on earth can you do that?' he asked. 'I know your computer skills, you can just about manage Facebook and e-mail. What do you propose to do?'

'Well, when I say I may be able to help you, what I mean is that I know that I can definitely direct you to somebody who can. Do you remember Kirsty Pepper from the WI? Her husband, Carlton, is a computer code whizz and strictly under the radar he's quite something of a hacker - for purely altruistic purposes, of course. He hasn't got a criminal bone in his body, which is quite a loss to the underworld I'm sure. If he decided to turn delinquent he'd be unbeatable.'

'I can't believe you're telling me this, Beth. Just how wide does your dubious network spread?'

'Well, do you want a peep inside that computer, or don't you?'

Beth's brother sat considering the proposal for some minutes before he replied. 'I think that it's high time I walked over to Brough's. While I'm out, if that lap-top becomes mysteriously unlocked I won't wonder too much about it. If we find nothing of interest the we can magically lock it away again and let it rot in a queue without further worry. If we find anything that proves useful then I can quietly pursue my lines of enquiry and when I need to reference the information I can date it back to our official access into John's computer system. That should cover it.'

Detective Chief Inspector James laced up his walking boots and made his way to the funeral directors. Hardly had the door closed behind him when Beth picked up the telephone and scrolled through the contacts list to select P for Pepper. 'Hello Carlton. I wonder if you're free to quickly help me out in something of a covert operation?' She explained the situation and it wasn't long before Carlton was sitting at the kitchen table. He looked as though he was absentmindedly tapping away at the keyboard in an haphazard manner as Drew walked into the kitchen for a tea break. Carlton began to plug an external hard drive into the lap-top and was soon sitting back contentedly in his chair as the files copied over. The atmosphere lightened at the prospect of a done deed and as the files flew across the cable Carlton and Beth made a joint effort of explaining the situation to Drew. Carlton explained that there was no need for him to actually see any of the content of the computer, in fact he had made sure not to read anything. He had merely created a carbon copy of what was on the computer and stored it onto the external device. Once he had shut everything down it would be as if he'd never been there.

'When your brother's finished with it all could he please return the hard drive. He could either wipe the contents before he sent it back or I'll do it without reading anything. There's no rush though. Tell him to take his time.' said Carlton.

'Goodness, such espionage at the humble breakfast table!' said Drew. 'I wash my hands of the lot of you'. He smiled as he said this, which belied his intention to get well and truly into the heart of the matter. 'I suppose that it's just a short cut, really. We know that Carlton is as discreet as they come. I guess it's OK. How's come your brother is involved in all of this? What's the to-do?' Beth explained the query regarding the cause of John's death and the appearance of the name of Jefferson in the diary.

'Conrad Jefferson you say? He's a decent enough fellow. He's got a massive property portfolio and runs a building company - elitist stuff, not your usual housing estate developer. I do artistic impressions of his architectural plans from time to time. He's very clever, a bit too smart sometimes and I think he was in prison for a while, but I've never had any trouble from him.'

'I thought I'd seen his face before. He came to the Fête with what I assumed was his wife. I didn't realise who he was though.' said Beth.

'I'll be hurrying along before your brother gets back, just for form's sake. We don't want any awkward overlap, do we? Nevertheless, tell him that I say "Hi".' said Carlton.

As Benedict was walking to Brough's his mobile phone bleeped to tell him that the Forensic team was nearly finished. In reality this comprised a few members of the department that were bursting to get out of the office. Just one person would have been sufficient but they cheekily assured Detective Chief Inspector James that more was necessary for protocol, and they wanted him to have the best service possible. They assured him that they fully understood his need for prompt action and had sensibly employed the flashing blue lights for the whole drive there - nothing was too much trouble.

'Well now, that's very reassuring. Just make sure you maintain the same attitude and get the results back to me with the same lightning speed.' said James.

'Of course, Sir. But you do realise that petri dishes don't have accelerators or blue lights.' replied Forbes, the bravest of the team.

'Silly me. Nevertheless, unless you want a long stint of office work I suggest that you invent some. Now that you've begun with such gusto I expect it to continue.' said James. He clapped the likeable rogue across the shoulders and walked with him to the funeral parlour's morgue.

Benedict James knew Fred Brough through many years of visiting his sister and joining in on the edge of village life. A round of conversational pleasantries was the precursor to the grittier aspect of the visit. Brough's staff were sensible, professional and the epitome of discretion. After being asked to leave John's body as it had been found they didn't need any further explanation. Nobody asked questions and they simply got on with their other work. Apart from moving John into a horizontal position everything had stayed as it was and had been left well alone until they were told to do otherwise. John was brought out to them on a stainless steel trolley. His eyelids were still open and his eyes were still gazing strangely upward. The flush of blood to his face, which had suggested a heart attack to Dr Wainwright, was still evident but had settled as he had lain. Forbes explained that samples of fibre from John's clothing and matter from under his nails had been bagged, more as a matter of form than for any particular reason.

'I thought that, as we don't really know what we're looking for, too many specimens is better than too few. We can discard what we don't need but we can't come back for more when it's too late.' he said.

'Good man. I don't know if we're looking for anything at all, but you're right. Log down anything at all that you find whether you think it's of interest or not.' said James.

'We've garnered what traces we could, even if they might now be contaminated and we've had to cut through garments so that we don't disturb the body. We've taken blood samples from the femoral artery and we've catheterised urine samples. We've also taken swabs from the mouth and nasal cavity, and some hair samples - including the roots. Other than that the only thing we can do is take some photographs with the clothing removed, after that it's a full autopsy. Do you want some snaps taking, Sir?'

'I think you might as well. If you've got what you need from the clothing there's no need to keep him in rags. You might as well take some pictures while you're at it. Let me know if you find anything of interest. I'm trusting you to apply the blue lights again, and I don't just mean as you drive home.'

'We'll do our best, Sir.'

James went to thank Fred for his help and to also ask for more. 'Can you keep him here for a bit longer please, Fred? I can't release the body for burial just yet but I don't really want him moved to the police morgue to then have to bring him straight back. I also don't want to set tongues wagging by carting the body off. If you start running out of space or if it becomes an inconvenience just call me.

Hopefully it won't be for too long, I just want to satisfy a few question marks for now.'

'We're not expecting to be busy at this time. You know how it gets busy at the end of winter, or during a particularly hot summer, but we're hoping to enjoy a bit of a lull for the moment. There's no rush at all as far as I'm concerned and I agree it's better John's body stays here. I presume that you want him untouched still. I'll side-step any questions and I don't think Jean is keen to view the body again, so all should be quiet on the home front.' said Fred.

'I really appreciate that, thank you Fred. The team have bagged up the clothing, so I'll leave it all in your capable hands to cover him appropriately. I'll try and let you the state of play as soon as I can.'

DCI James rallied his troops. He knew that some of these tests took weeks to garner results, but the sooner they could get started the sooner he'd know how matters stood. A thought struck him, it was a pity that Beth didn't know any toxicologists that she could conscript. She had always had an uncanny flair for networking people together and had made herself very popular by introducing friends and acquaintances. Quite a few marriages owed their origins to her subtly disguised guidance and no small number of business partners had met and materially flourished under her discreet influence. Now the criminal justice system was being fast tracked by her guiding hand. In the domestic setting her skills were overlooked but if she ever chose to move into more executive circles she would be a formidable force. Only Benedict and

Drew had ever openly discussed this with Beth but she always minimised her influence and said that village life suited her best. She said that she felt like the business world was a "let's pretend" environment and much preferred the grittier subject of village life as the arena to work within. Benedict thought of his Grandmother, after the war. All of her intellectual achievements were sunk from notoriety and acclaim was far from her mind. Who would ever really know how many lives she had saved through her perceptive reading of codes and systems within enemy communication? For the rest of her life all of her efforts were focussed around nurturing a healthy intellect and a passion for problem solving in her children. Beth was just like her Gran, using her skills for the benefit of others without tribute or applause. It was such strength that made him really respect the women he knew. He was sure that most of the men he worked with couldn't stand to work in such anonymity. He thought that his Gran would be pleased with her legacy. Thankfully they were no longer living in a time of war, but he hoped that they were still putting their skills to good use. The thought of another broken code quickened his pace as he hurried to see what awaited him at Beth's.

As he walked through the kitchen door Benedict's eyes fell onto the lap-top which, as far as he could tell, was exactly where he had left it. It's lid was down. Beth and Drew watched him as he raised the lid and begin to initiate the software. The same password encrypted screen greeted him as before and he looked at them in confusion.

'Did you have any visitors while I was out?' he asked.

'Were you expecting anyone?' said Beth. Unable to contain herself any longer she handed him the hard drive. Attempting nonchalance she said, 'You might like to look at this when you've a spare moment or two. Oh, and Carlton sends his best regards too.'

Benedict gave a hearty laugh and said, 'You had me there for sure. Go on then - off the record, tell me all.'

'There's hardly anything to tell, really. As far as I understood Carlton quickly by-passed the security screen and merely copied everything off the lap-top onto that external hard drive. Nobody has seen a single file.' said Beth.

'I took the wrong moment to take a tea break and now I'm "accessory after the fact" in a web of intrigue.' said Drew.

'In essence you have John's computer in your hand and nobody is any the wiser.' said Beth. Carlton politely requests that you return the hard drive when you've finished with it. He says that there's no rush and either you can wipe it clean before you return it or you can trust him to delete everything without looking - and you can trust him, I'm sure. He really isn't interested in looking, so you needn't worry.'

That's a most unusual character trait in a computer hacker. Are you sure he doesn't fancy a career change?' said Benedict.

They put aside the business of the day and settled into private family mode. They had planned to eat early in the evening so that Primrose could join in. The men retired to the lounge and Beth began the final touches to the meal. The mincemeat had eventually transformed into a Chilli con Carne as even Primrose was happy to eat a robust chilli dish. A rocket salad was draining in a colander in the sink and some nachos awaited a quick course in a hot oven once the family arrived. Some overripe tomatoes, green peppers and lemon juice converged in the blender to make a quick salsa dip and a tin of budget, tinned chilli mixed with a tub of cream cheese made a surprisingly tasty extra dip. One of the meringue bases had predictably crumbled so both were consigned to a plastic bag and were mistreated with a wooden spoon before being sandwiched between layers of strawberries and whipped cream in sundae dishes.

Jonti walked across the village holding Primrose's hand, having evidently enjoyed the privilege of being favourite Uncle for the afternoon. Nathaniel and Emma followed soon after. As they walked up to the house they could see that Matt had arrived too. When the family were gathered in the lounge poor Primrose couldn't choose which male relative to bestow her affections on first but drifted between hugs until it was time for the dinner bell to sound. It was her job to ring the bell and no amount of doting Uncles could diminish her pleasure in such a responsibility. At the meal table she combined attention as best she could by sitting between her two

Uncles with the promise that they would swap places with Grandad and Great Uncle Benji during dessert. The conversation around the meal table was a lively mixture of catching up on family news and pleasant banter over conflicting interests. The various merits of two and four wheeled vehicles were extensively covered and then front wheel and rear wheel drive got similar coverage. As expected the topic moved on to music and Jonti's harmless prejudice was given full voice. Uncle Benji kindly reminded Jonti that he had begun his career with the Silk Mill Brass Band at the Blackpool Winter Gardens brass band competitions, so any attempt at snobbery was futile. Jonti gracefully acknowledged that this was so and admitted that he'd enjoyed reliving his past by playing to a largely uninterested crowd in a field only yesterday.

Emma and Nathaniel observed that it was well past Primrose's bed time and stood up to leave. Benedict also got up from the table and volunteered to walk with them, saying he'd like to "stretch his legs" and they could enjoy a chat as they walked. So as to give them a little more time together Beth suggested a small alteration to the plan and took Primrose upstairs. She gave Primrose a wash, brushed her hair, cleaned her teeth and dressed her in a spare pair of pyjamas kept at the house. They then rejoined the party downstairs and she wrapped Primrose into a blanket and set her on Uncle Benji's lap with a warm drink of milk which she drank as the adults chatted. Once her mug was emptied Benedict picked her up in his great arms and, making sure that she was thoroughly tucked into the blanket and his chest, he walked towards "Lilac Cottage" and chatted quietly with Nathaniel about his business and the state of affairs at the dairy farm. Walking up to the cottage they were met by Walter at the gate. Primrose had been asleep for most of the time that they had been walking and talking so Benji carried her up the stairs and tucked her into her small bed. He came back downstairs and stayed chatting as Nathaniel kicked off his boots, waiting for Emma to finish settling Primrose into bed before he returned to Beth's house. Matt had volunteered to drive Jonti back to the city rather than taking him to the train station and they only waited for the return of Uncle Benji to say "good bye" before they left. Drew, Beth and Benji then sat comfortably in amicable silence for some time. Drew then suggested cracking open a bottle of his prize single malt whisky. It was a bottle of Longmorn from a 22 year old cask. He'd become quite a connoisseur since he'd discovered a dedicated website that catered for his little passion. Benji had originally planned to drive back home that night but the mention of a vintage single malt swiftly altered his thinking and he accepted the offer of staying over until the morning when he would make an early start.

Beth kissed each of the gents on the top of the head and said "goodnight" before quickly changing the bedding over and sprucing up the spare room after the guests from the night before. Drew had helped to clear most of the dishes whilst Benji was out walking Primrose home and she gratefully sank into bed.   The remaining dishes could wait until tomorrow.

Chapter Eight

DCI James sat in a squat, square chair set at an angle which directed his large frame towards the desk of Chief Superintendent Holloway. They chatted amiably and the cups of coffee and plate of digestives endorsed the friendly atmosphere. 'What's the situation with the death at Mossleigh then James? I gather that you've spoken to the coroner and have already got your finger well into the pie.' said Holloway.

'I was "on the spot" visiting my sister and thought that I'd have a word with Sgt Maddox and Dr Wainwright while I was there. The doctor wasn't very happy with the sudden demise of John Barlow and didn't feel he could give a satisfactory cause of death with good conscience, although he has no inkling of what the alternatives could be. I don't think that Sergeant Maddox would have had the courage of such convictions and might have encouraged the least line of resistance without intending any harm. It may all be a mare's nest, but I do think that the situation merits a closer look.' said James.

'You know that I trust your judgement, of course. It's better to be sure, but all the same I advise that you tread very carefully. These little villages aren't used to any whiff of real scandal and folks will scare easily.'

James thought of Beth coolly engaging the services of a seasoned computer hacker and suspected that this didn't conform to his boss's idea of the stereotype. Instead of rectifying his superior's misapprehension he said, 'I've asked Fred Brough, the funeral director, to keep the body there so as not to raise any alarm unduly. He's thoroughly discreet so there's no worry there. I agree with you that things shouldn't be blown out of proportion and with that thought in mind I thought it best to keep Sgt Maddox "front of house" for the time being to keep enquiries on a local level. I wanted to ask you if you'd let me oversee this case? Since I started the proceedings I'd like to keep an eye on things myself for as long as it runs - which most probably won't be any time at all. If it does turn out to be more serious it would be referred to us in the end anyway. I also think that it would be a good opportunity for Maddox to gain a bit of on the job mentoring - Continual Professional Development and all that. It'll do him far more good than any amount of courses and he can't get much of a variety of experience in the village.'

'I take your point James, but you have to consider your own workload. You also need to be very careful not to tread on their toes at Mossleigh. These provincial coppers don't like to think that the big boys have muscled onto their patch. Do you and Maddox work well together?'

'He's a nice chap and I think he could be a really good copper if given half a chance to do something other than rescue old ladies' cats. As for my other commitments, I don't see much of a problem as I'll be letting Maddox do all the work and I'll just keep a weather eye on him. I spoke to Inspector Buckley at Mossleigh on the day that I met with Maddox and Wainwright and she didn't seem too bothered, in fact I think she was glad not to have to bother with the Barlow case at all. I've reassured her that we would keep her well informed.'

'I think that settles it then. I'll just give the station at Mossleigh a courtesy call and trust you to keep me in the loop - bearing in mind that I do really mean that, unlike the village Inspector. What's your first port of call?'

'The toxicology report is the crux of the matter, but it'll take weeks to come through even if I lean on the lads in the lab a bit. If I work on the assumption that it's clear in the mean time I'll set Maddox on the trail of Barlow's business affairs. The only sensible explanation that Wainwright can give is that undue stress, owing to business worry, caused the heart attack. That's what we'll need to find evidence for, and already have a couple of leads to follow in that line.'

Over the weekend Primrose had developed a nasty cold and Emma made an appointment to take her to the Doctor's surgery. They took their seats in the waiting area and found themselves sitting next to Betty Barnsford.

'Hello Betty, I would say "How are you?" but that's not really an appropriate question in a doctors waiting room, is it?' said Emma.

'Oh dear, is Primrose poorly?' said Betty, as the reason for Emma's visit was obvious when you looked at the little girl's doleful expression and watery eyes. 'You do always say "How are you?" don't you? Thankfully I'm quite well, this is just a routine appointment. Since I started with my heart trouble I have to have a check up regularly.   I don't really bother to take the tablets Dr Wainwright prescribed for me, they don't make much difference anyway. I'm quite well really and a glass of whisky at bed time does just as much good - but don't tell Dr Wainwright I said that!'

Further conversation was curtailed by the receptionist signalling that Betty needed to move to the consulting room. As they waited their turn Emma cheered Primrose up by suggesting a trip to Gran's house after she'd been seen by the Doctor. When it was Primrose's turn to be seen all the force of Dr Wainwright's charm and bedside manner came into being. He gave her a break-down plastic model of the digestive system to play with as he discussed her symptoms with Emma and then placed the stethoscope on her chest and back. Primrose was unperturbed by these ministrations as she rearranged the digestive system to her own satisfaction. She was confused that the lower intestine wouldn't fit down the oesophagus despite her best efforts.

'I can't hear any signs of infection and we don't like to dole out tablets these days. If you just keep her warm and rested, and make sure that she drinks plenty of fluids she'll soon be on the mend. If you have any concerns though, or she takes a turn for the worse come back straight away.'   said Dr Wainwright. Before Primrose was allowed to leave Dr Wainwright helped Primrose to put the digestive system back to its rightful order, his professional ethics couldn't leave a student (no matter how young) with the misconception that the colon should be joined to the small intestine via the mouth.

Emma wrapped Primrose up in her coat and carried her from the surgery to Beth's house. As she walked into the kitchen Beth was sorting laundry into piles. Forgetting her cold Primrose took up her usual position at the table and began to play "Snap" with the socks. 'I'm sure that I learned my colours playing "Snap" with wet socks ready to peg them out onto the "sock trees" to dry.' said Emma.

'That's the best way to learn, isn't it 'Rose?' said Beth and huddled up closer to help Primrose to concentrate on the task.

At the same time that Primrose was attempting a creative re-design of the digestive system her Great Uncle was making his telephone calls. 'Good morning, Sergeant Maddox. It seems that you and I are going to make something of a team over the next week or two, that is if you don't have any objection. I've got the all-clear to poke my nose into everybody's business while we wait for the toxicology report.' said Detective Chief Inspector James.

'Thank you, Sir. I'd be delighted to work alongside you. I'll do as much as I can to be of help, though what I can do I really don't know." said Maddox.

'Great! That's settled then. I've got a few things to attend to here for a couple of days but I'll try and pop over and chat to you properly by the end of the week. We're just playing the waiting game now and if the results from toxicology are clear we need to help Wainwright by supporting the verdict of a stress induced heart attack. I need you to find out what state Barlow's affairs were really in. Go and see his accountant for a more specific idea of his finances. You could also look into his domestic affairs. We're presuming that everything was as it seems at home and also that Jean is now the beneficiary of his will - it's worth just checking. Your first job, however, is to pay Jefferson a visit. It's mighty fishy that his name should turn up. Physical violence simply isn't his style but he needs to explain his connection. That should keep you busy for the rest of the week. If you need any help call my mobile, I'll give you my number now so you don't have to get through the switchboard.'

'Right you are, Sir. I'll get onto it straight away. It's just general information about anything I can find out then really. I'll see what I can dig up.'

'You could even speak to Jean's cleaning lady. I'm sure you wouldn't mind doing that!' James laughed and then hung up.

Sergeant Maddox sat considerably taller at the end of the phone call than he was when it was first put through to him. It didn't matter that it was boring, routine enquiry - he was working with Detective Chief Inspector James! Everybody in the Cheshire police force, and probably even further afield, knew of DCI James - and he'd put Maddox in charge to get on with things. He'd give it all that he'd got, for however short a time he was working with James. It was an opportunity too good to miss.

Turning to his desktop computer Maddox drank his extremely sweet tea as he waited for the screens to load. Once onto the system he accessed the central database of previous convictions and looked up the domestic address of Conrad Jefferson. He then logged out of the police software and clicked onto Google Maps. He typed in the address of his destination and hit print. As the page was spooling to the printer in the reception area he walked across the corridor and knocked on the Superintendent's office door. It wasn't often that Maddox had ever crossed the threshold of his superior's office and when he did it was because he'd been summonsed. It was a mark of his newly elevated position that he now approached the doorway unbidden. As he raised his fist, poised to knock, he was no longer so sure of himself and he found that his mouth was dry - the moisture had evidently migrated to the palms of his hands. From around the corner the sound of approaching footsteps gave him the final nudge to make his fist make contact with the door. It wouldn't do to be caught dithering like a naughty schoolboy nervously waiting by the headmaster's door. If his next foray into door knocking was to be on the front door of an ex-convict he'd better get on with it now.

'Come.' The monosyllabic directive called Maddox and he walked tall into Superintendent Buckley's office . Looking up Buckley said, 'Ah, Maddox. I'm glad it's you. I've heard from Superintendent Holloway this morning about the Barlow situation. I gather that our Doctor isn't entirely satisfied and they've got the coroner's go ahead to fish around a bit. For goodness sake lad, keep that to yourself until you know there's good reason for it. I don't say that I disagree with him, I'm sure he knows what's right - just keep it under your hat for now or there'll be a hell of a hullaballoo! I gather you were at the meeting. Tell me what it's all about.'

Sergeant Maddox relayed the main points of the meeting with James and Wainwright and of the conversation he had just had with James, explaining that while they wait for the toxicology results it was his job to ferret out as much information as he could. 'I also need to go and pay a visit to Conrad Jefferson as his name was scribbled in John's diary.'

'Was it indeed? What's John Barlow doing fraternising with the big boys I wonder? Jefferson has only been convicted once, but that's only because he's too clever to get caught. He's had his finger in plenty of highly lucrative, but intrinsically rotten pies.'

'That brings me to the main point of why I came to see you, Ma'am. Please can I have the use of one of the station's vehicles? Jefferson lives in Harrisfield and I'd never get there on the bus. I'd like to get there as soon as possible.'

'Yes, I seem to remember that he has an impressive place in the middle of nowhere. He didn't buy that place legitimately I'm sure. You'd better see Janine in the office to sign for the keys. Just don't go playing "Starsky and Hutch" the second you're out of sight.'

'Of course not, Ma'am.' said Maddox. Collecting his map and keys he walked around the building to where two station cars were parked. It wasn't until he'd turned the corner that he threw the keys into the air and laughed out loud. Now this is being a policeman, he thought. The allocated car was only a small black Vauxhall Astra, but it represented a definite incline in the otherwise strictly linear progression of Maddox's career so far. He was acting as "sleuth" for DCI James and he was on his way to interview a criminal.

Maddox's enthusiasm was tempered slightly by the prospect of an intercom at the looming and definitely locked electric gates. Getting out of the car he pushed the buzzer and waited for a response. 'Name and business.' crackled a male voice without ceremony.

'Sergeant Maddox of Mossleigh police. I'd like to speak to Mr Jefferson, please.'

'Wait one moment.' The buzzer snapped off and Maddox was left to wait again. He reflected on his first steps in criminal investigation. On second thought he considered "I'd like to" lacked the necessary authority. It suggested the possibility that his wishes rested on the pleasure of Jefferson and could necessarily be refused. That gave Jefferson control and that wasn't right at all - he had the weight of the law behind him. He'd better change tack, he wasn't dealing with little old ladies now.

The intercom buzzed into action again. 'Jefferson here. What's your rank and business?'

'My name is Sergeant Maddox and I'm here on behalf of DCI James of Winsford HQ. Your name has appeared in a current enquiry and I need to ask you a few general questions.' That should do it, though it was perhaps a little cowardly to hide behind James's credentials. The intercom snapped off and Maddox was left to wait yet again. Before he could register annoyance the gates began to open inwards. He jumped into the car and quickly drove through as if he feared they would close before he was through. Once safely inside he steadied his pace to take in his surroundings. He whistled softly to himself as he took in the view. Either side of the meandering driveway lay elegantly manicured gardens and pristine flower beds displayed a riot of colour against the luscious green lawns. To the left, a little in the distance, a tennis court could be seen. It didn't look real but seemed more like a TV set. The house rose up before him. If Maddox had known his architectural history he would have seen that it was of Georgian design. Built of the expected Sandstone appropriate to the period it displayed the proportion and balance of the era in the symmetry of the many sash windows. The Greek inspiration behind the style was acknowledged in the simple Ionian columns that supported the triangular portico over the impressive front door. Maddox nevertheless clearly recognised that the house was tastefully built and, above all, impressive.

The front door opened as Maddox pulled the car over to the side of the driveway and he met Jefferson on the doorstep. 'Good morning, Sir. I'm sorry to disturb you but I need to ask you a few questions in connection with a man named John Barlow.' said Maddox. He curbed a deep seated desire to doff a non-existent cap and ask for directions to the servants' entrance.

Jefferson rolled his eyes. 'I knew that man would be nothing but trouble. You'd better come inside. I must say that I'm not very happy about you just turning up here. My wife is understandably jumpy after my brief holiday at Her Majesty's pleasure, and you can imagine the shock she got when the gardener starts yelling for me to tell me that the police are here. You could have telephoned me at work and asked me to come over to the station.'

'Would you have come?'

'Of course I would. What do you think I'd do, run for the nearest airport? I was a little foolish once, but now I'm down as a potential fugitive! Good grief, you watch too much TV.'

Feeling somewhat abashed Maddox apologised for his tactlessness. He could appreciate the secret of Jefferson's success, he certainly came across as the acme of respectability. Maddox was led into an opulent study. A large desk, probably responsible for the demise of a good chunk of endangered Amazonian rain forest, lay at an oblique angle and dominated the room. Rich burgundy leather chairs sat on the outskirts of the room in front of floor-to-ceiling bookcases. Quickly scanning the spines of some of the contents of the shelves Maddox saw that the topics covered were wide and varied, ranging from Art and History to Classic Literature and Music. Unable to contain his curiosity Maddox asked.

'Have you read all of these?'

Jefferson laughed. 'Maybe not all of them from cover to cover, but I've certainly dipped into nearly all of them. The gardening and music books are my wife's.''So, what's the matter with John Barlow? Is he in over his head?' asked Jefferson.

'You could say that.' said Maddox. 'He's dead.'

Jefferson stood as still as the marble statue that stood on his windowsill for long seconds before turning to Maddox. 'Well, I didn't expect you to say that. You'd better tell me all about it.'

'I think that really you'd better tell me, that's why I'm here. Your name is jotted down in John's diary on the page of the date that he died. He died at the Fête, did you see him when you were there?'

'I was at the Fête with my wife. She found the social stigma of me being in prison pretty tough and she's found it even harder since I've come home. She's very sensitive and the embarrassment has almost been too much for her. She has gradually been gaining confidence and she said she'd like to go to the Fête at Mossleigh. I was pleased that she would consider being seen with me again and I tried to make sure that she had a good time - though I was getting heartily sick of knitting, jams and cakes.'

'I see, Sir, but that doesn't explain why your name should be written in John's diary.'

'No, you're quite right. It doesn't.' Jefferson paused and seemed to be thinking what he should say next. He gave a deep sigh. 'The answer to that is simple and yet, maybe not so simple.'

'Go on.'

Jefferson indicated that Maddox take a seat in one of the leather chairs and he joined Maddox in an adjacent low armchair. 'John Barlow called me at my office about two months ago. I run a sizeable building company in Winsford and also have an office in Alder Leigh. I can only assume that he'd heard of my misdemeanour and had tracked down my business contact details. He'd e-mailed a couple of times and then he called me on the telephone. I have to admit that I had originally had no intention of replying to his e-mails. When my secretary told me that he was on the line, wanting to speak to me urgently, I decided to let her put the call through. I thought it was the best way to get rid of him in the end. He sounded pretty desperate and he said that he really needed my advice on some property holdings he had. He seemed to think that I was the key to some criminal underworld. He was very melodramatic and wanted me to help him out. It was laughable really, it was so seedy. However, if you're telling me that he's dead then it's not so laughable really, is it?'

'Not really, no. Can you tell me what was on his mind? Did he tell you what he needed help with? Did you ever meet with him?'

Jefferson paused for a moment before answering. He shrugged his shoulders and continued. 'I may as well tell you. It appears that I'm marked as a hardened criminal and you'll just keep hounding me until you've got every last drop of my privacy. I don't want that, for my wife's sake, so I'll do what I can to tell you what I know - but it's not very much I'm afraid.' Maddox smiled encouragingly and took out his notebook and pencil as Jefferson continued. 'As you are aware, I'm sure, I stayed at Her Majesty's pleasure as a result of a brief dip in my moral conduct and a few nifty alterations on my tax returns relating to certain property investments. In some measure John occupied a similar business world and held a small property portfolio with leases available in Greece and Spain. The property crash of recent years has hit us all hard, but you have to take the rough with the smooth in our line of business. You can't expect to ride the gravy train all the time. John Barlow had thought that he could and didn't like the prospect of a few bumpy years, or I should probably say that he thought that his wife wouldn't like it. He begged me to meet him and I could see that he was going to be a nuisance. The only way to deal with it was to meet him and try and talk some sense into him.'

'And so you met him at the Fête?'

'Yes. He concocted this ridiculous cloak and dagger meeting behind the village hall for two-thirty that afternoon and in the end, like a fool, I agreed. I tried to arrange a meeting with him in the office as we had done before but he said that it couldn't wait. I knew I could easily slip off for half an hour without any trouble. Ha! that's ironic - I'm in trouble now, that's for sure.'

'I'm not so sure that we're looking for trouble yet, Mr Jefferson, but it certainly is inconvenient for you. What did you discuss? I presume that he was alive and well when you went to meet him."

'Of course he was alive! I wouldn't leave a chap like that and not tell anybody. He was alive, but I'm not so sure that he was alive and well. As we talked he got progressively worse. He began to sweat and became more and more flushed and red in the face. In the end I asked him what the matter was and offered to go and get help. He'd made quite a drama of our meeting and I thought it was all getting a bit much for him. He told me that he'd be fine. He said he'd got diabetes and just needed a sweet cup of tea and a piece of toast and then he'd be as right as rain. He assured me that he was quite used to the symptoms and he'd soon be back to his usual self. He was so sure about it. I didn't think that he was ill enough to die or I'd have insisted upon getting help.'

'What did you discuss during your meeting? Was he in dire straits and under a severe burden of stress?'

'There was nothing unusual about his situation, we're all in the same boat and his dilemma was only to a small degree, relatively speaking. In short his income was down and his expenses were up. The Euro crash meant that tenants couldn't pay their rent or weren't taking on new leases whilst the Greek Government was trying to save its own economy by raising property tax to increasingly dizzy heights. The Spanish tourism trade was also falling off. Brits weren't holidaying abroad so much as the cost of living in Spain had risen so holidays there were becoming more and more expensive. The tenants of the bars he owned were struggling for business and were falling behind on their rent.'

'How did he expect you to help in all of this? What could you do about it? You could hardly negotiate with the Greek Tax authorities - could you?'

'Certainly not. I don't know whether John thought that because I'd been in prison I'd got daring contacts. He'd got very exaggerated ideas about my illicit past. His situation wasn't as bad as he made out. I suggested that he tighten his belt and ride it out like the rest of us. I told him that if he was feeling the pinch too much he could convert some of his assets by selling them. I know that property wasn't moving in Greece, or maybe even Spain but he could easily ease his budget by selling what he had in France.'

'What did he say to your advice?'

'He said that he didn't want to let his wife down, if he could help it. You know, the whole Alpha-male thing.   He wanted my so-called underworld contacts to help him. I told him that I didn't have such contacts and that he was foolish to look on these things as failure - this was business. If he'd never had to experience this before he had done well, extremely well. You know he actually laughed and suggested I speak to his wife.'

'What did you say to that?'

'I told him to stop being an idiot and to stop making mountains out of molehills. I also told him to look at my recent holiday in prison as a warning. Surely that's what his wife would like least of all. He just laughed again, but after that he seemed to take notice of what I'd said and I really thought I'd got through to him. He seemed to pick up a bit after that, he really did.'

'So you thought he seemed well enough when you left him?'

'I thought he looked tired and older - resigned, if you see what I mean. He knew he'd have to ride it out like I am. He didn't look too well, but he insisted he'd be fine once he'd had a drink and a bite to eat. He was adamant about that and didn't like me fussing. I believed him when he said he was OK, he seemed so unconcerned himself. I'm sorry that I was wrong about that, but I could only take his word, couldn't I?'

'I understand. So, in a nutshell, you say that he was making a dramatic fuss about a bit of economic inconvenience and, after speaking to you, he seemed to understand that foolish attempts to get around it were futile. You're saying that his situation wasn't critical and hardly really embarrassing but that he felt it too keenly. Perhaps knowing that others were in the same boat encouraged him and he just had to take the knocks like you all did. Have I understood correctly, Sir?'

'I should say that's about it. I think he told me everything. He was disconcertingly transparent. I felt so sorry for him that I offered to help him as much as I could. You could speak to his accountant to check what he told me, but I think he was telling me the truth. I wouldn't have said his situation was desperate.'

Maddox stood up to leave. He extended his right hand to shake hands. 'Thank you for your help, Sir. I'm sorry that I've unsettled your wife. If I need to speak to you again how would you prefer me to contact you?'

'I'd appreciate it if you'd call me at the office. If I'm not there my secretary will be able to get hold of me most of the time and I'll get straight back to you. Jefferson walked over to his desk and picked up a business card which he gave to Maddox.

'Thank you again for your time and help. Of course you know that if you think of anything,

anything at all which might help me, you can call me at the station.'

Maddox drove back to the station in a very sedate manner. His boss had warned him against driving too fast and so he drove slowly. The fact that he took the long, picturesque route back hardly entered into the equation.

Chapter Nine

The ladies met as usual for their regular Women's Institute meeting and the gents whiled away their loneliness at The Badger. Nathaniel had acted the gentleman in volunteering to stay home with Primrose for the entire evening so that Emma could accompany the ladies to the pub for the night. At the meeting the evening once again began with tea and cake before Mae called the ladies to order and asked them to take their seats for "Jerusalem" and the commencement of business.

'First of all I would like to thank everybody for all their hard work over the last few weeks, and probably even months. The Fête was a huge success. As ever, Darcy has been the model of efficiency and she has typed up an accounts sheet outlining all expenses and takings relating to the Fête. I'll leave a few copies here on the desk for those of you who would like a closer look at the figures and I'll just sum up the results by saying that we did better than ever. The committee will be meeting within the next week or so to discuss the matter of charity donations from this fund. However, before we continue with our evening I would like to express our deepest sympathy to Jean.' Looking across the room to speak directly to Jean, Mae said. 'We are so sorry for your loss, Jean. I want to assure you of our continued support over the next few weeks and months.' Then turning to the main assembly she continued, 'Surely this is the reason why we meet, ladies - to care and support each other through life's ups and downs. So please make use of your friends here, all of you.

Nobody should struggle unnecessarily.' Jean looked distinctly uncomfortable at being the centre of attention, but awkwardly nodded her thanks to Mae and her nearest neighbours. Moving on with the agenda for the evening Mae said. 'I have sitting beside me Robyn Denton from the Royal Horticultural Society who is going to present a slide-show of highlights from the Summer Flower Shows and explain the background to the RHS. Thank you Robyn.'

An enthusiastic round of applause encouraged Miss Denton to take the floor. 'Thank you for your kind hospitality. I'm so pleased to be able to speak to you tonight about a subject which is very special to me. I hope you enjoy the subject as much as I do.

'The Chelsea Flower Show is perhaps the most well known of our annual shows. This is most probably due to the fact that it is usually attended by members of The Royal Family and this may also explain why it boasts the highest quality gardens and exhibits. Here is a picture of the Renaissance Garden.' She clicked the slide projector into life and showed some pictures and then continued with slides of the Floral Marquee. 'This next photograph shows the Perfume Garden, which hardly does the subject justice. It's a pity that technology can't provide "Scratch and Sniff" pictures for us here. The assembled ladies laughed obligingly and were evidently enjoying the subject.

'The Hampton Flower Show is situated just off the Thames and the Long Water passes through the grounds of the show. It is a much larger show and the atmosphere is considerably more laid back. Maybe this is because we aren't expecting the surprise of an impromptu Royal visit, or maybe it's because of the larger area and the exhibits can be much further apart - the greater space between the plots makes for more relaxed browsing. I myself prefer the hustle and bustle of Chelsea, and the intimacy of being squashed close to the exhibits.'

Robyn then began to explain the various trophies awarded with photographic evidence of each prize-winning exhibit and finalist. Categories included Best Show Garden, Best Courtyard Garden and various junior trophies and scientific awards were illustrated. Nicola gained a few nudges of encouragement when the RHS Floral Arrangement trophies were shown. 'You could do that easily.' whispered Natalie conspiratorially into Nicola's ear. 'Yours are just as good as those slides she's showing.' Tatton Garden Show was whizzed through with eloquence and the delights of forthcoming Autumn Shows were hinted at. Robyn ended her presentation by offering a round of Q & A before she finished. Not surprisingly it was Kirsty who was the first to shoot her hand into the air.

'Do you suffer much with plant pilfering? Not just during the shows but generally in your public gardens too?' asked Kirsty.

Robyn shook her head and sighed dramatically. 'Ah yes, green-collar crime, so unnecessary and such a problem. We employ our own form of a dedicated police constabulary in an attempt to prevent this from happening, but it doesn't stop people from trying. Wanton damage is always a problem but I find it harder to bear when the damage is done by fellow gardeners.'

Betty gingerly raised her hand and asked. 'Why does it matter so much? If it's just a small cutting it'll grow back won't it?' Those sitting next to her later said that she definitely had a guilty look on her face.

'It may seem a petty state of affairs but it really is a serious matter.' said Robyn. 'Not only do you have to consider that if everybody kept on snipping bits off a plant there'd be no plant left, but you also need to bear in mind that just one ill-directed cut can kill a plant. This is especially true if a pruning is made at the wrong time of year or in the wrong place. It can be really harmful to the plant - it's like open heart surgery. It can even be true with trees too. If you cut the branches of a Copper Beech tree during the summer a harmful sap is released and those branches may never grow back. If too much damage is done the tree will just die. If you cut a plant at the wrong angle water can settle into the cut and the plant will rot. I know of a case where a seed had been nurtured for almost a decade and it was grafted onto a host plant to bring it on. It takes a long time for the graft to establish but it was ripped off by an uninformed enthusiast and brought my friend to tears.'

A series of sympathetic groans from the audience could be heard and later it was said that Betty blushed considerably under her rouge. Robyn was no idealist though and said, 'Of course we know that it happens and there exists a complex, unwritten code of honour when committing green-collar crimes. Some protagonists even carry pruning shears around with them on the off-chance, so that they don't harm a plant that they just can't resist pilfering from. Of course it is accepted that if you are going to sneak a cutting it has to be correctly done - not just randomly snipped. You need to know when in the season a little liberation can be managed. Out and out thievery is always a no-no. Never should you just dig up a plant outright. On the whole it is always better to ask permission, but never hesitate to ask - most gardeners are more than willing to share but will get a bit proprietorial when somebody else is wielding the clippers!'

The presentation ended on this lighter note and as the speaker was guided to resume her tea drinking before the journey home Beth rose to take her place at the piano for the closing National Anthem as the traditional ending to the meeting. The milder members of the group then headed for home whereas Beth, Emma and Kirsty quickened their pace towards The Badger where they knew that their chosen cups of poison awaited them. Beth was pleased to see that Jonti and Matt had come to join them for the evening and gave each of them a tight squeeze of appreciation before taking her seat next to Drew and picking up her waiting half pint of "Cheshire Set." She was soon joined by Natalie and Nicola, who managed to squeeze a couple of stools into the group and then began rehashing the topics of the evening to their own satisfaction.

'You really ought to consider entering one of these flower shows, Nicola. You really are just as good as those pictures we saw tonight. The promotion for your flower shop would be fantastic - you could double your prices if you won!' said Natalie.

'I'm not sure that I want to double my prices - I'd have no customers at that rate.' said Nicola.

'Maybe not, but the point remains. You should look into it.' said Natalie.

'I know a landscape gardener who entered, and he won a prize too.' said Beth. 'He was just an average kind of guy who ran his own landscaping business. You don't have to be anything special - just good at what you do. Natalie's right, you ought to think about it and do some research. It would definitely do you good.'

'It's not something that I'd have ever considered. I've visited shows, of course, but I've never thought of entering. I'll give it some thought. Will that satisfy you for now?' said Nicola.

'Just for now, but we won't let you conveniently forget. If you don't enter you'll have to give us a damned good reason for bowing out.' said Natalie.

'What made you ask about the plant crime, Kirsty?' asked Emma.

'It sounds really silly when you say it like that.' said Kirsty. 'The sinister green fingers of the Underworld, huh? It's not very funny really though, you know. My garden was ransacked on the day of the Fête. I can't think how they all did it though, I never left them alone. Between me and Jean there was always somebody on the lookout.'

'Oh your poor garden! What's been nicked?' asked Beth.

'Pretty much a bit of everything. That woman was right - I'm sure some of them were carrying secateurs with them as some of the cuttings are quite neat. That's annoying enough but some plants have had bits just ripped off any old how. Some of the plants are a real mess, especially the woody stemmed ones. Some bits have ripped right down the main stem. It makes my blood boil. Robyn Denton said it's like an open wound and she's right. There's nothing I can do about it either, I'll just have to chop off the damaged bits and let them recover. Some of the plants were really well established too and it'll really set them back in their flowering now. It happened last year, but this year was much worse. I've read that since the recession green-collar crime is really on the up.' said Kirsty.

The levity of Kirsty's predicament became apparent as sniggers broke out at the bizarre turn of conversation. 'I know it sounds ridiculous, but imagine if you owned a garden centre, or a flower shop like Nicola's. It takes on new meaning then, doesn't it? Apparently OAPs have taken to stowing away stolen seed packets in foil lined bags to dodge the shop's security systems. In my garden the bloom of the rosebushes is seriously diminished in some patches. Obviously somebody fancied an unofficially sponsored rose bowl. The herb garden got a pasting too. I suspect a load of the old dears were inspired to try sage as an alternative HRT and thought to give it a go pro-gratis. It's just downright lazy as it's as easy as anything to grow and it's cheap to buy too.'

'Well, city crime just can't beat this. Who thought living in a village could be so treacherous.' said Jonti. 'What are drive-by shootings compared to this?'

'I told you that village life has as much nastiness as the city, didn't I?' said Beth.

'I think I prefer the brashness of city crime.' said Matt. 'At least it's up-front and doesn't pretend to be nice. This is just small minded pettiness which I think is far more shabby.'

'I quite agree with you, Matt.' said Kirsty. 'It's just so futile and unnecessary. I've got my work cut out for me now and I've had to start trimming things back far sooner in the season than I'd wanted to. I've done all the emergency cases as best as I can but I'm waiting until I've got some time off work before I can get a proper look at everything and tidy it all up.'

Orders were being taken for the last round and Emma got up to leave not wanting to leave Nathaniel on his own for too long. She also wanted to get back to Primrose, as she still wasn't quite back to her usual self after her cold. The conversation fragmented into different topics and Beth turned to Gareth, Nicola's partner, sitting on her left.

'Didn't you deal with John Barlow's accounts? Are things a bit sticky for you after he died so suddenly?' said Beth.

'I can quite honestly say that we've been better prepared than this, shall we say.' said Gareth.

'I know that you can't break professional trust and I don't mean to pry into private information - it's just that it's pretty common knowledge that things were a bit sticky for John and now you must have your work cut out trying to wrap it all up. Do you think that the stress of it all could have pushed him over the edge?'

'That's a bit drastic, don't you think? You'd have to ask Dr Wainwright that - not that he'd tell you, I'm sure!' He gave Beth a wry wink that suggested she might be on forbidden territory.

'Oh, my brother's a Detective Chief Inspector. I'm the model of discretion, you know.' laughed Beth. 'Poor you, you've got to tidy up all the loose ends now and clear up the mess. Jean says that she doesn't understand business, but I suppose it will all go to her now. I suspect that she's shrewd enough to deal with it.

'I suppose that once everything is in order we'll be guided by her wishes. I've not troubled her with it for the moment as there's not much she can do just yet.' said Gareth. 'I know there's a lot of gossip, but John's situation wasn't anything like as bad as folks are making out. It's ironic really, there were a few things he could have done to smooth things over but he just didn't seem to want to take action. It's sad that now he's dead it'll probably all sort itself out anyway. We'll just have to wait and see. I think that John was too sensitive and seemed to think that lean times were shameful. It's not like that at all, but he couldn't see it.'

The bell sounded that drinking-up time was finished and gradually the bar emptied out into the street. Beth, Drew, Jonti and Matt made their way home. Once inside Beth made a saucepan of her

137

signature concoction of milk, cocoa powder, malt extract and vanilla for them to drink before bed. The four of them sat around the kitchen table in their pyjamas, nursing their bedtime drinks.

'I was just talking to Gareth about John Barlow's state of affairs.' said Beth.

'I'm not sure he should be talking to you about such things. Isn't that against the accountancy Hippocratic oath?' said Drew.

'Oh, I disarmed him by reassuring him that I wasn't digging for information.'

'But you were, though, weren't you?' said Jonti.

'You know me too well. Of course I was!' said Beth. ' I wasn't really lying though, what we discussed was more or less common knowledge anyway.'

'More or less.' said Matt.

'Gareth didn't reveal any facts or figures. It's only what we'd all guessed, but it did shed a different light on things. He pretty well said that John felt ashamed at business being a bit tight. I've had quite a disturbing thought - you don't think that John would commit suicide, do you?'

'Crikey, Beth! Whatever makes you say that?' said Drew.

'Well, people do - don't they? It's no use saying "He'd never do such a thing" because that's what everybody says and yet people do still go and kill themselves. Those left behind spend the rest of their life wondering why and still clinging to the hope that it didn't really happen when it obviously did. It's easy for others to say that matters are never that bad, but it's not really the facts that carry the weight. It's all about that person's perspective. We might say "Oh don't worry, you're still super rich" but it doesn't necessarily cut through, does it?' said Beth.

'I take your point Beth, but there must be more to your reasoning than just "it could happen." said Drew.

'As I said, Gareth hasn't told me anything new. I just got the impression that the problem was more to do with John's attitude that the actual financial situation. Although business wasn't booming it seems that there were measures he could have easily taken but didn't. Perhaps the fact that somehow everybody knew his affairs didn't exactly help matters either. He'd been actively advised to take certain steps but apparently he couldn't bring himself to do so. Gareth seemed to think that the imagined shame of failure was overwhelming John and action may have implied defeat or failure.'

'If you think about it, if money was tight then the obvious practical steps would be to sell off some property. That's quite a public thing, especially if it means selling off their own holiday home in France which Jean is so proud of. Do you think that he'd worry about his image in the village to that extent? It surely couldn't be just that! Maybe the thought of having to face Jean with the prospect of downsizing or selling the house in France was too humiliating for him. I suspect that's more likely. It's still not that drastic, though. They'd still be really well off from what I can gather.' said Beth.

'They are valid points, Mum.' said Jonti. 'I think that John could be quite sensitive. I do hope that you're wrong, he was such a lovely chap. He always used to make jokes about my trombone saying that it was just a penny whistle with too much ego.'

'I'd never given such an explanation a thought until just now, but something in Gareth's tone gave away the emotional struggle that John must have been facing. I don't think Gareth realised what he was saying and he didn't seem to think he was telling me anything new. I'll have to talk to Benji about it sometime, though I'm sure he'll have considered it.' said Beth.

They placed the empty mugs in the sink and said "Good night." to each other. Each sleepy individual then made their way to bed. Beth glanced into the kitchen and wished that she didn't have to face each new day with a sink full of last night's dirty dishes. As they'd been chatting Matt had made a plate of toast and had liberally smeared it with a jar of Emma's lemon curd. Now a chopping board and some sticky knives lay strewn across a crumb-ridden surface. It would be a matter of minutes to stash the dishes into the dishwasher, but the saucepan would have to soak in soapy water for a while to get rid of the burnt milk at the bottom of the pan. The dishwasher had finished its cycle while they were out at the pub and was now fully stocked with gleaming dishes to be put away and she wasn't starting that job at midnight. She shrugged her shoulders and switched off the lights. For once she'd make sure that she went to bed at the same time as her husband. In the grand scheme of things, it wasn't such a travesty. After cleaning her teeth Beth climbed into bed next to Drew and snuggled up close. 'Nothing can be that bad really, can it?' she asked. Drew didn't answer but kissed her forehead and put his arm around her to hug her as they both fell asleep.

Chapter Ten

Early the next morning Beth jumped out of bed with a new sense of purpose. After mulling the situation over through the night she'd decided to take action. Sitting at the breakfast table she stirred her cooling, lumpy porridge and chatted to Drew. 'The boys have decided to stay over for the day as they are both free today. Would you mind if I asked Nathaniel to join you all with Primrose so that I can whisk Emma off for a few hours? Primrose will have a lovely morning soaking up loads of positive male reinforcement and she knows she gets spoilt when the men are in charge. If Nathaniel has plans for the day would you look after 'Rose yourself?'

'That's fine by me, it'd be nice if Nathaniel could join us - we can have a movie session. If he's busy I'm sure we'll manage for a few hours without any female intervention. Noodle will help to keep Primrose occupied, won't you buddy?' said Drew, glancing towards the dog. A sleepy nose peered at Drew in response to hearing his name, which Drew interpreted as canine agreement. 'See, he can still take on a four year old girl. What are you planning on doing?'

'I'd like to muster a girly trip to the Blue Willow tea rooms. I haven't been for ages and I think Eileen is doing a super job there. It must be really hard work. If there are enough of you on duty how do you feel about having young Toby join in? Henrietta doesn't get many treats and I particularly want her to join in, if she can. I'm really pleased at the way she's getting along with Emma, it's good to see the friendship growing.'

'I should think that would be OK. Toby and 'Rose play nicely together and I'm sure that Toby would enjoy hanging around with the guys for the day. I'll hold the fort if the others are busy. I'm sure it'll be fine. I expect that we'll end up with a house full. What shall I feed them all on?'

'I'll ring around and see who's up for a party. When I've an idea of numbers I'll get some naan bread pizzas ready for you to shove in the oven when you're ready. They only take about four minutes so they'll be easy enough.'

Beth made her round of calls and it was arranged that all the men and children would meet at the house and the ladies would meet at the Blue Willow tea rooms. Beth also decided to invite Mae to join in her underlying scheme but before she could scroll down the phone's contact list the handset rang as she held it. The caller ID displayed Benji's name.

'Hello Benji, how nice to hear from you again so soon.'

'Hi, not only am I a regular caller, I'm going to be a regular visitor. I need to speak to young Maddox and rather than discuss things over the phone I've cleared my desk and I'm driving over to speak to him in person. I thought I'd come and see you guys as soon as I'm done.'

'How lovely, I hope we'll be seeing a bit more of you if you're working with Maddox. It's going to be quite a gathering. The boys are here and Nathaniel is coming over too. I think they're planning on watching movies. I'm nipping out for an hour or two but I'm sure I'll catch you before you go back. Is it anything particular that's bringing you to our fair village?'

'I want to speak to Maddox to see how he got on at the Jeffersons.'

'I don't think I mentioned it to you when you were here last, but Drew knows Jefferson. He does artwork for his company from time to time.'

'Does he now? I'll be grilling Drew too.'

'How terrifying! It's a small world, isn't it? The concentric circles of life have a knack of overlapping in the strangest places. Give my love to Lexi, you must bring her with you one time.'

'I will. I'll see if I can tear her away from the city.'

Having arranged the rendezvous at the Blue Willow tea rooms Beth set quickly to work in preparing food for the male entourage laying out packet naan breads over the entire work surface of the kitchen. She spread a blend of passata and tomato puree over each slice and then sprinkled dried mixed herbs over the tomato base. This was then topped with grated cheese and slices of pepperoni. Glancing at the clock Beth figured that it wasn't worth trying to store them in the fridge, they wouldn't have fitted anyway. Chances were that lunch would be early that day. To bolster the meal Beth then opened two packs of part-baked baguettes and sliced them at an angle into small chunks. In the fridge was a stock of home made garlic butter which she always made sure was to hand and this was quickly loaded between the chunks of bread to follow the pizzas into the oven. Kissing Drew good bye she headed towards Main Street in the centre of Mossleigh village. It boasted a post office which also doubled as a minor grocery store, a pet and animal foods store and Nicola's florist shop. It also housed the Blue Willow tea rooms. All of the buildings lay on the left hand side of the road as you walked towards Main Street from Beth's house. On the right hand side was a grassy expanse which gave way to a small natural lake. There weren't enough resident attractions to make Mossleigh into a tourist spot but cars driving through often chose it as a place to break their journey and visit the tea rooms or picnic by the lake.

The interior of the Blue Willow didn't hold any surprises, the main theme of the decor - along with its title - took its inspiration from the traditional Old Country Willow tableware pattern which was manufactured just over the Staffordshire border. The well-known pattern was mimicked in stencils all about the room and the colourway of the tablecloths and curtains maintained thematic unity. The school summer holidays often brought a lot of passing trade and the little room was quite full. Beth entered through the door in the centre of two large windows and scanned the tables for either a vacant table or one occupied with her chosen party. Towards the back of the room a raised arm gesticulated and was followed by the emerging head of Mae who beckoned Beth to join them. Dealing first with the matter of primary importance they selected sandwiches and tea to aid negotiations and then the group looked at Beth expectantly.

'Although it's very nice to meet you for tea and sandwiches, and we're happy to do so whenever you summon us, Emma seems to think that you have something up your sleeve. Is this a cloak and dagger rendezvous? Do we need a secret handshake before you'll tell us all?' said Mae.

'I'm so glad that you could all make it . Henrietta, I'm pleased that you've joined in our little conspiracy.' said Beth. The explanation was delayed by the arrival of an Old Country Willow tiered stand holding a stack of sandwiches and a huge Old Country Willow teapot with all the necessary accoutrements. It was unanimously agreed that under the circumstances it was necessary to both speak and eat and so talking with your mouth full was voted in as acceptable behaviour for their newly formed league. Duly reassured Beth bit into a salmon and cucumber sandwich and said, 'What I really want is to conscript your services. After listening to what is being said about John Barlow's death I gather that the officials aren't entirely satisfied but at present can offer no suitable explanation. I know that Benji and Bobby Maddox are pursuing what enquiries they can with vigour and I expect that Bobby is keen to show his worth to Winsford HQ. The problem there is that they are bound by what I think of as the "official perspective." Benji always tells me that he suffers from people unwittingly keeping information back purely because they give stifled "official answers." He says that they are only too aware that they are answering a policeman's questions and don't like to feel that they are gossiping. The problem is that relaxed gossip is just what he needs, that's where the little gems of information are to be found. People don't mean to hold back any important facts, it's just that you don't know what is or isn't important straight away. I read a book years ago, called "A Jury of her Peers" where the women of a small village solve the motive for a murder by looking into a sewing box and understanding the significance of unfinished kitchen chores. A woman's plight of loneliness was explained by the fact that she had to knot her quilting rather than sewing it in the usual way in a quilting bee. I appreciate that this is a melodramatic example but the point remains. All of us here are in just the right place to casually snoop around and pick up bits and bobs of important information in passing. It's so much more revealing when you're on the domestic level, don't you think?' said Beth.

'You mean that you get more inside people's lives when you see inside their kitchen cupboards, rather than just what you'd get shown as a visitor?' said Emma.

'That's precisely my point. Just like the women in the story could peep inside a sewing box we can peep around as opportunity provides and we just need to be aware and ready to take notice.' said Beth.

'What exactly is it that you think we'd be looking for? I'm not saying that I will, just yet, but if I did agree what do you hope for us to find?' said Henrietta. As cleaning lady at the home of the Barlows there was no doubt that this was directed particularly to her. 'Are you suggesting that John was murdered, if you're referring to your story?'

'I'm not suggesting that particularly, but nobody can easily explain why he died so suddenly. I realise that this might sound a little far-fetched but we all know that John was more than usually worried recently and I do have a concern that it's possible that he may have committed suicide.' said Beth.

'Oh, no! I'd never even considered that. Now you put it that way, I understand you wanting to snoop a bit.' said Mae.

'Do you see my concern?' asked Beth. 'I don't want to raise any official alarm until we feel that it's justified, but we can perhaps exert ourselves to find out if there is sufficient grounds for raising any alarm. I know that Benji will be bearing such a circumstance in mind, he's bound to. However, he can only get "official information." He can't go rummaging in cupboards without a search warrant but it's hardly conducive to gossip when you've been served a warrant, is it? We can find out a lot quite unofficially by paying a bit more attention and maybe contriving a few schemes. Henrietta is in the perfect position as cleaner - and especially as she helps Jean clear out John's things. You can tell an awful lot about a person by cleaning out their bathroom cabinet and sock drawer.'

'Surely John wouldn't consider such a thing.' said Henrietta. 'I hadn't known John for very long but I'd never have thought him capable of such a thing.'

'There's no point saying that though, is there?' said Beth. 'I'm sure that all the friends and relatives of suicide victims would say the same. If we're wrong then we've lost nothing and nobody is any the wiser - nobody is unduly upset. If we're right, well - we've helped speed the process along and we'll hand it all over to Benji to deal with properly. I'm not suggesting that we undermine the official process but I do suggest that we have unique insight and access that would help the official procedure if it came to that. We can look inside the proverbial sewing box without raising suspicion or alarm. If you agree in principle then we can make a more guided plan of how to work together. Do you agree that it's a valid suggestion?'

After some minutes quiet consideration agreement filtered through the mood of the group. 'I don't see any objections. Nobody will be offended if we keep it under our hat.' said Emma.

'Just so long as you don't expect us to do anything illegal' said Henrietta.

'Certainly not. I do think we need to manipulate circumstances to our purpose though.' said Beth.

'It sounds like you already have an idea as to what those purposes are. It appears that we are now getting to the crux of the matter - let's hear it Beth.' said Mae.

'I've only thought as far ahead as our first list of operations, after that we'll have to rely on our intuition.' Beth turned to Henrietta. 'I know that you've been helping Jean clear out John's things, and

I'm genuinely glad of that. I'm sure that she needs practical help and moral support just now and there's no doubt that you're a more calm source of help than the well meaning, but slightly irritating Betty and Eileen.' Here Beth cast a cautious glance around the tea rooms checking that the lady in question wasn't within hearing distance. The last thing they needed was Eileen, on hearing her name, joining in their discussion. Seeing that the coast was clear she continued. 'If you could make yourself as available as possible and then be unobtrusively inquisitive. See if you can find anything which might encourage further scrutiny. If we all gather little snippets who knows what sort of a picture we might find if we piece them all together. I did also wonder if Emma could be squeezed into the equation and could offer to come and lend a hand. Something along the lines of all those heavy bags to lift and high wardrobe shelves to clear and dust might do it. Two heads are better than one.'

'Ordinarily that would be fine, but as it's school holidays my hands are a bit tied with having Toby around. Emma has Toby for me once a week for my regular cleaning day there, but I don't think it would work with both of us there.' said Henrietta.

'Maybe you don't need to both be there at the same time, or if I'm around then I can have the children for you both to go sometimes. The logistics can easily be organised if the main idea is agreed upon. said Beth

Emma and Henrietta looked at each other and as no objections could be thought of they both acknowledged the plan as fundamentally workable.

'I can't imagine what you think we might find but it won't hurt to take a look and I'll pay more attention to what Jean says as she chatters while we work. I imagine that's the sort of thing that you mean.' said Henrietta.

'Super! That's exactly the right idea. Just keep an open mind and be on the alert.' said Beth.

'And what did you have in mind for me?' asked Mae. 'Jean certainly won't want me tidying out her bathroom cabinet.'

'I think that Emma and Henrietta will have that angle covered. You and I need to take a slightly more official approach.' said Beth.

'I thought you said that our success lay in being unofficial?' said Mae.

'Yes, from the policing perspective. I mean that we'll be official, or you will - in your role of Secretary of the WI. Just before I left the house Benji said that he needed to find out about a link with a man named Conrad Jefferson. He hopes to find out some business information that way. Drew has done some work for Jefferson in the past and I recognised him as being at the Fête with his wife. If you and I could call on Mrs Jefferson, I think her name is Hyacinth, we could see if she's interested in joining our WI and maybe get chatting to her generally. She's very shy. Conrad was sent to prison and she's naturally very embarrassed about it. Apart from digging for enlightenment I genuinely think that she's lonely - I'd like it if she could join our little WI group. The fact that we might pick up some hints that Jefferson would never think to say to Benji are just a happy by-product. Do you see what I mean? We can pick up bits of gossip as we go about our usual day to day stuff. If we are a bit more conniving about our usual routine so much the better.' Beth sat back pleased at finally unloading her plan and sharing her burden with her friends.

'I'm not sure what we'll achieve, if in fact there even is anything tangible to achieve, but as the girls have said there isn't really anything to lose.' said Mae. 'The worst case scenario is that it will all prove to be so much hot air and the next time we meet here (I presume that this will be our official headquarters) we'll all just feel a bit silly. I can live with that.'

'Benji is coming to the village today and I don't want to get under his feet if he wants to talk to Jefferson himself. Can you spare an hour first thing Monday morning, Mae?' asked Beth.

The newly formed alliance laid its plans and arranged to meet again over the next week or two, but sooner if anyone felt that they had anything to report. Mae then drove off towards home and the remaining three went to rejoin the others at Beth's house. As they walked into the kitchen it looked like a scene from the Mary Celeste. Scraps of pizza and tomato were strewn about the kitchen but all was quiet and no one was to be seen. Opening the door to the lounge they walked into almost complete darkness. The curtains were closed and bodies were strewn over the furniture and the floor. As predicted a movie was well underway. Nathaniel was asleep after an early morning at the farm and Primrose was also fast asleep in his lap. Almost in mirror image Drew and Toby were also sleeping. Matt and Jonti were quietly positioned on cushions on the floor, their attention captured by the flickering screen. Benedict looked up on their arrival and waved a silent greeting. He stood up and followed his sister quietly into the kitchen. Emma and Henrietta joined in watching the film with the others.

'Did you get any pizza, Benji, or are you hungry?' asked Beth

'I managed to fight for a few scraps, a coffee would be nice though.' said Benji.

Beth made the drinks and placed them on the kitchen table along with a box of flapjacks that she'd made the other day.

'It's a good thing that Lexi doesn't bake like you. I'd be the size of Jim's prize bull.' Nevertheless he took two.

'Did you speak to Maddox? Did he find out anything helpful?'

'I'm not sure that he learned much. I can't quite believe it but there are hints that John was trying to turn "con." Jefferson said that he told John not to be a fool. He also said that it was a bit extreme as his financial situation wasn't really all that bad. I gather that he'd done pretty well for himself on the whole. I'll have to get Maddox to speak to his accountant and solicitor. I just wish that somebody would say something definite. What I really want to hear is, "His business was in shreds, no wonder he had a heart attack - the strain must have been tremendous!" Instead I'm getting half measures, it's bad but not that bad. I just don't understand it.'

Beth wondered if she ought to mention her conversation with Gareth at The Badger the other night. She decided against it as Maddox would probably get more detailed information and could then form his own conclusion rather than being biased by hearsay.

Peeping through the doorway to the lounge Beth could see that the movie hadn't long to go. As Benji sat chatting about his own family news Beth cleared away the remnants of lunch and began an off-the-cuff early tea. She wasn't sure how many would want to stay and eat but didn't want to fracture the communal spirit by asking officially for numbers. Instead it seemed more hospitable to set out an informal buffet and then people could stay or leave as they preferred without awkwardness. She hoped that Henrietta would stay, it was good to see her settling into the gathering and sharing an informal meal together would help Henrietta to integrate further into family friendship. This was much more relaxed than being officially invited to a meal. As Beth set a pan of fusilli to boil she broached her concerns to her brother.

'I'm sure that you've already thought of this Benji, and I feel quite melodramatic saying this out loud, but do you think John may have committed suicide?'

'Well done you!' he said. 'It was the very first thing I thought of, although it doesn't seem to have crossed anybody else's mind - and I'm glad about that. The last thing we need right now is a hue and cry. Under the guise of finding out if the stress of his business matters could have been sufficient to cause a heart attack I'm also trying to get an idea of the state of John's mental health with that very thought in mind. There is one problem with that theory however. I've looked through the photographs from when John was found dead and there is so much general litter about I'll never know if John had a drink to take stuff with. There may have been a discarded cup or something quickly thrown into one of the nearby bins but I can't tell from the general mess. Never say never though - the toxicology report will answer that question for us in the end. I've a sneaking suspicion that there's more to this case than meets the eye. I honestly thought that Jefferson was on the straight and narrow until this. And yet, what do I really imagine his role in this could be? He doesn't strike me as the type to get physical and there's no evidence of that. Neither would he be a willing partner in crime to a relative stranger. Jefferson's weapon is his brain and he only uses it for his own good as a rule. I'll just have to play the waiting game and do what I can until the forensics boys turn something, or nothing, up.'

'I've only seen Conrad a couple of times and then only for a very brief time. From what I've heard Drew say he is a really clever man. Drew said that he thought that Conrad only played the financial system for a game - not that that makes it right. He certainly doesn't need the money. Because he was clever it was a sort of intellectual challenge and Drew thinks that once he got caught the game was over. He sees it as being bested more than being found out and that put an end to it. Drew has definitely got more commissions from him recently. I presumed that meant that he was now throwing all his energies into his legitimate business concerns.'

'Who knows? It's going to be a long and tedious process - I do know that!'

As the pasta cooked Beth chopped olives and parma ham. She then made a basil and pine nut pesto crushing the green leaves from a plant in the kitchen windowsill with a pestle and mortar and adding extra virgin olive oil. She sliced small paninis lengthways and spread a little of the pesto inside before adding the ham and fresh halves of vine tomato. Not owning a panini press didn't prove too much of an obstacle, instead Beth used a large George Foreman grill to quickly toast the filled paninis. She kept a steady feed going from the press to the oven to keep warm. Stirring in the rest of the pesto and tomato into the fusilli she emptied the mix into a large bowl.

The film ended and the party gradually came blinking back to life. Benedict and Beth carried the food into the dining area and Beth added a side salad of vine tomatoes and lettuce leaves drizzled in olive oil and a little mint. Nobody seemed in a hurry to get away and plates of food were soon balancing in hands and on chairs rather than a formal seating around the dining table. People ate and chatted and the rule of allowing speech with a less than empty mouth evidently prevailed amongst friends here too. Only as bed time for the youngsters approached did the gathering break up but once the group fragmented even the older members decided it was time to begin the drive home. Jonti and Matt left together and Benedict walked down the driveway to his own car with his nephews. Very soon Beth and Drew found themselves alone and left to face the mayhem left by the get-together. Drew assumed his natural role as expert dishwasher stacker and Beth hauled out the Dyson to deal with the crumbs broadcast over the carpet, thinking how glad she was that she wouldn't be waking up to this mess tomorrow.

Chapter Eleven

The beginning of the week saw the cars of Sergeant Maddox and Mae Holland both driving out of the village. At the junction on the end of Main Street they split off in opposite directions. Sergeant Maddox made his way to Alder Leigh, with considerable pleasure at the prospect of driving the Station's car once again. He was driving to keep his appointment with Gareth Foster who was overhauling John's business affairs. Mae, with Beth sitting beside her, was heading towards the home of Hyacinth and Conrad Jefferson. 'How do you propose to open the conversation?' asked Mae. 'What are you superficially there to talk about?'

'I thought that we could begin with the pretext of asking Hyacinth to join the WI. I'm not entirely sure that it's only a pretext either. I genuinely think that she'll be glad of some female conversation. I seem to remember that her son is a big businessman in America and although Conrad appeared to be genuinely trying to make sure she was having a nice time at the Fête I bet he spends most of his time on his business concerns. Drew says he never stops working.' said Beth.

'I guess that we'll just have to improvise then. I'll take your lead and if the conversation falls flat then we'll just have to drive away with our tails between our legs.'

They drew the car up to the tall, wrought iron electric gates and Beth got out of the car to walk to the intercom. Pressing the call button the tone buzzed for a minute until a lady's voice responded.

'Hello. Who is it, please?'

'Hello, Hyacinth. I'm Beth Williams from the WI. We met at the Fête.'

'Oh yes, I remember. How can I help?'

'I'm here with Mae, the WI Secretary. We thought we could come and say "Hi" if you're not too busy.'

'Oh, of course. I'm sorry, I'll open the gates.'

The intercom switched off and the gates slowly swung into life. Climbing back into the passenger seat Beth turned to Mae and said, 'Crikey, it's no wonder you said she seemed lonely. It's not exactly easy to nip in for a brew. I think you're right and we should have come - ulterior motive or no.'

As the car curved around the gravelled driveway the front door opened and Hyacinth stepped out, evidently happy to see them. 'Hello, Beth. It's good of you to come and visit. I hope the Fête was a success.' She faltered at the end of her sentence as if she'd suddenly realised her tactlessness, remembering that the day had ended with a death.

'I've been wanting to try and get to know you for ages, especially as Drew sees Conrad for work now and then. I thought that the Fête had given me sufficient introduction to warrant coming over. 'I've brought my friend, Mae, along. Mae is the Secretary of the WI and we've come to see if we can persuade you to swell our ranks.'

Beth introduced Mae to Hyacinth and she followed them through the hallway and into the kitchen. Although the kitchen was of undoubtedly expensive design the overall effect was surprisingly home-like and welcoming. A rich, dark oak table and chairs sat at an angle and this theme was carried out through leaded display cabinets and a vast oak dresser laden with Spode dinner ware. The ladies naturally gravitated towards the kitchen table and sat down as Hyacinth made the necessary preparations around the teapot. It was the rural rendition of some ancient Chinese tea ceremony and was a necessary part of the breaking down of barriers and getting to know each other. She set down a pot of green tea along with slices of lemon and earthenware mugs. Hyacinth was about 5′ 6″ tall and although in her early fifties she was still quite slim. A petite bone structure increased her sense of vulnerability. Her still blonde hair and sparkling green eyes made her a captivating sight. In a simple plain blue tee shirt, jeans and tan leather shoes she looked a million dollars. The ladies settled to amicable chit-chat and despite the tea being served with lemon and not milk the group fell into easy friendship.

'We were hoping that, if you enjoyed the Fête, you might consider joining our little group. You don't have to get involved with any duties or contributions - unless you want to of course. We're quite a friendly bunch, you know.' said Mae.

'Oh, how lovely of you to think of me. I'd never even considered the possibility, but I don't see why not! I'll consider it, certainly. I know that I've lived here for a few years but I've never really managed to make much effort socially. I suppose it would help me to get to know people better.' said Hyacinth.

Beth encouraged the conversation along by asking about Hyacinth's son in America and then complimenting her on the garden - it was difficult to do otherwise.

'I designed the gardens.' said Hyacinth with evident pride, even if it were hidden under a disarming blush. 'I do some of the maintenance work, but it's much too big for me to manage without help. I have a regular gardener who does a lot of the heavy manual work.'

'Could you imagine a garden party here? It'd be fantastic!' said Mae. 'You need to meet Kirsty, you'd get on famously. She's an avid gardener, you really ought to show her around here. I can admire and enjoy it but Kirsty would appreciate what you've done here to the full.'

'I know that Drew has worked with your husband in the past, he does the artistic realisations of architectural drawings, but I've never had the chance of properly getting to know you.' said Beth. 'I can't really muscle in on a business meeting, so it's been tricky to find an avenue of introduction. I didn't like to just barge in so I concocted this plan to come and see you - and of course, we really would like you to join our group.'

'I'm afraid that I've purposefully kept myself away from village life. I suppose that it's common knowledge that Conrad was sent to prison and I just hid myself away, really. It's so embarrassing thinking that everybody is staring at you or talking about you.' said Hyacinth.

'Yes, I take your point.' said Mae.   'It's hard enough to fit in with a small village set at the best of times.   Emma's friend, Henrietta, has found it difficult.   She has her own web of intrigue; she always wears a wedding ring but no man has ever been seen.   It's obviously a taboo subject which makes folks talk about it all the more. Don't worry if you feel like people are talking about you, and no doubt some are - but they talk about everybody without discrimination. There's no real malice in the gossips, they just don't have much else to think about. I really shouldn't let it worry you. It'll give them a spicy new subject for a brief season and then they'll run out of information and find a new topic. I think that you'll find that you're already old news, they've got plenty to gossip about since John died at the Fête.'

'Yes, I knew about that. A young policeman came to see Conrad about him the other day. It really frightened me, touching old wounds if you can understand. Hearing a policeman at the gate again was quite a shock. Conrad was really angry that he came here, although he was quite a nice young man.'

'That'd be Bobby Maddox. His name is Robert and it's the height of hilarity here for folks to call him Bobby - being a policeman. Small minds, huh?' said Beth. 'Poor you, I'm sure it did give you a shock. Maddox would never have come if he'd have thought it'd upset you. I suppose he has to do his job though. Why did he come here? Was it because you were at the Fête, or did Conrad know John?' said Mae.

'I'm not entirely sure, it's probably for a bit of both of those reasons. I really don't think there was much to say of help either way. I didn't like to think that Conrad was in for a session of questioning about a death for any reason. I suppose they have to ask around though, don't they?' said Hyacinth.

'I suppose I'll have to "come clean" and tell you that my twin brother is the policeman in charge of the case. I hope you won't hold it against me!' said Beth.

'The way you say "case" makes it all sound quite sinister, as if something untoward was going on.' said Hyacinth.

'Oh, I wouldn't go as far as that. I think it's just a matter of going through the motions until they are really sure that all is at it at first seems.' said Beth.

Catching the drift that Beth was steering the conversation towards Mae took up the cue to help drive it forward a little further still.

'I gather that John had got himself into something of a tizzy. I think there were queries about the nature of his business interests. Is that right?'

'That's the impression that I'm under. I wonder if it all got a bit too much for him? I understand that he was considering taking some pretty drastic measures.' said Beth. Hyacinth began to colour at this stage of the conversation as the subject matter was obviously getting a little too close to home. 'Oh, I am sorry!' said Beth. 'You mustn't think that we're bothered by your husband's colourful past - even if it was only one brief splash of colour. Don't forget that Drew works with Conrad at times. If we were bothered it would have surfaced in their business relationship. I guess we all just want a share in your spice - in exchange for an introduction into our rather placid lifestyle. Does that seem like a fair exchange?'

Beth's blunt appraisal of the situation was quite disarming. There was no need to attempt to hide anything and so Hyacinth was put completely at her ease. Her facial expression visibly changed as her muscles relaxed and the colour in her cheeks settled. She was positively radiant now. She didn't need to pretend, or present a rehearsed facade as her new friends knew the worst and yet still sought her friendship. 'You must excuse my skittishness. I'm afraid that I've rather got used to living in defensive mode.' said Hyacinth.

'Well, I'm glad that's cleared up then.' said Beth. 'Is there any more of that delicious green tea stuff, or are we in your way? I don't want to stop you from getting on.' There was no evidence of any need to "get on" with anything, in fact evidence suggested that Hyacinth's time was her own and she might just have a little too much of it hanging heavy on her hands. Although Beth was now convinced that Hyacinth was indeed lonely she couldn't help but envy the luxury that she enjoyed. Nevertheless, Beth could respect the strength and dignity with which Hyacinth had met her isolation and the resourceful way in which it was evident that she had spent her days. Breaking her train of thought Beth refocussed on the task in hand and raised her mug expectantly. 'I rather think that it's my brother that's in a bit of a tizzy. He needs to know exactly what

John's worries were and how they might have affected his health.'

Mae nodded emphatically and tried to add another factor to the conversation. 'I get the impression that Jean wasn't much support at times.'

'Yes, I think that's right.' said Hyacinth.

Both Beth and Mae were surprised to hear such confident affirmation about someone who, as far as they knew, she had never met. Their surprise must have shown in their shocked expressions. 'I didn't think you knew Jean. Is her reputation as bad as all that?' asked Mae.

'Oh, no. I didn't know her at all. It's just something that Conrad said. He spoke to John at the Fête, they must have known each other through some business connection. I think that's why the Sergeant came over to speak to Conrad. I liked him, by the way - once I'd got over the shock of a policeman ringing at the gate. He seems really cute, he must have all the girls after him.'

'I think he could have if he noticed them. Unfortunately he's too busy admiring Henrietta, the only young female in the village who hasn't shown any interest in him at all. It's that mysterious left hand ring at work again.' said Beth.

'I suppose that you had your work cut out for you in sticking next to Conrad through his recent tricky patch.' said Mae, getting back to the more needful topics.

'I don't know that you could really say that.' said Hyacinth. 'I'd never find it difficult to stick next to Conrad, we still love each other very much. It was everything else that was difficult - the worry of what people would think. Of course, I was shocked that he would cross the line between clever business and dodgy business and I was embarrassed that he had to go to prison. I think that Conrad had warned John from doing anything drastic in his recent worries and told him to learn from his own mistake. He said he'd told him to stop being stupid and to think of his wife.'

'That seems natural enough in the circumstances.' said Beth.

'It does, but John's response was very bizarre.' said Hyacinth. 'Conrad told me that John gave a sickening laugh and said, "My dear chap, that's exactly what I am thinking of." Apparently he shook himself off a bit after that little outburst and, pulling his act together, said that no doubt Conrad was right and he'd take heed of his kind advice.'

'What a weird thing to say.' said Beth. 'They seemed to get along OK. Maybe they weren't very demonstrative in their affection to each other, but that doesn't signify much. You don't think he wanted a spell inside just to get away from Jean, do you? Surely not!' said Mae.

'Poor Hyacinth. We're treading on your sore toes again. I'm sorry.' said Beth. 'But don't you worry, we've got plenty of sore patches ourselves, as you'll find once you get to know us.' They tactfully manoeuvred the conversation into less troubled waters and were soon engrossed in telling Hyacinth all about Kirsty's garden.

'Did you go on the guided tour around Kirsty's garden on the day of the Fête?' asked Mae. 'Of course, it isn't anything like as grand as your gardens here and she perhaps works towards a less manicured style than you'd like. Nevertheless, she is very knowledgeable and you might enjoy seeing each other's different style of approach.'

'I'm afraid I didn't make it onto the guided tour. I would have liked to, but I didn't think Conrad really wanted to go. I didn't want to drag him around unwillingly and I didn't want to go on my own, so I just didn't bother in the end. I wasn't sure what to expect either, so I didn't think it was worth making a fuss about.' said Hyacinth.

'That's just as well then, in the end. You can see it properly as a friend. We'll take you over as soon as you like. I know you two will get along famously, in fact I'm already regretting offering the introduction as once you two get started I think Mae and I will fall by the wayside.' said Beth.

Just then Conrad walked into the kitchen. They hadn't heard him come in and he seemed surprised to see his wife comfortably sitting at the kitchen table chatting away to people who were obviously new friends. He seemed genuinely pleased to see his wife so happy in new company and engaging in what should be a natural exchange between ladies but had eluded her since they had moved there. 'Have I missed a tea party?' he said.

'Hello darling!' said Hyacinth. She jumped up to kiss him on the cheek. Again Conrad seemed pleasantly surprised at the ease of her public display of affection, rather than embarrassment of him in company. 'I think you know Beth Williams. You work with her husband, Drew, sometimes and you also met at the Fête.' said Hyacinth, introducing her new friends. 'And this is Mae. They've come to ask me if I want to join the WI.'

'Hello. Of course, I thought I recognised Beth. That sounds like a good idea, it'd do you good.' said Conrad.

Conrad's arrival made a natural break in the conversation and so, with promises of further friendship and exchange of numbers, Beth and Mae made their excuses and headed for home. 'I really like her.' said Beth. 'And it proves the point of what I said on Saturday. Although I created the meeting to snoop out some information if I could, I am genuinely keen to make friends. I've been wanting to for ages but couldn't quite get the impetus to find an introduction. I'm not being dishonest or devious but I am creating and making the most of opportunities - and I do think that it was worth it, on all levels. What do you make of the strange conversation that John had with Conrad at the Fête?'

'I'm not sure what to think of it. Does that mean that John's concerns were driving him to dishonest measures? If not fraud, would it imply suicide? It certainly means something and I think you're right that we need to find out.'

'I'll tell you what I am sure of. Conrad won't have told the police that little bit of gossip. I felt like a real fishwife with so much "I heard" and "he said" going on, but I'm sure that's where the real answers lie. If there is anything to discover this is how we'll find it and this is why Benji will struggle. Two men aren't going to swap idle gossip like that, it won't seem important enough, and it's those very details that will give us the clues that we need.' said Beth.

Back at Mossleigh police station Maddox sat at his desk feeling disgruntled after a very unsatisfactory morning with Gareth Foster. He was now talking on the telephone to Detective Chief Inspector James. 'How did you get along, Maddox? Did you find out anything of interest?' asked James.

'Oh, I got along famously.' said Maddox. 'Gareth was extremely helpful. Too helpful! There wasn't much he didn't tell me. I heard about John's entire business history and roll of accounts, if I had the brains to understand what was being said to me. I got an immense download of information and a very technical explanation of what the financial consequences would, or could be. However, when I finally got it wrapped up in layman's terms there's nothing new and we're no wiser. In short things were sticky but not as bad as they could be.'

'There's nothing worse than an earnest accountant. I presume that you came back with a small rainforest of paperwork which we could look through at our leisure?'

'Of course. If you want to get your boffins onto it maybe they could translate it for me, but I don't think it'll lead us anywhere new. We can only hope that there's something on the lap-top that can give us a clue.'

'Ah, you may have something there. I've made a start on that and it's interesting enough, but it can keep for a bit. I'll tell you about it when we meet up.

So, the official stance is that John's business was as Conrad said - a bit of a mess, but workable.'

'And that's just what we don't need. Something, but nothing. Typical. It certainly doesn't explain a massive coronary, does it?'

'Probably not. I take it that the estate now passes to Jean? You need to speak to John's solicitor to make sure. As they didn't have kids it's unlikely that the estate would be split. Better just check that he didn't have a Scandinavian lover and has left it all to her. His solicitor might just give us a different slant on his general state of affairs. It's worth a shot. In the meantime I'll wander over to the toxicology lab and breathe down their necks a bit - although I won't breathe in again until I'm out of the room!'

'Right you are, Sir. I'll make an appointment with Sheppard and Moss in Alder Leigh and see where that takes us.'

'I think that I might just track down some of the authorities in Greece or Spain to make sure everything is as it seems. I don't suppose I can justify a business trip to Spain, do you think? I guess I'll just have to telephone and do my best.'

'Well, if you change your mind, Sir, don't you worry. You can call on me at any time. I can pack my suitcase in a jiffy - no trouble at all!'

'Now, that's very kind of you, Maddox. I'll bear it in mind.'

Being the regular morning for cleaning at the Barlows' house Henrietta took Toby to play at Emma's and then walked to Jean's to begin work. 'What would you like me to do today, Jean?' she asked. 'Do you want to keep some of his things? Maybe some of his books, or some other mementoes? We can leave those until last, so you can think about it. Perhaps I could carry on sorting out the clothes for now?'

'Yes, I think that's the best way. I don't think that there's anything that I particularly want to keep. I don't think it helps in the long run. Do you?' said Jean.

'I expect everybody finds their own way of coping, but I'm inclined to agree with you, that's my way: Clear out and start afresh is my motto, but sometimes it's easier said than done.'

'Goodness, there's such a lot, though! Eileen has offered to help, and Betty too. It seems so ungrateful, but I just can't cope with them being around for too long. I know that they mean to be kind and don't want me to be lonely, but they just get on my nerves after a while. They do fuss!'

'Mmm, I can imagine. Maybe next time, if you think it would help, perhaps Emma could pitch in? I'm sure she would, and she'd make quick work of it, without fuss and bother. She's not one for sentimental attachment to things and she always tells me, "If you haven't used it - chuck it!" She'd be glad to help.'

'That would be great! Betty keeps on suggesting that I keep this or that, and then tuts disapprovingly when I tell her to bag it up for the charity shop. I think they'd only be happy if I turned the house into a shrine to John. But that just holds you back. I won't forget John but I don't want reminding of him every time I turn my head. It sounds harsh, I know, but I have to try and move on. You two are busy enough with your own families though, don't spend longer on me than you can manage. I can't deny that it'd be a load off my mind, I just don't know where to start. A bit of young, businesslike efficiency is what I need.'

'Oh, we'll manage just fine. Don't you worry. We quite like to get stuck into a project and it's easier somehow when it's somebody else's stuff. Just you make sure you put by anything you're sure you want to keep otherwise it'll go if Emma's got anything to do with it. She says it's because she lives in a tiny cottage and so there isn't room for sentimentality. She says that if she hung onto stuff they wouldn't be able to move. What will you do with the space? Do you fancy a sewing room, or maybe a cinema room? You could go mad!'

'I haven't thought that far ahead, I'm afraid. I can't think past just packing things away. I'm hoping that after that I can think of fresh starts, but not yet. Nothing seems quite real just now. It's purely psychological but I don't think it'll properly sink in until after the funeral. I hope it won't be too long before I can start to get all the funeral arrangements organised. I can't explain why, but it's really important to me to get that started - it'll make it real, I think.'

Chapter Twelve

Beth finished the final octave of her scales practice. It hadn't gone well that day and she just couldn't concentrate. Scales in 4ths kept becoming scales in 5ths, which is not a nice sound. More miraculously the scales in 6ths had mysteriously mutated into impressive 7ths. They sounded particularly nasty. She closed the lid on the piano and moved to the kitchen to prepare an early tea before Mae picked her up for choir rehearsal. Once the fajitas were ready she banged on the service bell and she could soon hear the tinkling sound of Drew cleaning his brushes ready to come for his meal.

'What will you be up to while I'm out tonight?' Beth asked.

'I think I'll go back into the studio for a bit to try and get this artwork finished for Conrad. A restaurant in Macclesfield is having a massive extension built and there is to be a huge conservatory around two sides of the building. I've got all of the architectural lines down but I really want to crack on with the painting. The reflection marks on all that glass will take me ages.'

'It sounds very grand. What sort of restaurant is it?'

'I think it's a traditional English place. It looks a Country House type of building set in the outskirts of the town. Perhaps I'll take you there when it's finished? I get the idea that we might have to save up a bit first, so let's hope that the building work doesn't progress too quickly.'

'Now, that sounds like a plan! Don't wait up for me tonight. I'm not sure if we'll go on to The Badger after choir or not. I guess it depends upon how rehearsal goes.'

As they were stacking the dishes into the dishwasher a horn tooted from the driveway. Beth kissed Drew good bye and left him to finish the clearing up.

The Templeton Singers were rehearsing for a concert programme entitled "Merely Mozart" which promised to be particularly delicious. Mae had had a quiet word with Betty's first soprano neighbours warning them to be ready with a judicious elbow during the "Gloria" of The Coronation Mass to make sure that Betty didn't launch into the soloists part. The guest soprano probably wouldn't be willing to share the limelight and especially not with Betty. The second sopranos sat at the back of the rehearsal hall where Beth and Mae had managed to secure seats on the last row of the second soprano section. Of course there could be no chattering during rehearsal but they filled the predictably long periods of time in which the Musical Director was laboriously note-bashing with the bass section by scribbling notes to each other on notepads secreted within their musical scores until it was time for them to sing again. As deputy conductor Mae knew that this could go on for a very long time. Years ago they'd been so tired of sitting idle until the second basses could understand their part they'd both composed an "Ode to Brock the Badger" who had died during an episode of "The Archers" aired at that time. They noticed that this week one of the second altos sitting at the back of the opposite side of the rehearsal room had just got her knitting out. Why was it always the bass section who insisted upon making up the notes and were persistently - no, doggedly dropping octaves? Of course everybody struggled with the music at some point but it was as if the trudging quality of the bass choral lines affected amateur bass's brains and their musical skills became equally lumbering. Perhaps, if they would just sit up straight and not slouch, then maybe their musical rendition wouldn't sag quite so much either. In fairness, the basses probably wondered why on earth the first sopranos found it necessary to screech like so many hags. Beth often wondered the same herself. Nevertheless, even The Templeton Singers couldn't quite kill "Ave Verum Corpus" and the text "in mortis examine" seemed especially poignant with the death of John Barlow hanging over them.

During the break Mae broke ranks and crossed over into first soprano territory to thank Betty's neighbour for doing such a great job as incognito voice coach and to see that all was well. The secret of her success was immediately evident by the unoccupied chair where Betty usually sat. The space was disconcerting as Betty had never been known to miss a rehearsal. As Mae approached she could hear that the topic of conversation buzzing along the row was concern over Betty's absence. Eileen usually brought Betty to rehearsal and so Mae and Natalie sought information from the alto section where Eileen sang. No news was forthcoming as Eileen's seat was also vacant. Nobody had heard why she was absent. The Musical Director was picking up his baton to begin the second half of the rehearsal and everybody scurried back to their positions and prepared to start singing. The rehearsal was productive and the programme progressed with relative ease during the second half. A slight tinge of guilt that Betty's absence was at least partially responsible for the success of the rehearsal was only just held at bay.

Not quite satisfied to leave things hanging Mae and Beth drove to Eileen's house as soon as rehearsal ended only to find the place in darkness and all locked up. The only logical next step was to drive on to Betty's house. The scene which awaited them there was quite different. All the lights were on, cars were parked up and down the road outside and the front door stood open. Mae gingerly knocked on the door and walked on into the house. Neither she nor Beth were prepared for what they next saw. Eileen was sitting in the tall armchair with red eyes from prolonged crying. Dr Wainwright was stooping to comfort her and sprawled across the sofa, in what looked a most uncomfortable pose, lay Betty - dead.

Dr Wainwright looked up as they approached and rose to greet them. He appeared relieved at their arrival and was glad to hand over the care of Eileen to the ladies. It transpired that Eileen had come to collect Betty to take her to choir and had found her like this. Not knowing what else to do she had called Bobby Maddox who in turn called Dr Wainwright. It was he who then suggested DCI James be called and that very person was now on his way to the scene.

After a brief discussion it was decided that Beth and Mae would escort Eileen back home and then later, regardless of the time, the doctor and the police would rendezvous back at Beth's house for nutritional sustenance once they had completed the necessary official procedures. Back in her own house Eileen let the wave of sadness overcome her and her tears flowed freely. It was evident that she had been genuinely fond of Betty. It was touching to behold. The three women sat nursing mugs of hot chocolate and Eileen reminisced over the years that she had known Betty. Mae and Beth were surprised to learn how long and deep the friendship had been. 'I remember when I went to my first WI meeting, all those years ago.' said Eileen. 'Gerald, my husband, had just died and Betty was the one who picked me up and took me along back then. She was a real lifeline and I never can forget her kindness to me. I know that she was getting a bit dotty lately but you could still see the kind-hearted, funny Betty shining through. Do you know what she said to me the other day?' Beth and Mae gave appropriately quizzical expressions and encouraged Eileen to continue. 'She was really upset because she'd heard that her Grandson's brother-in-law was critically ill. She tearfully told me how he'd been "seduced" into a coma. I just kept as straight a face as I could and suggested that I thought that this was surely the best way to go that I could think of.' The ladies laughed and now they all had tears in their eyes, of laughter and of sorrow.

'I know she often confused her words.' said Beth. 'She once told me how painful her "various veins" could be.'

They chatted some more but as conversation became more fragmented Beth suggested that Eileen might now need to go to bed. With promises of help should she call, at any time of the day or night, they made sure that she was cosy and warm and then left her for the time being. Mae dropped Beth at home and then made her way back to her own home where Richard would be waiting for her.

Seeing lights still on in the studio Beth shouted "Hello" to Drew and joined him as he sat still painting. 'I'm surprised that you're still up.' she said.

'I'd got a late night motorbike race, live from abroad playing on the computer, so I thought I'd just keep on painting while it was on. Did you have a good evening?'

'I've had a very strange evening. Rehearsal went well, apart from the basses making up notes as usual. I think that Mozart knew his stuff better the men in that section - not that they'd recognise the fact! I do wish they'd stop meddling with the harmonies! Neither Betty or Eileen were at rehearsal which was most unusual, so Mae and I went on a mission of discovery once practice was over. We drove around and finally found Eileen at Betty's house. I still can't quite believe it, it hasn't quite sunk in yet but Eileen went to pick Betty up as usual and found her at home, dead! I know that she was getting on a bit but all the same, it's quite a shock.

Bobby Maddox and Dr Wainwright were there when we arrived and apparently Benji is on his way right now. He's probably at Betty's house as we speak. We've been calming Eileen down and settling her in at home.'

'Goodness, what a night you've had.' Drew walked over to Beth and hugged and kissed her. 'Well done for looking after Eileen. She must be quite shaken.'

'You know, I'm quite humbled at the depth of the friendship those two shared. They've been such good friends and for more years than I imagined. I've always presumed that Eileen was just being kind in taking Betty under her wing, in a patronising sort of way. If anything it was initially Betty who took Eileen in hand years ago. When Eileen's husband died Betty was patient and kind with her and took her along to the WI to try and get Eileen to look about her in her grief. You just never can tell what's going on in people's lives, can you?'

'Well, we're always told not to judge a book by its cover. It's heartening to hear though, it quite gives hope in mankind, doesn't it?'

'Yes, it does. I'll tell you what does bother me, though. Why on earth does this warrant Benji travelling over? The death of an old lady, albeit a very lovely old lady, doesn't normally concern a Detective Chief Inspector from Police HQ.'

'Hmm. That does raise a few concerns. I suppose you'll find out soon enough. Your brother is bound to tell you as much as he can and probably a little more than that besides. With discretion, of course!'

'Speaking of which, I'd better get cracking! I thought they'd be bound to be hungry when they've finished with all the red tape and so I invited them back here when they've finished. I also wanted to know exactly what was going on.'

'Ooh, you're a sly one. You buy information in exchange for food.'

'It always works, doesn't it? I was always taught that the way to a man's heart was through his stomach. I'm just taking the premise a few steps further.'

Walking to the fridge Beth removed the fajita leftovers from their earlier meal and set them to steam in the wok. She bolstered the remnants by adding more courgette and green pepper. Turning the oven to a high heat she sprayed olive oil onto a large, stainless steel tray and sliced potatoes into wedges before spraying them with more olive oil and coating them liberally with All Spice mix and setting them into a hot oven. Not many minutes before all was ready the kitchen suddenly filled with the arrival of the Doctor and the policemen. Beth gave her brother a hug and set to pouring out tea and coffee.

'Now why on earth would the death of a little old lady bring a Detective Chief Inspector hurtling away from headquarters?' asked Beth.

'I'd like to point out, first and foremost, that I never "hurtle" anywhere. I'm far too dignified for that. I'd also like to point out that I don't actually live at HQ. I was at home when the good doctor called.' said James.

'I am sorry for disturbing you from your evening's rest, James. Nevertheless, I really did think that I should keep you informed. Ordinarily I'd have completed the paperwork with no qualms whatsoever - Betty had obviously had a heart attack. She was a regular patient of mine and she had a known and mismanaged heart condition. I know that she took her medication in a haphazard manner - if at all. Although her complaint wasn't acute her age and general feebleness would easily account for her succumbing to even the smallest heart tremor. However, the similarities between Betty's death and John's, and in such a small space of time were striking - far too alike to be ignored. I thought it best to notify you straight away. However, I must point out that you came "hurtling" here entirely by your own choice.' said Dr Wainwright.

'Of course I did. You know me, I'm a nosey-parker to the last.' said James.

'I'd like to say that I'm mighty glad, Sir.' said Maddox. 'I'd hate to be in the same position that I was on the day of the Fête. If it wasn't for what happened then I'm sure that none of us would trouble overmuch about Betty's death. It's a bit too close for comfort though and I'm delighted that you did "hurtle" down here.'

'It's nice to know that I'm appreciated.' said James. 'As I have "hurtled" myself here get on and dish out the rations Beth. I'm starving! None of us think too well on an empty stomach.' said James. Beth cast a wry glance at Drew and they exchanged a knowing smile. The five of them sat around the kitchen table and chatted over a midnight supper.

'I'm presuming that, as we're here among friends. Can I speak freely and without reserve?' said Dr Wainwright. An encouraging nod from Inspector James indicated that this was so. Seeing that permission was granted Wainwright continued. 'I think that we all know that Betty didn't take her medication as prescribed. I didn't worry too much as I knew that it would be a case of her not bothering to take her pills at all, rather than her taking too many at once as a result of absent minded muddling. Ultimately I couldn't do much else other than encourage her to take the tablets as directed. I don't think her mismanagement was particularly due to forgetfulness. I rather thought that it was more a case of wanton stubbornness and a throwback of the old-school pride in never swallowing a pill but trusting to more abstract remedies such as goose grease or some other old wives cure.'

'You're right there.' said Beth. 'When Emma brought Primrose to see you with her cold Betty was chatting to her and quite freely admitted that she never bothered with the tablets. Apparently she seemed almost girlishly proud of her boldness.'

'That settles it then.' said Wainwright. I'd got my suspicions but now we've confirmed it from source. However, I'm afraid that things don't stay as simple as that.' said Wainwright. 'Once Maddox came on the scene I had a scout around for the tablet bottles. I looked in all the obvious places that tablets might be kept; the bathroom cabinet, dressing table drawers, the bedside table and so on. I didn't move anything but just had a look. I even used a hanky so I didn't leave any prints. I found a few bottles that

I'd recently prescribed but they were mostly all empty. Now it may be that she'd flushed them down the loo. These old dears refuse to get out of the habit of doing this, no matter how much I beg them not to. If she didn't flush them away did she just suddenly take them all? I think that if this was the case then the bottles would all be stashed together and probably near to hand where she died. If they disappeared by other means then that's a matter for you boys in blue to look into. I don't want to put two and two together and make five but I rather think that we've something of a problem on our hands.'

'I think that now is as good a time as any for us all to lay our cards on the table. I'm wide awake if it suits you all the same?' James looked around the table. Nobody seemed inclined to disagree. He gave a nod of assent and Beth made a fresh round of drinks. 'I really can't imagine how the death of dear old Betty could be related to the death of John Barlow. I've had a good look around John's lap-top contents, thanks to Beth's dubious network of friends. I was really surprised to see just how much was on there. He wasn't your average "silver surfer." I'm definitely going to need to justify official access to the contents of that computer - his whole life is on there! He even kept a sort of diary-cum-journal on it. I did wonder if he felt that it was the only place where his wife wouldn't be inclined to look. He really put his heart and most private thoughts down at times. It was embarrassing to read, I can tell you, and I felt really shoddy for doing so. We've all got our job to do though.'

'Can you give us the gist of what you found? You can keep the personal stuff to yourself.' asked Wainwright.

'Well, on a personal level it's sufficient to say that he refers to his concerns about Jean's reaction to having to make necessary economies. This was reinforced by e-mails and letters to his accountant refusing to sell their own personal property in the South of France which would have sold quickly and raised the much needed capital. He mentions in the correspondence that he couldn't face Jean with the proposition and it appears that he was too ashamed to broach the subject. It seems a bit extreme to me. He suggested that he would be willing to sell any of the Greek or Spanish properties but the market there was too strangled to be of any immediate use. In his personal diary he does give vent, quite rightly to my mind, to his feelings about Jean's response to having to cut back a little. I don't think that it's inappropriate to expect to have to eat in and wash your own dishes for the most part - and neither did John. It seems that she objected to having to adopt these basic domestic duties even if John offered to help out.' said James.

'Poor John. He suffered from his own generosity. She'd had it so good and spent so many years on the gravy train that when she came to need to live a bit more like the rest of us she couldn't hack it. I'll bet they were still exceptionally well off by our standards. I guess it's all relative. What a shame Jean couldn't enjoy the good that she still had. That begins to explain a strange comment that Hyacinth made. When talking to Conrad, John mentioned that it was actually the thought of Jean that was driving him to less honest business rather than away from it. He should have just told her to "man up" and tighten her belt. He was too soft for his own good.' said Beth.

'Now that's very interesting. It brings me to the weirdest part of what I read. I know that John owned a night club, or at least some sort of bar in Spain, which I doubt was common knowledge.' said James.

'I can't imagine Jean giving her consent to that. It'd be far too seedy for her sensibilities.' said Wainwright.

'There were a couple of e-mails to Spanish names that I didn't like the sound of. I'll have to do some digging around but, believe it or not, I've a feeling that they belong to a protection racket group. If I'm right then this takes us into very troubled waters. I can't think of any way imaginable how the death of an old lady like Betty can have any links with the likes of this. I find it crazy enough to see how John could have anything to do with these guys. I'll have to see where the road takes me as I scout around.' said James.

'Hyacinth said that Conrad had told him not to be stupid, but I don't think that she had any idea that it went that far.' said Beth.

'We don't know that these deaths are linked at all but I think we're going to have to approach both of them as suspicious for the time being. I've got Forbes and his chums from the Forensics lab on the job as we speak and Brough is already in the loop as far as necessary.' said James. 'Maddox, first thing tomorrow I need you to have a good look through Barlow's bank accounts. I'm specifically after any large and unexplained withdrawals or deposits. I also want you to have another word with Jefferson. See if he has any light to shed on these dodgy characters.' James handed Maddox a list of names. They looked like they belonged in an old gangster movie. 'Don't give too much away about the whole Mafioso thing, just see what he'll offer voluntarily.'

'Righto, Sir. I'll ask him to come to the station. He didn't like me upsetting his wife when I turned up unannounced last time.' said Maddox.

'What a shame that you had to hurt his feelings. Well it never does to upset the ladies, sort it out as you like.' said James.

'I have an awkward point of enquiry.' said Drew. 'I'm working on a project with Conrad. It's on the easel right now. Does that pose a problem for you, Benji?'

'I don't see that it does. Thankfully, under British law an individual is innocent until proven guilty. I'm not even sure what it is that he could be guilty of - not bumping off old ladies, of that I'm sure. Carry on as normal, Drew, but listen out for anything of interest. That goes for all of us.' said James. 'In the meantime I'm going to squeeze something from the toxicology lab. They must have some droplets of wisdom for me by now, even if the tests aren't completed in duplicate and triplicate. That's the trouble with these scientific types, they're so keen on absolute accuracy - which is all well and good in its place, but they can't step outside the red tape for a millisecond. I bet they've probably got a good idea and could tell me a good deal already but daren't break the mould by chatting to me before I've got the papers in my hand.'

Chapter Thirteen

Emma and Henrietta took the children to Beth's as arranged and then together they walked through the village to Jean's house. 'I know that we're supposed to be making use of this opportunity and that we need to keep our eyes open, but I think we need to make sure that the priority of our going to Jean's today is really to help her. Do you agree, Hetty?' asked Emma.

'Yes, I do. Your mum was quite clear that our intentions should be genuine but we were to be wise to the opportunity.'

'I think it has a more wholesome feel about it if we think about it that way. I'm not just saying that to make myself feel better. I don't think we're doing anything shabby, but it's best to define the grey areas, don't you think?'

'You're right. If after a morning's hard work we've nothing to show for our efforts but a more organised Jean then so much the better.'

'Exactly. Well, here we are. Let's roll up our sleeves and get stuck in.' Emma rang the doorbell and they were quickly inside the spacious hallway planning their morning's work.

'I've had a think about how we might best work things this morning.' said Henrietta. 'What do you think, Jean, if Emma gets on with the clearing out and bagging up while I do a bit of my usual cleaning? It's a while since I did any of my usual chores and once I get them done I can help Emma.'

'That sounds like a good idea. I'm so grateful to you girls. I really haven't the energy for any more crawling into cupboards and climbing to the top of wardrobes. John would normally do the heavy lifting, though I suppose that if he were here to do it then the job wouldn't need doing at all. I guess that's the way of it now.' said Jean. 'I'll make sure that I'm on hand so you can come and ask me if you're not sure of anything. As far as I can tell I've moved away any items that I definitely want to keep, so it should be just wholesale bagging up.'

The next hour or so was spent industriously. Jean sat knitting in the lounge as Emma cleared out and bagged up clothes, belts, shoes and other paraphernalia from John's separate bedroom. Henrietta polished and vacuumed throughout the house, humming as she worked. At 11 o'clock Jean put aside her knitting and called the girls into the kitchen for a drink. She made a pot of tea and put out a plate of biscuits which soon needed replenishing. 'Do you have any paracetamol, Jean? I think I've got a headache coming on.' said Emma.

'Oh, I hope you haven't overdone it and tired yourself out. I'm so sorry but I don't have any at all. I'm afraid that I never take any tablets and neither did John. You must go home if you're not well.' said Jean.

Emma brushed aside Jean's concerns. 'Oh, it's nothing really. It's hardly there at all, in fact that cup of tea and some biscuits have set me to rights again. I'll have another cup out of the pot and then I'm raring to go again. How's your knitting coming on?'

Jean walked into the lounge to fetch her knitting to show to the girls and as soon as her back was turned Henrietta threw Emma an enquiring glance. In reply Emma wrinkled her brow and shrugged her shoulders. Further explanation was impossible as Jean came bustling into the kitchen with her arms full of aran wool in various stages of completion. She explained that she was knitting a large cabled throw and the younger ladies were eager and generous with their praise. Jean blushed with the enjoyment of their approval, obviously unaccustomed to such admiration, and proceeded to try and explain the cabling method.

As the only employee of the group Henrietta felt that she had finished her stipulated break and now needed to get back to work. Not wanting to miss out on the knitting lesson she decided to tackle what job she could in that room and began to clean out the fridge as they chatted. Running a bowl of hot water she tipped a splash of distilled white vinegar into the bowl. After emptying the contents of the fridge onto the kitchen surface she dipped the cloth into the bowl of water and vinegar and then sprinkled bicarbonate of soda onto the cloth before beginning to wipe down the shelves. She wiped the shelves with a dry cloth and placed a clean piece of kitchen towel under where the milk bottle stood before restoring the contents of the fridge back to their rightful place. 'I'm not sure that you're looking after yourself properly, Jean. It's not like you to have such an empty fridge. These contents have hardly changed since I last cleaned before the Fête. I know that cooking for one hardly seems worth the effort - I know it well, but you really do need to eat properly and look after yourself.' Jean looked up at Henrietta and gave her a sheepishly embarrassed look. 'You know, if you really can't stand the thought of just cooking for yourself all the time you ought to make a daily lunch date at Eileen's tea rooms. Her prices are very reasonable and it's quite acceptable to sit on your own if you don't want to make it into a social occasion. I understand that you might not want to be off on a jolly every time you want to eat your lunch. I can't afford to go very often, but sometimes when Toby's in school I treat myself to lunch out and I enjoy going on my own. People soon get used to the fact that you like to sit by yourself and they soon stop even noticing, it's just a matter of establishing a pattern. I find that I feel less conspicuous if I take a book to read but it's not strictly necessary. You could take your knitting, although I suppose you can't really knit and eat.'

'What a good idea, Hetty. It'd get you out of the house each day too. You should really consider it, Jean. You could have a standing reservation and get privileged treatment. I'm quite jealous. You need never peel a potato again if you didn't want to! All you'd need to worry about is your breakfast and a light tea or supper in an evening. How civilised.' said Emma.

'It'd be a waste of this fantastic kitchen though.' said Henrietta. 'You'd have to have a mammoth baking session now and then, when the mood strikes, just to justify this magnificent cooking range.'

'You're right, I've not been eating proper meals. There's something in what you say, you girls make it sound quite appealing. I've not been out as I'm not really in the mood for sociable outings just now, and I certainly wouldn't want that every day. I'd never considered going on my own, merely to eat. If you say that you do that sometimes Henrietta, then I suppose it must be all right. I'd never thought of it that way. I think it's just a matter of confidence. Once I've been I imagine it would soon be accepted without comment. I might just try - if I dare!' said Jean.

'Of course you dare. Hide behind a knitting pattern or a book at first, you'll soon settle down to it.' said Emma.

As the conversation progressed Henrietta finished checking dates and clearing out old jars. At the back of the fridge she found a jar of Jean's prize-winning rhubarb and rose petal jam. She opened the lid to check the rim and noticed signs of mould forming on the sides of the jar. Wiping her finger across the lid, she tasted the jam. "This jam's going off, Jean." said Henrietta. "What shall I do with it? Shall I just scrape away the mould?"

'I'd forgotten that it was there, that was John's jam.' said Jean. 'I'd better throw it away, I don't want to eat it now. I've blamed myself for John's death thinking that in giving him a treat I'd actually caused him to die by upsetting his diabetes. Dr Wainwright tells me that it's utter nonsense, but you do dwell on such things, don't you?' Jean took the jar from Henrietta and after tipping the remnants into the waste bin she rinsed the jar and set it to dry on the drainer.

'Oh, Jean!' said Emma. 'Nobody ever sticks to their diet as they should. You really need to stop thinking like that.'

'You're right, I'm sure.' said Jean. 'Even so, I'm sick of the stuff. I can't believe that Darcy hadn't got the guts to choose a proper first place and gave a joint first prize at the Fête. That's worse than coming second, don't you think?'

'I just thought that both yours and Phoebe's jams were top notch and they both deserved first place. I honestly think that was the case and Darcy was really brave to stick to her guns in saying so.' said Emma as she stood up to resume sorting and bagging duties upstairs.

By the end of the morning the two younger ladies had made a thorough job and Jean's hallway was now full of bags of clothes stashed in piles. 'I'll get Nathaniel to call round in his truck later today, if you can cope with these here for a few hours. That's upstairs finished I think.' said Emma.

'There isn't much more left to do, in fact I'd say that you're almost done apart from some little bits and bobs which you'll need to look through first, to check if there's anything you want to keep.' said Henrietta.

'Please thank Nathaniel for collecting all of these bags. If you take them to the church hall they'll decide what's best to send where. As there's too much to carry now will you be walking straight back to Beth's?' said Jean.

'Yes, we'd better go and rescue her from the kids - or vice versa.' said Henrietta.

'If you don't mind, I think I'll walk with you. I'm going to strike while the iron's hot and go to The Blue Willow tea rooms for my lunch. You two can bolster my courage as we walk.' said Jean.

The last thing that Emma and Henrietta wanted just now was Jean's company. They had so much that they wanted to talk about after their morning's work but that would now have to wait. Nevertheless, they were glad that Jean had taken their advice and was acting on it so quickly.

'Good for you!' said Henrietta. 'Take a book, or something, just for the first time. I found that it really helped me. Nobody else cares I'm sure, but it just covered my shyness.'

'I'm so glad that you understand. I'll take this book of knitting patterns as I want to figure out the next pattern panel. I feel quite rebellious at the thought of reading and eating at the same time. I was always taught that it was bad manners to take a book to the table.' said Jean.

'Oh, you rebel!' said Emma.

The three of them walked happily towards Main Street and then Emma and Henrietta continued to Beth's house. The distance left was too short to allow any lengthy conversation and they didn't want to linger and be later than they already were in picking up the children. 'It's a shame that Jean walked back with us, though I'm glad that she'll be having a proper meal today. Well done you, for spotting that she wasn't shopping or eating properly.' said Emma.

'I'm surprised at her really. I thought that she'd be more practical than that.'

'We've obviously got plenty to talk about and to think over, but it'll have to wait until we all meet together to discuss all of our findings. What was all that funny business about you having a headache? I know that you carry the contents of a chemist's shop wherever you go.'

'The answer to that will have to wait, I'm afraid. I can see mum with Toby and Primrose walking to meet us.'

Beth had been in the garden with the children and had seen Emma and Henrietta as they walked towards the house. She had quickly picked two bunches of mismatched flowers and these were now in the clutches of two pairs of small, grubby hands. The children were now running to give their posies to their mum. Simultaneously Emma and Henrietta stooped to catch a running child. Appropriate smiles and sniffing gestures were directed to the proffered posies and they thanked Beth for her kind attention to the children and for the flowers. An enquiring glance from Beth was understood. 'I don't think that our efforts have been entirely wasted this morning. Jean is nicely organised at home and, thanks to Henrietta's powers of observation, she is probably eating her first decent meal since John died. Henrietta sent her to Eileen's tea rooms to make sure she has some quality food. We definitely need to go there ourselves, as soon as we possibly can.' said Emma. She gave special emphasis to the latter part of her sentence.

Without need for further comment Beth gave a decisive nod, fully understanding the implication. After a round of hugs Emma and Henrietta took charge of their own children and they parted company.

Sergeant Maddox had spent a dreary morning ploughing through reams of pages of John Barlow's accounts and bank statements. It was a tedious business and he frequently needed to revisit pages once he realised that his attention had waned and he hadn't actually registered any of the figures he'd been glancing over. James had told him to look for large or unexplained sums of deposit or expenditure, but as far as Maddox was concerned almost all of the amounts that he was reading were to be considered "large" and many of them didn't make a great deal of sense. In the run of his own financial dealings he certainly didn't deal in figures with this many digits. There were the usual payments to official bodies such as tax payments, National Insurance contributions and other legal necessities. Payments had come in from foreign banks but these had continued over long periods of time and, although he couldn't make a great deal of sense of them, he discounted them as regular and therefore acceptable. Maybe it was rental agreements from his property abroad. These deposits had slowed down more recently and this bolstered the theory that they were the rental payments which were now in jeopardy. Only in the most recent accounting quarter did any item of interest appear, and even this was only a singular deposit of a relatively small amount, although to the wallet of Sergeant Maddox it was still a sizeable sum. It was the name of the payee that primarily gave rise to interest. Earlier that summer the ledger showed a singled payment of fifteen thousand pounds from Jefferson Properties Ltd. and once the cash was cleared the sum had been transferred into John's personal bank account. Maddox had arranged to meet Jefferson at his company's office later that day and he would be sure to ask him about this payment. As far as Maddox was aware John hadn't dealt with Jefferson Properties on a business level. If the transaction was business related why then was the money transferred to John's own personal bank account?

A brief meeting with John's solicitor revealed that all of Barlow's property portfolio was now up for sale, excepting their residential address in Mossleigh. Even the holiday home in France was now on the market. It was ironic; if John had done this some months ago he wouldn't have been in such financial difficulty just before he died. It transpired that although Jean was now quite a wealthy lady from a long-standing life insurance policy and didn't now need the capital releasing from the properties she had instructed the sales to go ahead as she didn't want the hassle and didn't understand how to deal with all the business affairs. This seemed reasonable enough. The meeting with Jefferson couldn't be described as a signal success. When confronted with the subject of depositing a lump sum into John Barlow's bank account he was totally unabashed. 'I didn't realise that it was a topic worthy of consideration. I knew that you'd have gone over Barlow's accounts with a fine tooth comb so I just presumed that you'd know all about it. It's a trifling sum and I didn't think you'd find it worthy of speculation.' said Jefferson.

'I'm afraid that the financial world in which you live is very different from the one which I'm accustomed to, Sir. In my world fifteen thousand pounds would never be referred to as a "trifling sum" and would always be of interest to me. What was the payment for?' said Maddox.

'I told John to think of it as a penance payment - a secular act of contrition. I've made a lot of money by dancing on the edge of legality, and over the edge of it too. John was in such a state for ready cash and he was pitiable. He was in such a blind panic that he simply wasn't thinking clearly. He couldn't accept that he'd have to take the rough with the smooth like the rest of us. He kept talking of being a failure and worrying about what Jean would think. I offered a lump sum to buy him some thinking time. Of course, he said that he couldn't accept such an offer, he's of the old-school like that. I'd seen his bank details before when he was asking my advice and I've a good memory when it comes to numbers. I instructed my secretary to transfer the money into John's account. I assumed that he'd swallowed his pride and accepted the cash as he never returned it. When he spoke to me on the day of the Fête I think he tried to thank me in his own stumbling, awkward way. It had obviously stung him to have to accept it, mumbling about appreciating my generosity. I brushed over it quickly to help him save face.'

'So, you're asking me to believe that the cash was a gift, to appease your conscience?'

'Indeed I am. Whether you believe it or not it's the only explanation that I can offer. I suppose I could have told you that it was a loan - I may even have hinted that John could think of it that way if it helped him to accept it more easily. From my point of view I never expected it back. I've never conducted any business with John so I can't give any other explanation than the one that I just have. It's the truth.'

'I think I believe you! Perhaps the business world isn't as harsh as I'd thought.'

'Oh, I think you'll find that it is just that. It takes a holiday at Her Majesty's Pleasure to make you see a different side - that and a steadfast wife.'

'While you're in your "Good Samaritan" phase, perhaps you could help me with this list of names. What can you tell me about any of the people on this list?'

'Hhmm. This looks like an exotic bunch. Frankos, Alexi Spiros, Salvatore and Migella, I've heard of the last two I think. I think these last two are linked to the Spanish property market, although much more than that I can't tell you. I know that you've got me down as a hardened criminal but my misdemeanour runs to being too clever with numbers for my own good. I've no knowledge of what you'd personally consider as out and out bad guys and I'm certainly not one. Even when I was in prison I didn't mix with the "criminals" other than was absolutely necessary. I helped the officers prepare their accounts - legitimately - and I set up spread sheets for the wardens and the prison librarian. I didn't make any "underground connections." I only know of these last two enough to know that if their names show up on any business transaction it pays to walk away, fast. No matter how lucrative the deal I know to avoid any further negotiation, they're not good news. After that I'm afraid that I'm in the dark and choose to remain so.' As Maddox was similarly in the dark there wasn't much he could say on the subject and was unable to attempt to coax any further information out of Jefferson, presuming that he knew more than he had said. Either this set of leads had led him down an investigative cul-de-sac or Jefferson was such a charming and consummate liar that Maddox had met his match. If there was more to be learned here he would have to hand over to DCI James.

Chapter Fourteen

Beth was sitting in Emma's lounge as Primrose played with her teddy bear. 'We've spent so much time and attention looking out for Jean and trying to figure out about John that I'm afraid that we've ignored what's under our nose. Hetty has just told me that towards the end of term Toby has been suffering from taunts from his school mates. They've been picking on him because nobody has ever seen his dad and only his mum walks him to and from school.' said Emma.

'As if it isn't bad enough having the adults of the village wondering about the mysterious wedding ring, it now seems that the children aren't deaf to their parent's gossip either. I bet the little lad can't even answer the questions himself, or he's wise enough not to.' said Beth.

'I think that it's really crass. It's the adults who are at fault. The children are just copying what they see and hear. As if people haven't got enough worries of their own without needing to mull over other folk's troubles.'

'There's not a lot we can do about it during the holidays. We'll have to just keep an eye on Henrietta and Toby, meanwhile I'll have a think about. We need to meet up at The Blue Willow as soon as we can. Can you arrange it with Hetty? We'll save what we've got to discuss until then, rather than go over everything twice.'

'I'm not sure what you'll make of our findings but we definitely need to put our heads together.'

In his office at Police HQ Detective Chief Inspector James had consumed several cups of strong black coffee in the process of cross referencing the names found in the correspondence on John Barlow's lap top against the police database system. The subject matter of John's e-mails had guided him to a certain point and then, not being proud, he allowed a Google search to play a part in helping to piece together an idea of what was going on. Although it looked as though John hadn't committed himself at the point of the last e-mail contact, it was evident that he had dipped his toes into very turbulent waters and would soon be past the point of no return if he hadn't already crossed that line. It was certainly very worrying and it seemed quite unreal when you connected the names he had just researched with the quiet village life of Mossleigh and the gentle figure of John Barlow. He logged out of all the systems on his screen and unplugged the hard drive surreptitiously accessed by Carlton Pepper. Draining the dregs of his coffee cup he grimaced at the bitterness of the cold coffee and of the situation in general. His thoughts were interrupted by a knock on the door and the entrance of Forbes. 'Ah, Forbes. How good of you to grace me with your illustrious presence.' Forbes raised his eyebrows and looked up at the ceiling. 'I do hope that you've come with more in mind than merely brightening my day with your boyish good looks.'

'Very funny, Sir. I know that you're in a tight place with the Mossleigh case and so I thought I'd give you the heads-up on our first round of results. It's all unofficial of course, until we've run all the checks and counter tests. Off the record there's little doubt that we're wrong though. We'll have more to say next week but I thought you'd want to know as soon as possible.'

'Yes, yes. I won't quote you until you give me the official say-so. Take a seat and do tell all.'

Forbes sat opposite to James and casting an inward glance he formulated his thoughts. Before he began his discourse he began with a series of questions. 'Just to clarify, did the chap have a known heart condition and did he suffer with diabetes?'

'No, and yes. Do go on.'

'Rather than unload a stream of abstract jargon I'll uncharacteristically put my neck on the line and interpret the lab findings. We've only got partial results yet, but for what it's worth - here goes. It would appear that the poor chap died of a heart attack as a result of an insulin spike. The spike is the grey area in this case as it can occur from many and varied stimuli. In this case it was a direct result of the presence of a form of digitoxin. The drug digitoxin contains cardiac glycosides and the derivative digitoxin can produce an insulin release. Also, in the presence of glucose digitoxin can produce an insulin spike. As such the cause of death can accurately be termed a Myocardial Infarction as a result of Diabetes Mellitus (Type II). This seems straightforward enough, but if you say that the chap wasn't known to have a heart problem then there is no explanation for the presence of digitoxin in any form. We can pin down the strain of the drug more specifically with more tests but I thought that this in itself was enough for now and better than nothing.'

'That's very interesting, Forbes. What else can you tell me?'

'The matter of the insulin spike could easily have been explained by diabetes and superficially this would have been the case, if the presence of digitoxin wasn't discovered. The tricky part here is to define the quantity of each and I think that will be vitally important. Various forms are absorbed at different rates in the gastrointestinal tract and for a diabetic sufferer only a small amount of digitoxin could prove fatal as the resultant insulin spike would be more pronounced than for a non-diabetic. You'd need to talk to the bloke's GP to get a better idea about that. In short, the presence of digitoxin - in whatever form - needs explaining. I'm not sure that I can imagine how that could happen by accident, though there have been cases with muddled tablet bottles or confusion on similar themes.'

'Forbes, I owe you! Don't worry, your secret is safe with me. I'll make sure that nobody in the force ever gets to hear that the Forensics department can be helpful or imaginative. Next time I need someone to put their foot down with all the lights flashing I'll make sure the call comes to you.'

'Oh, I do that anyway, as well you know. But it'd be nice to be official about it. When we whizzed down to Mossleigh we were pretty thorough over this chap, not being keen to tear ourselves away from the idyllic scenery. I think there might be bits of incidental material which we could look at if needed, but I guess that this is the main thrust.'

'It's certainly enough to be getting along with. I know that you've other things on the go but if you can keep going with this I think I'll be coming back for more. See what you can find for me. This case has taken some surprising turns and the concept of quiet village life is tainted for ever for me now. I'll never believe the facâde of a rural idyll again.'

Forbes raised his eyebrows. 'I'll be interested to hear your news. We'll keep this one going then and we'll keep each other posted.'

James liked Forbes. He had just the right mix of professional standing and kind humanity. The way he referred to the subject of his gruesome findings in terms of "the chap" or "the bloke" was reassuring. Despite the unthinkable methods which were necessary in his job he had never referred to "the body" as long as James had known him. The additional bonus was that Forbes could stretch to some creative thinking along with precise scientific method. He liked him a lot. As Forbes left the office James picked up the telephone and called Dr Wainwright, judging him to be between surgery and house visits at this time. This being the case the doctor's secretary put his call straight through.

'James, how good to hear from you. How's it going?' asked Wainwright.

'I'm finding myself caught deeper and deeper in a complex web. I feel like I'm lost in a labyrinth. I must be a magnet for trouble because as soon as I'd heard about John's death when I telephoned Beth that night I must have smelled trouble from afar. Certainly nothing is as it at first seemed.'

'Ah, it's like that then, is it?'

'This morning has brought me some bizarre and puzzling information. I'd like to talk with you about it all. We could meet at Mossleigh police station as I need Maddox in on our little chat, but I don't feel inclined to rough it there. The local Inspector doesn't seem inclined to stick her nose in and for that I'm grateful. How would it suit you to set up a temporary case room in Beth's kitchen again? I rather fancy that she'll have some bits of information to throw into the mix herself too if I'm not mistaken. She'll have got her underground network busy I'm sure. I can pop over to the police station and give a polite update to Inspector Buckley afterwards. She'll appreciate the formality and want nothing more, sensible woman.'

'Sounds good to me, if you're happy to keep it that way. You're the boss.'

'Beth and Drew are used to it by now, they know to be discreet. You need to think of them as a type of undercover officer. If Beth ever went "pro" we'd all have to look to our laurels. Do you mind losing part of your Sunday? That way we won't interrupt your surgery hours.'

'Don't worry about that, it suits me fine.'

Knowing that her brother was arranging a meeting for the coming Sunday Beth decided that a meeting of their own at The Blue Willow tea rooms was now a matter of urgency. She rang around and arranged a hasty meeting. It was as busy as ever there but as it was only mid-morning there were several tables still vacant. This was the perfect ambience. If the place was too empty their conversation would be conspicuous and Eileen might feel inclined to join them for a chat while business was quiet. As it was she was kept busy and there was sufficient background noise to cover their own conversation. They ordered a selection of cakes and pots of tea an as the instigator of the meeting Beth opened the proceedings. 'Benji has arranged a meeting with Bobby Maddox and Dr Wainwright for tomorrow morning. I think we can all guess that something is amiss in the death of John Barlow. I don't know if Betty's death has anything to do with the case but I do know that Benji is keeping an open mind. If we've anything at all that we think might prove helpful, however insignificant it might seem, then let's hear it and I can tell Benji what we've found. We'll let him choose what's relevant, so don't be shy. Mae, please tell the girls how we got on at the Jefferson residence - my toasted teacake is getting cold.'

'OK but feel free to pitch in as I go if you think I miss anything out.' said Mae. 'First of all I'd like to say that I really think that we've found a new friend. Hyacinth struck me as being genuinely pleased that we'd bothered to call on her and her openness to the friendship was quite disarming. We're taking her to meet Kirsty next week and I'm really looking forward to them meeting each other. I think that once we've made the introduction and helped to break the ice Beth and I will be redundant as Kirsty and Hyacinth will be engrossed in each other and plant lore.'

'Like you said, Beth, we'll start out with genuinely honourable aims but be wise to make the most of the possibilities to find out what we can.' said Henrietta.

'Exactly.' said Beth, her mouth full of teacake and a cup halfway to her lips.

'On another level the conversation did reveal something of interest.' said Mae. 'It seems that John sought help and advice from Conrad and was quite desperate about it. I don't know what he was thinking of exactly but extreme measures were referred to. When Conrad advised John to steer clear of anything dishonest and to think of the implications for his wife Hyacinth told us that John's response was extremely strange. Conrad was obviously thinking of the suffering and shame his incarceration had caused Hyacinth, but apparently John just barked out a strangled laugh and said "That's exactly what I am thinking of." What on earth could that mean?'

'We wondered a lot about that comment.' said Beth. 'Does it mean that he intended to go to prison specifically to get away from Jean, or to cause her embarrassment? Did he want revenge for something? It just doesn't make sense.'

'That's a bit harsh on Jean.' said Henrietta. 'She's more vulnerable than she seems. She isn't eating properly. I noticed that she hadn't been shopping since I last cleaned the fridge out before John died so she can't be eating properly.'

'Oh don't talk to me about cleaning out fridges. Mine is in such a state and I keep putting the job off.' said Mae.

'You did a good turn in spotting that and making sure that she eats at least one good meal a day here'. said Emma. 'I don't think that we've quite realised how hard Jean has taken it all. I don't think she's coping as well as we at first thought.'

'The contents of her fridge haven't changed at all since John died. There was all sorts of stuff going mouldy and out of date. She'd pushed John's jam to the back of the fridge in an attempt to forget about it because she blames herself for upsetting his diabetes and feels responsible for his death.' said Henrietta.

'Goodness!' explained Mae. 'Is she still nursing a sense of guilt about that dratted jam? To be honest we all thought that John was something of an old woman about his diet. He only had the mild onset of diabetes and didn't need medication but just needed to watch his food intake a bit. He was such a fuss-pot.'

'I think it was more to do with the fact that Jean was annoyed at not winning first prize outright.' said Henrietta. 'I had a taste of it and I can't see what all the fuss is about - it didn't taste so wonderful to me. I suppose it was just starting to go moldy though.'

'After his death we all felt bad about deriding his fussy ways.' said Beth. We all wondered if he'd suffered more than we'd given him credit for and thought that maybe his pedantic ways were more important than we'd realised. I don't think that's an issue now and we all guess that there's more to it than that. I know that Dr Wainwright wasn't satisfied from the start but couldn't say more than that. Benji obviously isn't satisfied. I think that it will be interesting to see what next week will reveal.'

'All this makes my little discovery even more confusing.' said Emma. 'I made quite a show of pretending that I'd got a headache at Jean's. Although I always carry paracetamol with me I asked if she had any. I'd heard before that neither of them ever took tablets but I wanted to be sure that I'd got my facts right there. The reason that I asked is because whilst ridding out John's wardrobe I found an absolute stash of both paracetamol and aspirin hidden away behind some shoes. There were about ten boxes of each and I figured that if they were for normal use they'd be in a more conventional place of storage. What this could mean I can't guess. If it's suicide that we're thinking killed John then, despite the stock of tablets, the theory doesn't work. If he'd overdosed on paracetamol and aspirin the stash would no longer be there. It may well indicate intent but that still doesn't help us.' said Emma.

'Now that is interesting.' said Beth. 'I wonder if he found a more thorough method?'

They pooled all of their findings and by the end of the morning they couldn't form a clear picture from the information they had to date. Rather than keep going around in circles they decided to leave things as they stood. Everybody agreed to keep their eyes and ears open and said they would meet again shortly.

Chapter Fifteen

DCI James, Sergeant Maddox and Dr Wainwright sat around the kitchen table and Beth stood by the toaster feeding crumpets into the slots and buttering them. Drew emerged from his studio and joined the group for the food and conversation.

'I organised this little "pow-wow" because quite a minefield of information has come to light and we need to get our heads together.' said James. 'I think you'll find that once you join me in this "Alice in Wonderland" type journey down the rabbit hole all sense of perspective will fall strangely away. When John Barlow died and Dr Wainwright here so perceptively felt that he couldn't satisfactorily issue the necessary death certificate little did we realise how bizarre the trail would become. I'm not entirely sure where to begin, so perhaps Sergeant Maddox could set the ball rolling and tell us how his second meeting with Conrad Jefferson went?'

Sergeant Maddox blushed a little and hastily swallowed his mouthful of buttered crumpet. With a glug of his signature sweet tea he described the outcome of his meeting. 'I'm afraid that there's not a lot to tell. I asked Jefferson about the money that he deposited into John's account straight off the bat and he didn't flinch a bit. He seemed to presume that, having access to John's accounts, it was something that we'd always known. Do you know that he could remember John's bank number and sort code after just glancing over some statements that John showed him when he was asking Jefferson's advice? I'll tell you, that's worrying! Also, he referred to fifteen thousand pounds as a paltry amount. He didn't seem to think it was enough to signify in our investigation. When I informed him that it did figure in our thinking, if you'll pardon the pun, he was quite ready to offer an explanation - though it's not what you'd have expected. Jefferson said that the money was a goodwill gesture to buy John a bit of thinking time. He said that John wasn't thinking straight and thought it would take the pressure off a bit so that he could clear his head. Jefferson admitted that he'd made a tidy sum out of his recent tangle with alternative accounting and as he could remember John's bank account details he instructed his secretary to make the deposit. She confirms that this was the case and that Jefferson gave her the necessary bank numbers out of his head. This was quite normal apparently. Jefferson did say that John seemed too embarrassed to accept the money and so he suggested that it be considered a loan, though he didn't expect to see the money again. As the money wasn't returned he presumed that John had swallowed his pride and accepted the gift. For what it's worth, I have to say that I believed him, sir. He never conducted any business with John, or not as far as we know, so how else can we account for it?'

'I guess anything is possible. We'll leave it as it stands for now. What else is there that you can tell us?' asked James.

'I've spoken to Barlow's solicitor.' continued Maddox. 'We'd already guessed that Jean is now a very rich woman owing to a long standing life insurance policy. Even though she doesn't now need the ready cash she's instructed that all properties except the home here in Mossleigh be put up for sale. Her reasoning is that she can't cope with the hassle and doesn't understand business.'

'That seems fair enough.' said James. 'It's a part of John's life that she never had any dealings in and it's a bit late in the day to try and learn now, even if she had the inclination. Even so, there's a sad irony to it. She's now selling the house in France, which is quite a magnificent structure, if what I hear is true. This was the very property that John didn't dare venture to suggest should be sold for Jean's sake. A quick sale there would have been more likely and highly profitable. The property market in that part of Europe is quite vigorous and they would have made more than enough to tide him over this recent bumpy patch.'

'You can't really expect Jean to go there now though, can you? She's not likely to want to go on her own, is she?' said Drew. 'It's a sorry state of affairs, however you view it.'

'I gave young Maddox here a list of names to see if Jefferson could, or would, shed any light on them.' said James. 'Now this is where things get very surreal and my mind still boggles when I link what I'm about to tell you with the name of John Barlow.'

Maddox interrupted James' flow. 'I'm sorry sir, I clean forgot to tell you about that. I did show the list to Jefferson. He said that he didn't know the top two names on the list but he knew the last two names enough to know that if you saw those names attached to a business deal you walked away. He said that it didn't matter how lucrative the deal was, it was a matter of self preservation to leave well alone.'

'That fits with my findings.' said James. 'Salvatore and Migella are a dastardly duo in the Spanish property market. I can see how John's troubles could edge into their territory as their names are associated with the recent "property bubble" and subsequent financial crisis. As far as I can understand property investment in Spain has been out of control for some time now. I'm sure we're all aware that not so many years ago simply loads of retired UK residents were using their golden-handshake retirement funds to buy property in Spain so that they could live the high life and watch EastEnders sitting outside on the balcony or by the pool during the winter months. Whole villages in Spain became colonised by "ex-pats." As a prime tourist spot real estate companies made Spain into an important place for investment. This would be where Jefferson's company would come in and Barlow was hanging onto the shirt tails of the big fish like Jefferson.' James took a gulp of his coffee before he continued. 'At about this time a change in Spanish legislation allowed local communities to have a greater involvement in town planning. On the surface this would appear to be a good thing. It allowed the locals to have a say in what was or was not built in their own towns. This is where our terrible twosome comes in. Using their contacts they manoeuvred themselves onto various committees and your average fisherman was no match against the Mafioso officials who could manipulate sales and development to their own ends. At the same time these undesirables maintained their usual business of low-level tobacco smuggling into the UK and had even progressed to the sale of more serious narcotics. Business of this kind is usually conducted in bars and night clubs so John's business interests overlap here on both the property and the smuggling fronts. He may even have got entangled against his own wishes as he wouldn't necessarily know about the day to day dealings of his bar manager in Spain until it was too late.'

'Crikey, he really was in over his head.' said Maddox.

'We don't know that he was definitely involved, but he was certainly beginning to sail a little close to the wind.' said James. 'The first two names on the list that I gave you, Frankos and Alexi Spiros, are known as the Greek Mafia. We know that John had rental properties in Greece but the recent Euro crash had rendered these obsolete for the time being. Nobody could afford the rent. These two unsavouries are part of a group known as "The Godfathers of the Night" if you'll believe it, because of their association with night clubs from where they base their smuggling operations. They run a protection racket over the businessmen in the area as well as the usual tobacco and narcotics line. They've never been convicted as it's rumoured that they have links on the inside of the police force there who keep them ahead of the game. It may be that John was considering, or being persuaded to convert his empty property into a bar or night club for their purposes. We know that they have contacts in New York, but it's not known if they operate in the UK.'

'I see what you mean about shattering any sense of perspective. It'd be laughable if it weren't actually happening.' said Drew. 'It all sounds so far-fetched. The man was out of his league!'

'It would certainly justify the theory of a stress induced coronary.' said Wainwright.

'Indeed it would, but I'm afraid that the case is no longer so straightforward.' said James.

'If you consider that as straightforward then I dread to think what's next on the agenda.' said Beth.

James coated a fresh batch of buttered crumpets with Phoebe's renowned damson jam and continued to explain his findings. 'If we'd learned all of this earlier we'd have readily deduced stress as the contributing factor. This is where you come in Dr. Wainwright. Forbes has broken the mould and given me a heads-up on toxicology's preliminary findings. In short, evidence of a form of digitoxin has been found in John's body. Whether he took it on purpose, by accident or via a third party is left for us to decide. The lab is doing more tests to pinpoint exactly what form was taken, but the fact that he'd ingested a dubious and unexplained substance is beyond doubt.'

'That surely provides a tentative link between the death of Betty and John. Both deaths display similar symptoms of cause of death and the timing of the deaths are so close together.' said Wainwright. 'Could that explain the missing tablets from Betty's house? The situation with the business heavies would also support that, presuming the theory of suicide is still valid.'

'Stereotypically you would expect to find a note.' said James. 'It's part of the human condition to want to share your burdens, even when you think all is beyond hope and you're at the uttermost end of your tether. There are of course always odd exceptions to the rule. I'm not entirely convinced of the theory of suicide myself. Although there was plenty of litter about the place where John died; bottles, cans and so forth, there's no vessel on the table where he sat. He could have discarded his drink soon after he'd swallowed, but it's not usual to tidy away after committing suicide. There wasn't anything next to him was there, Maddox?'

'I don't remember there being any sign of a cup, but I can check the photos just to make sure.' said Maddox.

'Good man. You did a first rate job that day. Wainwright, what can you tell us about digitoxin in general? Purely for argument's sake, would it take many of Betty's tablets to commit suicide? Could he have taken something much earlier and there was a delayed reaction? That would explain the lack of suicide note on the scene.' said James.

'Without knowing the exact form of digitoxin and exactly how much was ingested it's impossible to say for sure. Generally speaking anything is possible. I would hazard the opinion that I think it would be mighty tricky to take a fatal dose by accident. Regardless of what is seen on the TV a fatal dose of digitoxin is quite substantial, unless you took it in a concentrated form. Even then you'd have to take quite a lot of the stuff, which you wouldn't easily do by mistake.' said Wainwright.

'Well, that's good enough for me.' said James. 'I think that we can rule out accidental death from what Wainwright says. Do we all agree?' Unanimous nods of assent assured him that this was the case.

'Don't discount anything utterly on my general advice. Until we know the details of the concoction taken it's not feasible to rule anything out completely. That being said I would still suggest that it's highly unlikely.' said Wainwright.

'Spoken like a true scientist! I take your point though. nevertheless, I still endorse suicide or murder as our most likely solutions.' said James.

'Sir, do you realise that, just then, that was the first time that anybody has actually vocalised the word "murder." I think that it's been at the back of all our minds but now that you've said it out loud it makes me feel quite queer.' said Maddox.

'Nothing seems queer after the Spanish and Greek Mafia cropped up in the conversation.' Everybody looked up as Drew spoke. They'd forgotten that he was still listening. In answer to their shocked expressions he said, 'It's true though, isn't it? Now that we've entered into that sort of territory anything is possible, isn't it?'

'That bolsters my point that taking the stuff by accident is extremely unlikely. That being so, let's consider the alternatives in turn. Wainwright, you guide the way. What can you tell us?' asked James.

'I've been thinking about John's symptoms on the few occasions that he came to see me at the surgery in the preceding weeks before the Fête. The symptoms he came to see me with were consistent with diabetes. However, in hindsight, it is possible that the very same symptoms could match a slow release of digitoxin poisoning. Taken over a prolonged period of time the symptoms would look just like an insulin high. Prescribed drugs are measured minutely to match a patient's needs so if someone who didn't medically need them took another's prescription drugs, those same drugs could create disastrous results. Digitoxin creates a slowing of the heart rate which, if maintained over a period of time, or taken in a large enough single dose would result in a massive heart attack as the heart struggled to supply oxygen to the brain. Alternatively, it has to be said that those very same symptoms could be attributed to a combination of diabetes and stress. If he took a significant amount of the drug at once the result could be quite quick.'

'Would that explain him dying in such an out-of-the way place, do you think?' asked Beth.

'Possibly, but that brings us back to the point that there is no supporting evidence to show that they were definitely taken in that place.' said James.

'If the drug was taken over a longer period of time the end result would be the same but there would be a delay in actual death. It's possible that if he took an insufficient dose then the resultant death could be prolonged. Death could be delayed by many hours, even days.' said Wainwright.

'Then that would explain the lack of note and the odd time and place that he died.' said Beth.

'It happens more often than you'd realise. People think that suicide is quick and easy. The TV has a lot to do with that. Contrary to popular opinion an overdose of paracetamol is a very precarious way to attempt suicide and then, if you do manage to pull it off it really isn't a pretty way to go. Your internal organs gradually shut down one at a time and your brain is usually the last to switch off - not quick and certainly not painless. None of this brings us much further forward though.' said James.

Wainwright thought for a moment or two before he spoke again. 'Digitoxin is a glycoside and in the presence of sugar it creates a massive insulin high creating symptoms very similar to a diabetic episode. If John's sugar levels were a bit on the high side the resultant reaction to the drug would be intensified. I'd have to properly consult my notes but I'm almost sure that when John came to see me a week or so before he died he complained of feeling sick and that he was very tired and got dizzy at times. He also said that he felt a bit headachy. His blood pressure was a little on the high side which could account for the headaches and he did acknowledge that he was much more stressed than usual. I don't go dishing out prescription drugs after just one isolated incident of high blood pressure and I suggested that he came back to me if the symptoms didn't ease off soon. The sickness and dizziness could be attributed to a combination of high blood pressure, slightly raised insulin levels and stress in general. These very same symptoms could also be attributed to prolonged exposure to digitoxin. This would suggest that the drug was in his system in some small measure over a long period of time, if it was in fact that which was making him feel ill. It's ambiguous and only sure knowledge of the presence of the stuff at that time could pinpoint the exact reason for such symptoms. It's not something you look for as a matter of course in general practice here.'

'Of course not, nobody is thinking you were at fault. We're just hoping that in retrospect there might be something to help us find our way now.' said James.

'Correct me if I'm wrong, Benji.' said Beth. 'I'm right in presuming that it's not normal for someone to try and commit suicide slowly, aren't I?'

'I've never come across it before.' said James. 'You're quite right, Beth, which leads me to think that if what the doctor here says is possible is actually what was happening then we have to acknowledge that we have a definite case of murder on our hands. We may even have to consider that it's now double murder, if sufficient evidence supports that theory.'

A shocked silence held for long seconds as the reality of the situation sunk in. It was Maddox that broke the spell. 'Let's face it, we've all been thinking it but we've never really dared to voice the possibility. We've kept looking for alternative theories from day one. Each time that we've tried to provide some explanation we've known that it didn't quite fit - right from when Dr Wainwright couldn't fill out the death certificate with a clear conscience. Although he had no alternative to offer he knew that he wasn't satisfied that all was as it seemed. Now we've come to the end of the road and there are no more other options left.'

'You're quite right, Maddox.' said James. 'We have to face facts and pursue this most obvious line of enquiry, but while we are doing so let's make sure that we don't now get blinkered. Let's try to keep an open mind.'

'As we're in the mood for facing brutal facts, do I need to point out that even I know that statistically the most obvious suspect is the wife?' said Beth.

'I'm afraid that's quite true.' said James. 'It's very unimaginative and, sordid as it seems, it's usually the case. The fact that Jean is now a very rich lady, even before all the properties sell, merely adds weight to the presumption.'

'Why now, though? I spoke to their solicitor and the policy that is now being claimed was set in place years ago. It's been paid into for decades, so why now?' said Maddox.

'If we're casting Jean in the role of prime suspect how did she get him to swallow any heart tablets at all?' asked Beth. 'I know that they never take pills and she can't have slipped them into his food? Surely he'd taste them? I don't see how it was possible. From what Dr Wainwright says he'd have to have swallowed a fair amount and at regular intervals to be sure of success. Are we presuming that Betty's tablets were the culprit and if so how strong were they?'

'For the present we're guessing that Betty's missing tablets were responsible, simply because we have no alternative at present.' said James. 'It would certainly link the two deaths. We need to remember though that this may not be the case. It's just as likely that Betty flushed all the tablets down the loo. It's a starting point, that's all.'

'If you're thinking that it was Betty's tablets which were used then he'd have to have taken quite a lot, and fairly regularly to reach a sure conclusion.' explained Wainwright. 'His diabetes could have increased their potency to a point but it wasn't an extremely strong prescription. John's diabetes wasn't acute either, so although it would exacerbate the effects this would only be accurate to a point. I would have expected much more exaggerated symptoms before death. He would have had episodes of fainting and serious illness if the poison was working slowly over a long period of time.'

'Do you honestly suspect Jean?' asked Drew. 'Is she a genuine suspect or are you just postulating to discount her after having dealt with the statistical probability of her being the culprit?'

'I've had my eye on Jean for a while.' said James. 'But it's more to do with dealing with the obvious. I don't really suspect anybody particularly as things stand. There's no doubt that Jean had the most obvious motive of financial gain and she had the easiest access.' said James.

'Is financial gain a satisfactory motive?' asked Maddox. 'We know that they were still well off, relatively speaking. If John hadn't dithered about selling the house in France they'd have ready cash coming out of their ears. We know that John made a great fuss saying that he couldn't face Jean with such a prospect and yet the evidence is that Jean is quite willing to sell up and is in fact doing just that. She's been set up as quite the bad guy but there's no real evidence to support the idea. All we've got is what John's been telling anybody who'll listen.'

'Well, if the motive is dodgy then ease of access is just as tricky.' said Wainwright. 'It'd be jolly difficult to keep cramming crushed pills into his mugs of tea. They'd taste nasty too. If they didn't take pills as a rule it'd be a risk to pretend that she was giving him vitamin pills each day all of a sudden, although it's possible.'

'Fair enough. We've discounted the obvious. We'll have to look elsewhere for something less obvious.' said James.

'There is an elephant in the room, you know.' said Drew. 'You've made a direct reference to the involvement of two different Mafia connections and then proceeded to talk about wilful murder. Surely that association is more obvious than anything.'

'And this is where everything gets way too big for the likes of us.' said James. 'There was no sign of a struggle and so we assume that it's a form of digitoxin poisoning from Betty's tablets as they are helpfully missing at about the same time. These Mafia guys are professionals, it's true, but poisoning just isn't their style. I still say that this whole thing has a local feel to it. Nevertheless Drew, you're right to point out that we simply can't ignore the ridiculously obvious. From what I read in John's correspondence I didn't get the impression that he was in very deep, if he was in fact "in" at all. He may have been considering turning a blind eye to a bit of smuggling but I don't gather that it went any further than that. The e-mails didn't suggest that it had progressed into actual business dealings. Perhaps he got cold feet and changed his mind.'

'Or perhaps he went right ahead with it all and became much more careful in covering his tracks.' said Maddox.

'What about Conrad Jefferson?' said Drew. 'He's on the local scene but he's also in the world of big business. He says he doesn't know that list of names, but does he? Could he have bumped John off? He says that John was alive when he left him, but it's only on his say-so that John wasn't dead by the time he left. Did he clear away vital evidence from the scene of the crime? Even if he didn't actually do the dirty work he might have been part of the clean-up operation.'

Wainwright picked up on the theme that Drew suggested. 'He could have been responsible for getting the poison into John's system. He could have cleared away some drinks cups after their meeting, one of which might be carrying the remnants of digitoxin in it. Or could it have been injected?'

'Conrad Jefferson struck me as a genuinely nice guy. It's a strange thing to say of someone who's just come out of prison but I can't imagine him killing anybody. Mind you, I've never seen a murderer before.' said Maddox.

'I'm afraid that there isn't really an archetypal murderer.' said James. 'Most murderers are really nice people save that one flaw in their ethics. We've obviously got to be on our guard. We've got a wide range of hypotheses and we need to keep open minds. There's plenty for us to be thinking over. Just take care and be extremely discreet. Needless to say, all of the things that we've discussed are to go no further than ourselves. Do you understand, Beth? Not even your underground network of buddies is to know, it's too dangerous.'

Beth nodded her head to show that she understood the situation. Quietly, under her breath she said, 'Poor Hyacinth, she's got it all to come again, I think.'

Chapter Sixteen

Wainwright and Maddox stood up to leave and James walked down the driveway in his stockinged feet as they walked to their cars. 'We'll keep each other posted.' said James. 'Thank you for giving up your free morning. Wainwright. I'm grateful for your input.' Wainwright nodded his acknowledgement and drove off, waving his arm out of the window as he went.

'Should I pull him over for careless driving?' said Maddox. 'You can see he's only got one hand on the wheel.'

James laughed aloud. He liked Maddox. They'd spent the last hour and a half submerged in the seedier side of humanity and Maddox could do a good job and yet keep it all at arms length. He could quickly revert back to the cheery village PC. It was a safety valve and it was good for them all. Nevertheless, they had a job to do and so James returned once more to the task in hand. 'We need to go right back to the day of the Fête. We don't know what time frame we're looking at and so we're searching in the dark, but at least we now know that we do need to be searching. I need to be sure that we can place exactly where everyone was throughout that day and what they were doing. I don't know what I hope we'll achieve but we've got to start somewhere. You're the local lad so you're the man for this job. Do your thing and chat to people. People clam up when I ask them questions, that's one of the drawbacks of promotion.'

'I'm sure you manage somehow, sir.' said Maddox.

James gave him a wry smile. 'I'll see what I can find out from Beth and Drew. A lot of water has gone under the bridge since then, but I don't know that we're so badly off. Because the Fête was held that day it fixes it in people's mind. We'll get a full toxicology report in soon and that will spearhead our enquiries. In the meantime make the best start that you can here.'

Back inside the house Beth and Drew cleared away the mugs and plates as they waited for Benji to come back. They knew that the official meeting, such as it was, had ended but they guessed that there was more to say to each other privately.

'Do you need to head straight back home or would you like to stay for lunch?' asked Beth.

'I'm in no rush to get home. Lexi knew that I was coming here and so she's made plans for the day.' said Benedict.

'Why don't you two go and relax for half an hour and I'll get lunch ready. I know that there's lots still to discuss but it can wait until after we've eaten.' said Beth. She was finding that the occasional bouts of insomnia that she suffered from could be turned to profitable use and she knew that Noodle would be happy to join her in a snooze later that day if she needed it. In the small hours of that morning instead of tossing and turning in bed she'd put a gammon joint into the slow cooker with a litre of fizzy cola. There was a tray of cooked potato wedges left over from yesterday which she crushed with the bottom of a heavy saucepan before frying them in a seasoned, cast iron pan. Although there were eggs in the storage rack Beth brought fresh eggs from the hen house as she knew how much Benji loved really new eggs. One was still warm and you couldn't get fresher than that. Once the peas had finished boiling she banged on the service bell to call the men to lunch. During lunch they restricted the topics of conversation to catching up on family news and general village gossip. Beth described the troubles that she'd heard that Toby was having at school.

'You can't help but wonder what Henrietta has had to live through, she carries an aura of dignified suffering.' said Benji. 'There's a sad tale to tell there, I'm sure. I can't help but notice that our young Sergeant Maddox thinks quite a lot of that girl. Who wouldn't? I gather that he's got his own fair share of admirers but I think that he's only got eyes for Henrietta. A few weeks ago I'd have said that he was wasting his time, but I do believe that she's thawing a little. I can imagine that he'd be good with the laddie too. The big question is whether or not she's already spoken for. I think that he's wise enough to be patient and find out gradually what the score is. He won't force his hand and waste his chance. Good luck to him!'

When the meal was finished they carried their coffee through to the lounge. Benji lounged on the sofa and Noodle nestled into the crook of his long legs with just the tip of his nose peeping from under a knee. Absentmindedly stroking the dog he opened the proceedings. 'Well, like Miss Marple we've left the unsavoury topic of murder until we've finished eating, but I think that we can speak freely between ourselves. If we just talk off the top of our heads it doesn't matter if we're mighty wide of the mark, we're amongst friends.'

'OK. You set the tone Benedict. Tell us freely what your suspicions are - not what you have evidence for or what seems logical. What do you really think?' said Drew.

'It sounds crass but it usually is the most obvious suspect who really is guilty and that means Jean. The means and the motive are both there and people have killed for far less than she's gained from John's death.' said Benedict.

'Do you still think that now that more information has come to light? asked Beth.

'I've not entirely given her up, but I'll agree that my enthusiasm for her as prime suspect is waning.' said Benedict.

'Is that because of the sudden appearance of all of these foreign heavies?' asked Drew.

'To a point, yes. I have to admit that it all has something of a "phoney" flavour to it, it just seems so unreal when you connect it to this little village and John Barlow. I still think that this case has a local flavour to it and not only because of Betty's missing heart tablets. I'm adamant that poison isn't the Mafia's weapon of choice.' said Benedict.

'There is another link between the deaths of Betty and John though, isn't there?' said Beth. 'Don't forget that it was Betty who found John's body. If somebody had killed him at the Fête they'd know that the body would soon be found, but maybe she found him before the stage was quite set. What if she saw something and the scene changed by the time she brought Dr Wainwright into the picture? She mightn't realise straight away but if she did she'd need silencing.' said Beth.

'You've got a point there. However, that again implies that the murderer is a local here. How else would anybody know that Betty had seen something? Either that or the foreign heavies had an envoy in your midst.' said Benji.

'Strangers stand out a mile in this village. There were plenty of visitors on the day of the Fête but if they'd hung around after then the whole village would be alive to the fact.' said Drew.

'Of course, there's always Conrad Jefferson.' said James. 'He's my best shot at present. He's local, he met John on the day that he died and he's a big noise in the property market. He could easily fit into their gangster world - you're not telling me that massive house was bought by entirely honest measures.' said Benedict.

'Oh Benji, I've just made good friends with Hyacinth. She's so lovely. This will tear her apart. Conrad himself seemed a genuinely nice guy too. Oh!' Beth stopped suddenly and passed her hand over her face. 'Did you mention that these "Godfathers of the Night" also operated in America?'

'Yes, that's right. New York, I think.' said Benedict.

'I'm sure that Hyacinth said that their son is a big shot in America. He took a branch of Conrad's business over there and then it grew and flourished into a mighty oak, from what she was telling me. Apparently he's expanded into other forms of business, but Hyacinth didn't really know much about it specifically. She was really proud of him and told me all about the business giants that he now mixed with and what fantastic contacts he'd made. It would look impressive on the surface though, wouldn't it? It could even be that it was the son who got the dad involved rather than the other way around.' said Beth.

'That's rather interesting. Do you know his name Beth?' asked Benji.

'I'm sorry, but I'm afraid I don't. I could find out though.' said Beth.

'His name is Quentin.' said Drew. 'There's something else which is rather an odd coincidence. I'm pretty sure that Conrad told me that Quentin has a girlfriend he's been going steady with for some time now. I've an idea he said that she was Greek. Her family still live in Greece but she moved to America to manage their business interests there, like Quentin did for Conrad. I gather they met at a business networking function - one of these monthly business breakfast meetings, but so far up the social ladder that we couldn't see it for clouds.'

'There's an awful lot of overlapping coincidence occurring within the Jefferson family at the moment, isn't there?' said Benedict. 'They definitely warrant a closer look. I'll let Maddox conduct the first round but I think I'm going to have to step in sooner or later.'

'Are you seriously suggesting that John Barlow became willingly entangled with some Mafia group and then did something which warranted him being "got out of the way?" Do you think that Jefferson had to do the dirty work for these people?' asked Beth.

'It's not a matter of what I personally think here, it's to do with where the facts are leading us. The case could well be that John didn't willingly get involved, or maybe he got cold feet and changed his mind. I'm afraid the pieces fit rather too well to be safely ignored, despite the fact that it sounds ludicrous.' said Benedict. 'If John took the bait in his vulnerable state and then became privy to goodness knows what they'd hardly let him just walk away, would they?'

'But didn't you say that poison simply wasn't their style?' said Drew.

'I did, but I've been thinking about that. Their signature method would be to make a particularly nasty example of a recalcitrant member to warn others not to be tempted to act likewise. However, let's face it - who is there in Mossleigh to set an example to?' said Benedict.

'Conrad Jefferson, maybe?' said Drew.

'Accepting that he is involved he'd be the ambassador, not a lackey at the bottom that might need teaching a lesson. I suspect that John was an embarrassing mistake who needed to be quietly let slip away.' said Benedict.

'He really was out of his depth, wasn't he?' said Beth. 'He tried to play with the big boys and when he didn't like it, well - it was too late. I still can't take it in.'

'It does take a good stretch of the imagination, I'll grant you. We did say that we'd let our fantasy roam. It may still be nothing more than our imaginations running wild but at present I have no better alternative. Something might turn up which will lead us in a completely different direction. Who can tell?' said Benji. 'An alarming percentage of our success rate is due to chance and happenstance. All we can do is hope that something presents itself.'

Beth gave a tremendous yawn. 'Like you said, Benji, everyone is innocent until proven guilty. Let's hope that something else crops up.'

'Beth's really tired, she didn't sleep well last night.' said Drew. 'I want to shake off all of this talk of murder, it's making me feel grimy. Shall we take a walk to The Badger, Benji? A walk in the sunshine and a pint of Cheshire Set will go a good way to restoring my faith in humanity. We can leave Beth and Noodle to a bit of peace and quiet.'

Maddox realised that matters had become serious and he decided that he'd get to work that very afternoon. He enjoyed working with DCI James and knew that the temporary partnership was a massive boost to his career profile. He didn't want to waste time if there was profitable work to be done. A Sunday afternoon would be the best time to catch people at home too. Keen as he was to get started he made sure that he gave his mum's roast dinner the proper attention that it deserved and he even made a start on clearing away the dishes. His mum was used to the subtle undertones in a policeman's thinking, she'd been married to a policeman and knew the signs long before Bobby followed in his dad's footsteps. 'You're itching to be off, I can tell.' she said. 'No need to tell me what it's all about - I can guess well enough and don't need to hear the details. Be off with you and I'll finish up here.' Hugging his mum Maddox then reached for his trainers. He figured that as today was Sunday he could keep his visits relatively unofficial and didn't bother with his uniform. During lunch he'd been wondering where would be best to start. James had asked him to find out where everyone was on the day of the Fête to start with. He couldn't go pestering Beth again, she'd had enough of them all that morning. Emma had been at the Fête all day and so had Nathaniel. They'd been in different parts of the field too so he would get a wider picture straight away. He kept pushing to the back of his mind the notion that he also thought he'd heard that Henrietta was visiting them for lunch today too. If he acknowledged the thought at all he cloaked it with the notion that he'd get even more information at the same time, so it had to be a good idea. Knocking on the door of "Lilac Cottage" Maddox began to have second thoughts. He'd no idea what questions he might ask and he suddenly wondered if meeting Henrietta by apparent coincidence was such a good idea. The option to turn away was taken from him when Emma opened the front door.

'Hello Bobby! Come in.' said Emma. As he stepped into the lounge the feeling of a content family atmosphere was physically tangible. Nathaniel was sitting in the easy chair with his legs stretched out before him and Emma resumed her place sitting on the floor by his feet, leaning back on his chair. Henrietta was comfortably stretched out on the sofa and Walter, the Labradoodle, sat on the floor while she scratched behind his ears. The children were nowhere to be seen as he first scanned the room. 'I'll put the kettle on. It's tea with about 20 sugars, isn't it?' said Emma.

'I'm afraid you're quite right, to my shame.' said Maddox. He sat down and took in the details of the room. Under the open-plan stair case, in the recess of the lounge, a small teepee housed some muffled shrieks of laughter and the flap then opened to reveal two small faces. Emma and Nathaniel had pooled their skills to make this impressive construction. Nathaniel had secured five sturdy canes into a wig-wam shape and then attached the top to the underside of a stair tread. Emma had sewn a mixture of flower print and polka dot fabric to cover the frame and had fastened a series of ribbons to the opening flaps. The shades echoed the gold and lilac decor of the lounge and also the name of the cottage. Nathaniel explained that the endeavour had been well worth the time they'd invested as Primrose spent all the time that she could in there. On special occasions she'd even slept in there while Nathaniel slept on the sofa so as to be close at hand. Primrose was evidently proud of her residence and Maddox was honoured by a request to join them.

When Emma brought the tray of drinks through Maddox wasn't to be found in the chair where she'd left him but his feet could be seen sticking out from the fabric door of the teepee. He seemed quite at home there so she placed his drink within arms' reach of the entrance flap. Maddox peeped his head out of the door flap to talk to the others. 'I am sorry to disturb your afternoon and I'm afraid that this isn't exactly a social visit.'

'If this is official hadn't you better come and sit here?' said Henrietta, motioning to the space next to her.

Maddox blushed a little. 'I'll finish my colouring first and when my back can't stand it any longer I'll come and join the grown-ups.'

Emma laughed. 'You've made some good friends there if they've consented to share the pencil crayons with you. Just make sure that you don't go over the lines.'

'I was hoping that you could help me out.' began Maddox. 'Your Uncle has said that we need to go right back to the day of the Fête and find out what everybody was doing. I know that it was a while ago now but I need to find out who did what and when throughout that day. I was hoping that you could get me started.' said Maddox.

'I've brought some cakes through. Hurry up and finish your colouring so that you can eat some and we can talk to you properly.' said Emma.

'I won't be long now.' Maddox crawled most of his frame back into the teepee and sat colouring and whispering with the children for a few minutes. When he appeared out of the tent he needed a moment to click and stretch his back. Without thinking he handed a picture of a teddy bear holding a bunch of flowers to Henrietta.

Henrietta laughed. 'You're quite the artist, aren't you!'

'I don't like to brag.' replied Maddox. Sitting more comfortably in the easy chair he helped himself to cake and prepared to get down to business.

Chapter Seventeen

'I'll be glad when these Summer holidays are over. It's been so busy that I'm ready to start teaching again just for a rest.' said Beth. She was sitting in the passenger seat of Mae's car heading towards the Jefferson residence. Hyacinth and Kirsty were finally due to be introduced to each other and instant friendship was an absolute certainty. They were both such gentle, lovely characters and their shared passion for horticulture was cement the bond.

'I know what you mean. I hope that all this police business gets sorted out soon. The start of term isn't far away and we'd all like a clear start.' said Mae.

'I'm afraid that it doesn't look like plain sailing at all. The more Benji finds out the more confusing it all gets!'

'I think that I can safely guess that we're looking at death by misadventure. I'll do anything that I can to help. Don't worry about telling me what it's all about, just tell me what to do.'

Beth didn't reply but gave Mae a grateful smile as she got out of the car to deal with the intercom. As the car drove along the gravelled driveway they could see Hyacinth standing at the door waiting for them. 'Don't bother about the gates.' said Hyacinth. 'Conrad said that he'd deal with them without the intercom. I'm so grateful for you introducing me to your friend, I've been looking forward to this all week. I'm sure that I'll learn lots from Kirsty, she sounds so knowledgeable.'

Leading Hyacinth quite literally down the garden path Beth led the way to the bench where Kirsty and Carlton were sitting. The group had arrived punctually and refreshments were prepared for them. 'Carlton, you've made your delicious carrot cake! What an honour.' said Beth. With a mouthful of cake Beth made the necessary introductions. The business of pouring tea and dividing cake covered any initial awkwardness and the group were soon chatting comfortably.

'Shall I give you the WI Fête tour, Hyacinth?' asked Kirsty.

Everybody agreed that this would be a good idea. Beth and Mae joined in as they never tired of Kirsty's enthusiasm and new morsels would always appear. With two enthusiastic gardeners and no time constraints today's tour promised to be especially interesting. Carlton explained that he'd got work to do and took the dishes back into the house.

The group wandered amicably around the segments of Kirsty's garden and the two enthusiasts soon became engrossed in earnest conversation. Beth and Mae were content to merely look and listen. They knew that they were in the presence of experts and now that Kirsty had a more informed audience she could enjoy the conversation without reservation. Although it was totally beyond Beth's sphere of knowledge she found it inspiring nevertheless. As she'd predicted the introduction was a huge success and Hyacinth was positively glowing. They were all standing next to the rose garden and the conversation had turned to the devastation wrought by itching fingers on the day of the Fête. 'We don't like to admit it but roses can withstand pretty much any pruning regime, especially hybrid teas. It's just so annoying because it means that I'll have a poor show for the rest of the summer.' said Kirsty.

'You'll be all right by next season, so long as no serious damage has been done.' said Hyacinth.

'There's not too much serious damage, but look at this.' said Kirsty showing a nasty gash down the stem of one bush. 'It's like an open wound.'

'At least the weather is warm. It should heal before the frost comes, or do you think that you need to "amputate?" said Hyacinth. The two gardeners moved through the rose bushes with the air of a medical team walking through a leper colony. They sought to bind and heal but hardly knew where to begin. 'I see what you mean, all the pruning is in the wrong places.'

'Excuse my ignorance, but what difference does it make where you cut? It looks neat enough here.' said Mae.

Bursting with the desire to educate Kirsty explained the science of good pruning. 'When you dead-head hybrid tea roses you should cut just above a set of five leaflets, that way you should get a hundred percent re-growth. If you prune by a set of three leaflets that growth is limited to a fifty percent chance of new bloom. In effect the meddling has reduced my floral display by half for the rest of this summer.'

'It's not something that I've suffered from, it must be so annoying for you. I don't get many visitors to my garden and any of the people who do come would never dream of helping themselves.' said Hyacinth.

'The real crime there is that nobody gets to see your beautiful garden, Hyacinth.' said Beth. 'You really do need to visit, Kirsty. It'll take your breath away.'

'I'm not sure that it's quite as impressive as that, but I'd love you to come. I'd like some fresh ideas and advice. My gardener is very knowledgeable but is too subservient to give me an honest opinion. Conrad tries to be interested but just says, "That'd be nice." to anything that I suggest.

The group wandered away from the tragic tale of the roses and walked over to the herb garden. A new botanical subject reinvigorated the animation of the enthusiasts. 'I've never considered a herb garden as a feature at home. I've got a few pots and shrubs next to the veg patch for use in the kitchen, but this is quite something.' said Hyacinth.

'I love the quintessential "Britishness" of a formal herb garden. I know that there have been herb gardens all over the world for hundreds of years, but it's the typical sixteenth century English herb garden that I mean.' said Kirsty.

'Yes, you automatically picture gravelled walks with clipped miniature mazes and symmetrical designs. What was it that Francis Bacon said about his idea of an ideal herb garden? Something like, "The breath of flowers is far sweeter in the air ... it comes and goes like the warbling of flowers." It conjures quite a picture, doesn't it?' said Hyacinth.

'I'm not sure that I agree with him. Lavender gives me a cracking headache.' said Beth.

'Well, at least the pruning here isn't giving me a headache.' said Kirsty. 'Not so many people felt inclined to help themselves here except a few dears who thought they'd try some alternative HRT.'

'You can at least understand why they didn't ask for some cuttings.' said Mae.

As they walked over to the natural garden Kirsty explained that this was her favourite part of the garden. 'If I'm honest, I like it best here because there's a quality of untamed beauty and it doesn't require much work. It brings out the little girl in me too. I imagine that this is a fairy garden where the gnomes live in the magic mushrooms and the fairies live in the bells of the foxgloves. I keep getting the urge to put up some outside lights here, to make it more fairy-like, but it wouldn't be so natural then would it?'

'It would be lovely though. You could have a little seat in that corner and create a cosy little arbour.' said Hyacinth.

'I've kept this corner a bit more overgrown than usual as a few hedgehogs made their home here over the winter and a frog is a regular visitor. He was here not long ago .' said Kirsty.

The ladies began to disperse and wander at will. Kirsty had gone foraging deeper into the undergrowth to see if the frog was still resting there. 'That's strange.' she said. She stood up and stared at the ground.

'What's the matter, Kirsty?' asked Beth.

'Some people, huh? You'd never believe it! I thought I'd be safe from pillaging here.' said Kirsty.

'What have you found?' asked Hyacinth.

'Somebody has even been pinching cuttings here! Not that it matters - everything grows like weeds here. In fact everything here could be described as a weed, which is why I thought it'd be safe from over eager shears. Who'd have thought it?' said Kirsty. 'Even so, I'd said more about the uses of nettles here than foxgloves. They've no practical use whatsoever domestically. Mind you, they're hardly likely to steal nettles - they sting. Well, if they've taken foxgloves I hope they washed their hands.'

'I don't. It serves them right if they get a stomach ache.' said Hyacinth.

'How can you tell Kirsty?' asked Beth. 'You can't be sure in this rough patch?'

'But that's just it, I can be absolutely sure. If I need to thin things out at all I rip them out. I'd never make a cut here. It's a little foible of mine never to use secateurs or a blade in this section because it doesn't maintain the spirit of the garden. I like to keep it as rugged as possible here just to please my own fancy.' said Kirsty.

'It's your garden and you can work it however you like. How rude!' said Hyacinth. She'd not noticed the sudden interest that Beth had shown and was annoyed on a merely artistic level. Beth had deeper concerns.

'What did you mention about foxgloves in your tour? Why would anybody be tempted to take some?' asked Beth.

'I hardly mentioned them at all. I probably warned people to wash their hands, though that would be mostly directed to the mushrooms here.

Foxgloves don't have any domestic use apart from ornamental purposes.' said Kirstly.

'How much has been taken Kirsty? Can you tell?' said Beth. She was trying to keep her voice casual but Mae detected a new seriousness in Beth's questions. When Mae finally made eye contact Beth didn't respond to her questioning glances. Bending down to examine the rendered stalks in the undergrowth Kirsty counted out six or seven chopped stems. Glancing up the stem Beth estimated how many flowers and leaves each spike would hold. It was a lot. Each of the tall spikes held a profusion of tubular bell-like flowers and downy, green leaves.

'I don't understand why they've been cut. I know they grow like weeds - they are weeds, but you can't cut them and transplant them. The only reason would be for cut flowers in a vase but even then they'd soon die.' said Kirsty.

Picking up the thread of Beth's reasoning Mae began her own line of enquiry. 'You said that you advised people to wash their hands. Are they very poisonous? Has the thief endangered themselves by taking these flowers?'

'I always say that, just to cover myself. The mushrooms are the most potently harmful but for any of the plants here just touching them isn't too serious.' said Kirsty.

This marked the end of the frivolities and they all began to wander back to the house. Mae and Hyacinth lagged behind a little as Hyacinth browsed through the garden as she returned. Kirsty walked more quickly to get to the kitchen to prepare more refreshments for the guests. 'I'll explain later, but would you help me out?' asked Beth. Kirsty looked enquiringly at Beth. Seeing the serious expression on Beth's face she just nodded her willingness and allowed Beth to continue. 'Can you spare me an hour or so as soon as you have the time? Either first thing this weekend, or earlier if you have a day off? In the meantime I need you to find out all that you can about foxgloves. Find out about their uses and what effects various stages of ingestion, or contamination of sorts, would ensue. I'm not really sure what I'm asking for, so just do your best, please.'

'I've got a pretty good general knowledge but I'll try and fill in the gaps. I'm off on Friday. Carlton and I are travelling to visit family in Manchester that day but we won't be leaving until mid afternoon. I can meet you for an hour or so on Friday morning if that's any use.' said Kirsty.

'Super! I really appreciate it. If you can be at The Blue Willow tea rooms for half past nine I shan't take up too much of your morning. There'll be a few of us there and I'll tell you all about it then. It's really important, so thank you.' said Beth. Everyone had gathered in the kitchen by this point and so she left any further questions for the time being. Tea and cake did it's usual job of cementing friendships, and telephone numbers and promises of return visits were exchanged.

On the return journey from Hyacinth's house back to Mossleigh Mae gave way to her inquisitiveness. 'What's going on Beth? The foxglove misdemeanour seriously troubled you and I'm sure that it's not because you think that it spoiled Kirsty's lovely garden.'

'I don't understand how, but I know that it's important. You know that we've contrived a few scenarios so that we could try and find some helpful information to help explain John's death? I think that we've just witnessed something very important without even trying. Can you meet up again this Friday morning?

'I can if you think we need to.'

'If we pool all the information then perhaps it will make a clearer picture. Hopefully, if we put our heads together, something will make sense somewhere.'

'You know that I'll be there, but I don't see how this can be helpful.'

'I need to think things over first. I'll tell you what I can on Friday when I've had chance to gather my thoughts.'

'All right, if you say it's important then we'll look into it. Until then, if there's anything that you need just give me a call.'

They drove the rest of the way home in silence. Beth sat trying to think of how the significance of what she'd just seen could be explained. Mae drove while wondering what on earth was going on. She supposed that she'd have to wait and find out.

Beth walked into the kitchen and gave Noodle an absentminded pat on the head as he looked up to her from his basket. Drew was busy in the studio and she didn't bother to shout to him but walked straight to the telephone. Benji's number was logged into the handset and it was a matter of seconds to scroll through the B entries and hit "dial."

'Hello, James speaking'

'Benji, it's Beth. I'm sorry to disturb you at work, but it's a work related call so I guess it's OK. I'm so glad to find you at your desk. Can you spare me a few minutes?'

'Of course. What's worrying you Beth?'

'Do you remember all the things that we discussed the other day - you know, about the heart tablets?'

'Certainly I do. What of it?'

'We've just stumbled upon something very strange and I think that it's important.' Beth proceeded to tell her brother about the green-collar crime from the day of the Fête and her more sinister suspicion that the theft of the foxglove plant caused. 'It's too much of a coincidence, isn't it?'

'It's certainly very interesting. I'll speak to Forbes about the specific form, he might know by now. Even so Beth, it still doesn't help us much with the method. That's where we're really stuck. If it does turn out to be genus this or that we're still no nearer to who or why, even if we know specifically what.'

'I've got the inkling of an idea there. I'm hardly sure what I mean myself yet, it's just on the edge of my thinking - you know, in the corner of my mind's eye. I've got a glimpse of something that I can't quite catch hold of. Can you pop down over the weekend? Let's see if we can tease out the end of this thread between us.'

'Yes, I'll come at the weekend if you want, or do you need me to come now? I can if you think it's urgent.'

'No, there's no need for that. I need to let my thoughts settle first. You know when you can't think of a crossword solution? You leave it for a bit and then when you come back to it fresh the answer usually hits you. I feel a bit like that's what's needed now.'

'If you're quite sure. But be careful Beth, we're not talking about solving a polite crossword puzzle here. Somebody out there means business. For goodness sake keep your cards close to your chest.'

'I understand, Benji. Thanks for saying you'll come, we'll sort it out then. I'll see you soon.'

Beth poured out two glasses of lemonade from the jug she'd made earlier. Carrying them through to the studio she sat herself down behind Drew's raised drawing table. Still painting Drew asked how her morning had been.

'I'm not sure, Drew. I'm just not sure.'

Realising that this wasn't the usual response he put his brush into a jar of water and swivelled his chair round to face Beth. Seeing the stern look on Beth's face he knew that there was more to this than a morning spent discussing plants. 'What's going on Beth? What's wrong?'

Beth told him of her concerns and of the sinister implications that the unofficial pruning held. 'Isn't foxglove the base form of digitalis?'

'I believe so. I think you need to tell your brother.'

249

'I've called him just now. It doesn't take us much further yet, but I'm sure that this is the key to the whole problem. I just can't see how.'

'You'd better wait until you speak to Benji. Don't go getting yourself too mixed up in this. You need to be very careful how you tread. For goodness sake Beth, steer clear of trouble!'

'I know, it's not funny, is it? I just want to think over a few things. Kirsty is giving us a botany lesson on Friday, but other than that there's not a lot else that we can do.'

'I'm glad about that! Leave it to Benji, please.'

'Well, there's nothing that I can do about it now. I'll find something to do to take my mind off things.'

Chapter Eighteen

Beth brought the wheelbarrow around from the side of the garage and loaded up all the hen house cleaning paraphernalia. Today she intended to be extra thorough and so also picked up the allocated wallpaper scraper. She always felt calmer when she was stomping around in her wellies. There was a therapeutic, calming effect in shovelling piles of dirty shavings into a bag and replacing them with a liberal scattering of fresh, clean ones. The bright scent of the clean shavings was a restorative to the soul. On top of the reloaded wheelbarrow she carefully placed today's fresh eggs and wheeled happily back to the house. As she'd cleared away the mess of the hens the busyness of her hands had allowed her mind the time and space it needed to clear her thoughts. She had a pretty clear idea of the whole picture now. Although she needed a few facts officially confirming there was little doubt in her mind that she was wrong. There really was nothing much for her to do now but wait. She carried the eggs through to the kitchen and met Drew as she reached for the egg rack. 'I suppose that I'll have omelette for tea again.' he said. 'These eggs are stacking up again. We've got far too many.'

'I really can't face eggs again. I know they're delicious, but you can have too much of a good thing. Leave those eggs and I'll make some lemon curd later. I'll poach Emma's recipe - if you'll pardon the pun - and I'll ring around to scavenge a few extra jars. Let's eat something else.'

'I'm so glad you said that. I was trying to be honourable but I'm sick of eggs for now. What shall we eat?'

Beth rummaged in the fridge and they settled on smoked bacon with pancakes and syrup - not a boiled, fried or poached egg on the menu at all.

That evening Beth raided her own supply of jars and rang a few people to borrow extra just in case she needed them. A quick drive around the village brought her back home with a good supply. In each case she was told that they'd been rinsed but would need a proper wash before re-using them. Drew was finishing the last stages of artwork for Conrad and was working the night shift which left Beth the whole evening to fill jars to her heart's content. She'd a seemingly limitless supply of eggs and plenty of lemons left over from her earlier lemonade making session. Following Emma's microwave method Beth could make just a few jars at a time and when the mixture was in the microwave she could catch up on the next stage instead of standing and stirring the whole time. By the time that she'd run out of lemons (not eggs) a row of bright yellow jars stood along the kitchen work top. Drew walked in from the studio pleased with his night's work. He'd finished this latest commission and knew that the artwork was good. 'Crikey, it's making my mouth water just walking through the door. There's certainly a zesty freshness in the kitchen tonight.'

'Would you like some toast and lemon curd for supper? It's eggs again, but they're cleverly camouflaged so you won't notice them.'

'I can see that you've stocked us up nicely. Did you run out of jars - or eggs?'

'Of course I didn't run out of eggs. I didn't run out of jars in the end either. I used all of my jars and a few of Phoebe's but I didn't need Jean's at all in the end. They're still in the bag there.'

'And what do you think of the Twenty-first Century method of preserving? Are you converted to the modern microwave after all the debating for the competition?'

'It's certainly a pleasant change not standing and stirring for an age. I also appreciated not getting molten liquid spattered up my arms. I'm tired now though, I've been on my feet all day.'

DCI James picked up the telephone and first dialled an internal number. 'Forbes, good day to you. We've had an interesting turn of events which look likely to rearrange the Barlow case.' He continued to explain Beth's news from Kirsty's garden.

'It's so much quicker and easier to look for a particular thing instead of conducting a blank search. We'll tailor our tests to see if we can isolate that particular strain. Do you want us to check the results for the old dear too?'

'I guess it wouldn't hurt to try for a short cut there. Don't get too blinkered though. Concentrate mainly on John for now. You said that you had plenty of material to go at - see if you can uncover anything out of the ordinary. Be creative!'

'I'm not sure what you mean, but I'll try. You'll have to tell me all about it, quaint village life isn't all it seems is it?'

'I'll tell you when I know myself. Thanks Forbes. Good bye for now.'

He replaced the handset and paused to think before dialling for an outside line. 'Maddox, my man. I've had some interesting news from the ladies. I'm hoping that you've managed to get an idea of who was where that day.'

After listening to the story of the unlicensed pruning Maddox gave a low whistle. 'It makes sense though, doesn't it? Somebody has been very crafty!'

'Wasn't Jean on ticket duty in that garden all that day? She could have snipped away at any time between visiting parties. I'll bet there was plenty of opportunity.'

'That's right sir, but I'm afraid it won't do. She never left her post that day. I have it from more than one person that she stayed at Kirsty's from early morning until after John was dead. She may have had time to pick a few poisonous leaves but she'd never have had the time to walk over to the Fête and persuade him to eat a light salad. Sorry about that sir.'

'What about Jefferson? Did he and his wife go on a garden tour?'

'I'm afraid not. Apparently his wife told the girls that she wanted to go but didn't venture to ask for fear of boring her husband. That's why she was there with your sister - she'd never met Kirsty before but now they're all set to be solid friends.'

'It's never easy, is it? Perhaps you should visit Nicola Farrington at the flower shop. Go and see if she can remember who she sold tour tickets to. I'm coming to Mossleigh at the weekend so we'll put our thinking caps on then. If you can re-direct this call I'll speak to your Super. I'll give her an idea of what's going on and get you cleared of any other duties this week. This case is hotting up and I need your eyes and ears.'

Using the premise of needing a coffee James stretched his legs and walked the long way through the corridors to the cafeteria. What he really needed was to give vent to his frustration and walking was the best that he could do. He guessed that he'd soon have all the facts at his fingertips but he knew that, for now, all he could do was to sit tight and wait for the final pieces of the puzzle to slot into place. Benedict James wasn't very good at doing nothing and so he returned to his desk and, fortified by the strong coffee, attacked a lingering pile of paperwork. By the end of the afternoon his desk was a model of ferocious efficiency and he was sufficiently tired from the mental exertion to properly sleep that night despite the myriad of questions running through the back of his mind.

Maddox walked into the flower shop and was surprised to see Henrietta talking to Nicola. Toby was bending over, dipping his fingers into the buckets of water which fed the flowers. As the door bell jangled both of the ladies looked up. 'Hello

Bobby. Have you come to buy me some flowers? said Henrietta. Confused and flustered Maddox mumbled something about him not thinking of it, but he would if she wanted him to. Fortunately he was saved by Toby getting a little too exuberant in his bucket ministrations and one of the buckets toppled over, sloshing water onto the floor. As luck would have it the bucket only held a little water and so disaster was averted on both counts. As Henrietta walked off to find the mop Nicola approached Maddox to see what he wanted. 'If it's not flowers that you're after then I assume that you're here on police business. How can I help?'

'It's something of a long shot but I'm hoping that you can remember who bought tickets for Kirsty's garden tours on the day of the Fête.' said Maddox.

'Now you're asking me!' Nicola sat down on a stool and casting her mind back she checked off a list of names which came to her in fits and starts. After about half a dozen names had been written into Maddox's notepad Nicola stemmed the tide and paused. 'I think that it would be easier for me to try and list those that didn't buy tickets. After that I'll try and think of anybody who bought tickets that stood out from the main community here.'

Maddox underlined the section that he'd been writing in his notepad and began a new filing system for the next set of names. Henrietta came into the shop carrying three mugs of tea and Toby trundled behind her carrying a plate of biscuits. He pulled up a small stool to sit next to Maddox and closely watched him taking notes. Maddox accepted such camaraderie without question and absentmindedly shuffled aside to make room for him.

'I think that nearly all of the ladies of the village bought tickets, except for those of us who were tied to a duty at the Fête.' said Nicola. 'If you leave it with me I can make a list of those of us who were tied to a stall or busy in the refreshments hall. Of the men of the village Mike Simmonds was one of the first. He'd be waiting to cast his expert eye over the proceedings and he'd be early so as to be ready for the poultry competition. Drew, Nathaniel and Terry were busy with their vehicle display and I doubt that Jonti or Matt were very interested in flowers. When they weren't busy they'd be in The Badger, as were most of the other men.'

'Were there any strangers? Can you tell me anything about any of the unknown visitors?' said Maddox.

'That's just it, isn't it? They're unknown. Oh, there were a couple of tourists that bought a ticket quite early on in the day I think. They said that they were having a driving holiday around the Midland Shires and were staying at The Raven in Harrisfield. They were thrilled at happening to be here on the day of the Fête. They said it gave their holiday an authentic feel - much better than an organised coach trip.'

'If they were staying at The Raven I should be able to find their names. They only have a couple of guest rooms so it shouldn't be difficult. Can you describe them to me?'

'The man might be in his mid-forties but his wife seemed a lot younger. They sounded American but they didn't look it.'

'What did they look like?'

'They both had tanned skin, a natural tan, and they both had dark hair. I suspect his hair colour came out of a bottle, but it matched. He would have had dark hair when he was younger. They looked kind of Turkish or Greek. They were probably Greek, he had a big nose.'

Maddox tried to keep his excitement hidden and asked Nicola if she could think of anything else, if only to deflect attention from his expression and to give himself time to think. As soon as there was a natural pause in the conversation Maddox thanked Nicola for her help and, after arranging to collect the list he stood up to leave.

'Are you going back to the station? If you are I'll walk back with you.' said Henrietta.

Saying that this was so the three of them left the shop together. Unbidden, Toby walked up to Maddox and grasped his hand ready to walk with him. Maddox looked at Henrietta in surprise and then shrugged his shoulders and walked on. Inwardly he was bursting with joy. 'Where are you off to now? Are you heading home?' asked Maddox.

'I'm just calling back for a few things but then we're going to catch a bus to Harrisfield. The holidays are nearly over and I promised Toby that we'd take a picnic to the park there. I know that The Green here is lovely but sometimes you just need a change, don't you?' said Henrietta.

'I'm going to Harrisfield too. I need to check up on the names of those guests. If you just give me twenty minutes I can give you a lift if you like. I'm due to go off duty in a bit so I was going to change before I pick up the station car.'

'That's really kind of you but Toby was looking forward to a ride on the bus. I know it takes three times as long to get there, but that's part of the fun I'm afraid.'

Feeling rebuffed Maddox concealed his disappointment. 'Of course, I didn't think about that. I used to love a bus ride myself.'

'If you're going off duty and you don't need to rush, why don't you come on the bus with us?'

Within seconds Maddox's emotions had plummeted to the depths to then be immediately restored to the heights. 'I haven't been on a bus for ages. I'd like that' he said. 'Shall I meet you at your house in about half an hour?'

The next thirty minutes saw Maddox tearing around at home as he sought to quickly change his clothes as he swapped his outfit about three times before hastily hugging his mum good bye and leaving again. He ran to Henrietta's house but stopped to catch his breath before he turned the corner into her street. Maddox knocked on the front door but a call from the kitchen brought him round to the back.

'I've made a couple of extra sandwiches. There should be enough to go around.' said Henrietta.

'I didn't realise that you'd thought of me joining your picnic. Don't let me steal your food!'

'It's only a few nibbles, it's just a gesture. Toby will be far too excited to want to eat much.'

They waited at the edge of Main Street until the bus which ran straight through to Harrisfield pulled up. There were only a couple of other passengers and Toby insisted that they all sit together at the back of the bus. In between commenting on the passing scenery and playing I-spy (which got rather confused owing to Toby's limited comprehension of spelling) Henrietta asked about Maddox's reason for going to Harrisfield.

'It's difficult to know what I can and can't say I'm afraid.' said Maddox.

'Oh, don't worry about telling me all the details. Just tell me what you can. If it makes you feel any better I know the whole John Barlow thing has taken another turn. Beth has called us all to another meeting at The Blue Willow tea rooms this Friday. I gather that something rather sensational has cropped up.'

Maddox was quite adept at holding two independent conversations at once and answered Toby's questions about the cows they had just passed before seamlessly returning to his conversation with Henrietta. 'I'd forgotten that you were one of Beth's underground agents. You probably know more about things than I do. James has asked me to find out who was where but this foreign couple could be the missing link to a bit of a puzzle we've got. Either that or I'm on a wild goose chase.'

'Oh well, at least you'll get a couple of ham sandwiches for your trouble.'

The bus stopped by the play area and Maddox hauled the picnic rucksack onto his back to carry it over to a grassy area. As Henrietta laid out the rug and food Maddox ran around with Toby and pushed him on the swings. They both went down the slide together and would have gone on playing indefinitely if Henrietta hadn't called them over to eat. 'You've saved me a lot of running about this afternoon, you must be exhausted. I think you've even managed to out-play Toby and that's saying something.' After eating their picnic in peace and quiet, as Toby was too tired to interrupt them, they packed away and walked to The Raven to attend to business. Maddox gave Toby a piggy back as he was too tired to walk. At the pub, despite remonstrance from Henrietta, Maddox bought a glass of squash, a wine spritzer and a pint of pale ale.

'We're in a holiday mood, so let's have a drink!' he said. Henrietta and Toby sat in the beer garden while Maddox conducted his enquiries and a short time later he joined them outside to enjoy his pint. 'I've got a couple of names. Whether they'll be of any use remains to be seen. I'll try and follow up where they live and see if I can speak to them. I'll see what Inspector James makes of them, or maybe I should just give them to you and let you lot sort it out at your Blue Willow meeting.'

'We're not in competition, you know. Beth just suggested that we might be able to help because we could access certain things more easily, not being bound by all the red-tape that you have to deal with.'

'You've got a point there. I can't breathe until I've got the correct form signed!'

The bus journey home was quiet, but it was a contented silence rather than an awkward lack of conversation. Maddox carried the sleeping Toby back home but he handed him over to Henrietta as they approached the door. He made no attempt to imply that he wanted to be invited in but made it clear that he now intended to go home. He didn't want to overdo things. He was grateful for the afternoon that they'd just had and didn't intend to push his luck. There was a delicate situation here and he had no intention of spoiling his chances by rough management now.

Chapter Nineteen

Breakfast was organised and orders were placed as Kirsty was enlightened regarding the group's manifesto. As the expert guest speaker she was invited to "take the floor" and explain what her research had revealed. 'It didn't take too much thinking to join the dots together and realise that this is to do with the recent mortality madness in Mossleigh. Putting aside wonder and dismay I tailored my research to the subject and its more sinister uses. There is a strange conspiracy theory that suggests the digitalis poisoning is responsible for Van Gogh's yellow phase. Prolonged exposure can create symptoms of visual disturbance and create a golden halo effect around objects. The most obvious use of foxglove is to the pharmaceutical industry where it's farmed and harvested for the base form of heart medication. Digitalis gives the foundation for digitoxin and digoxin steroids which slow the heart rate. If we're looking at poisoning with the natural plant then it's quite tricky as the raw plant material acts as an emetic. I read of a case in which somebody tried to commit murder by mixing foxglove leaves in a salad. The victim was desperately sick and this saved his life. Also, the plant material apparently doesn't taste good at all so it's difficult to imagine how someone could be induced to eat it.' said Kirsty.

'There's no evidence to support the theory that John took whatever it was willingly, but if it was forced upon him then how was he made to take the stuff? If it tasted so disgusting how could he have eaten it unwittingly?' said Mae.

'I think that I have an idea of how to explain matters but I'll save my theories until I'm sure. I need to check some things with Benji first, just to get my facts straight.' said Beth. The others looked at her in wonder. Had she really solved the mystery? Beth dismissed their inquisitiveness and encouraged Kirsty to continue.

'From what I understand, if small amounts are ingested over a period of time the result could be fatal if the symptoms are ignored. This isn't as strange as it may seem as the symptoms are very general and can be attributed to various common ailments. If the leaves are eaten in sufficient quantity over a relatively long period of time the heart would slow to such a pace that the result would inevitably be a heart attack. Taking an overdose of prescribed digitoxin would have the same effect, but in its natural form the digitalis compound is more concentrated and much more effective.' said Kirsty.

'The crucial point here is when were the plants actually taken? If they were cut on the day of the Fête during one of the garden tours then that would pinpoint the date of the poisoning and narrow the window of opportunity.' said Beth.

'I've been thinking about that.' said Kirsty. 'I'm really sorry, but I just can't be sure. The cuts are obviously old now as the stems have wilted and died but more than that I can't say. If it weren't for you coming the other day and me looking for that frog I wouldn't have noticed even now. I didn't spend much time at all preparing the natural garden for the tours as you'd imagine, so I can't be sure that I looked closely at it for some weeks before the Fête. I'm really sorry.'

'I know that I often let myself into your garden to come and see you but do you lock the gate when you're out? asked Beth.

'I never lock the gate. Anybody could get into the garden if they wanted to. I've never bothered as there isn't anything of value and we don't get much theft of any sort here. I'm sorry but it could be anyone at anytime over the last month or two.' said Kirsty.

'Don't worry about it, Kirsty. I think I have all that I need now, thank you. Does anybody have anything else of interest to tell?' asked Beth.

'I may do, I'm not sure.' said Henrietta. 'I met Bobby Maddox at Nicola's the other day. He was asking for a list of who had bought tickets for your garden tours. He was very interested in a couple of holiday makers who visited the Fête and probably came on a tour. We went to Harrisfield where they'd said they were staying and got their names to give to your brother. He seemed very excited when Nicola mentioned that she thought they were Greek but with American accents and he spent his afternoon off chasing down their names.'

Everybody had heard the "we" in Henrietta's sentence but nobody made reference to it, except for a few sly glances here and there. 'Now I wonder what that could mean?' said Beth.

'Are you going to share you thoughts with us, mum?' asked Emma.

'I'm afraid not. Not just now. I promised Benji that I wouldn't start casting aspersions hither and thither and it's only just a hunch I have at present. Don't worry, I'll tell you all as soon as I safely can - if I'm right, of course!'

At Winsford HQ a telephone rang. 'James speaking.' A long silence ensued as James sat listening attentively. 'Yes, that's very interesting Forbes. It makes a great deal of sense to me.' Another period of listening again followed. 'That's very thorough. Under his fingernails you say? Well, I guess that's only natural. Yes, I think I've got what I need. Thank you. Try the same tests on the old lady, will you? It should be a lot quicker now you know what you're looking for. Good job that man! I'll buy you a pint when it's all over.' Inspector James then walked over to his Chief Superintendent's office and knocked on the door.

'Come in. Ah, James. What's going on?' said Holloway.

'The Mossleigh case is hotting up. I was going to go there tomorrow but I've just heard all I need from Forbes so I'm going to head off now. My desk is clear and you can call me if you need me.' said James.

'Do you think that you can get it all cleared up now?'

'I'm not quite there at present but I'm going to go and see someone who I think can help me.'

'Do you need to take anybody with you?'

'No thank you, Sir. I've got Maddox once I get there. I know I could deal with matters but we'll keep it local. It's good for a community to see its own force clearing up.'

'That's very big of you, James. I'm sure you're right. Keep me posted, I hope you get things tidied up quickly.'

James got into his car and began a leisurely drive to Mossleigh. The sun was shining, he was going to see his sister and he could tell that this case was coming to a close. Although this would mean that somebody would soon be revealed as a disgrace and the usual shock and dismay would hit the community, it did mean closure. It also meant that justice would prevail. He also knew that, if he was honest with himself, it was that he experienced the thrill of successfully solving a puzzle. Beth was of the same mind. It looked as if they had both come to the same conclusion, albeit by two very different routes. He had used the official channels whereas Beth had used her village network and her own knowledge on the domestic front. If they had both come to the same conclusion then he knew that he was onto a winner. Between the two of them they should have all angles covered and they'd get the complete picture.

Toby and Primrose had spent the morning with Nathaniel and so Beth expected to return to a quiet house. As she approached the back door resounding laughter greeted her as she entered the kitchen. She opened the door to see Drew and Benji sitting at their ease at the kitchen table.

'Benji! I thought you were coming tomorrow. I didn't know you were here, where's your car?'

'I've left it at Mossleigh Police Station. I've just spent half an hour swapping notes with Maddox and as it's such a lovely day I thought I'd walk here and surprise you.'

'How lovely to see you. I suppose that you're here on business. Shall I join you and we'll get our heads together?'

Beth sat at the table and got down to business while Drew made a fresh round of drinks. They spent a good hour exchanging information and it was soon evident that they'd both come to the same conclusion.

'The problem here is that I don't think that I can prove all of this. Despite popular opinion most murderers aren't likely to confess. What I need is hard, tangible evidence. I've only got a good idea and that's not enough to stand up in court.' said Benji.

'I just might be able to help you out there. I'd got my suspicions a while ago and I think I've managed to get what I think you need. I had to tell some half truths I'm afraid but I hope that the end justifies the means. There's only likely to be a trace - if we're lucky.' said Beth

'You're too circumspect Beth, but it's to your credit.' said Benji.

'What do we do now? Is it enough to start official proceedings? asked Drew.

'I think that, between us we've got enough for me to be quite sure of my way. I'm going to call Maddox - it's his patch. He can take the limelight here. I'll call Forbes first and give him his chance to blaze a trail. All you two need to do is just sit back and enjoy.' said Benji.

Benedict reached for his mobile phone. 'Forbes, my man. This is the moment that you've been waiting for - are you listening? I want you to secure a car and get all the lights flashing because I need you to hurry here and collect what I'm hoping will be some vital evidence. I then need you to quickly hurry back to the lab as fast as you can, with all due caution of course. If you can run some preliminary tests immediately - you'll know exactly what you're looking for as soon as you see the evidence. As soon as you've done call me back with what results you can. Just a basic "yes" or "no" will do to be going on with.' Smiling he turned to Beth and Drew. 'Now there's a scientist who, in his boyish heart, wishes he could be in a SWAT team. This should cheer him up a bit.' He picked up his phone again. 'Now for young Maddox. Let's teach him to stand tall in his uniform. Mind you he seemed particularly chirpy this morning.'

'I think you'll find that that's due to a certain dark haired, olive skinned young lady rather than any sense of job satisfaction.' said Beth.

'All the better. Let's give him something else to crow about.' Benedict hit the speed dial and tapped his fingers happily on the kitchen table as he waited for an answer. 'Maddox, it's time to play ball. Are you ready?'

'I don't know sir, am I?' said Maddox.

'Oh, I think so.' James gave Maddox a series of short, concise orders and then concluded by saying,

'I'll come and join you in about an hour when you've got everybody nicely settled in, then we'll conduct the interview together.'

'I guess that's that. Now what?' said Beth.

'I'm afraid that for today Beth all you can do is sit tight. Perhaps you should call together your little underground network and arrange a meeting for tomorrow morning. Ask everyone who has played even the smallest part to come along. Don't worry about keeping the kiddies out of the way, it's never too early for them to hear the truth and I don't want anybody to miss out. It's up to you where you arrange everybody to congregate, though perhaps we should maintain tradition and meet at your famous tea room headquarters. There's likely to be a lot of us so maybe you'd better make a reservation.' said Benji.

After making the necessary arrangements there really was nothing more for Beth to do but wait. In an effort to occupy her hands and her mind Beth locked herself away in the music room. She was playing with such vigour that Drew could hear her in his studio at the opposite side of the house. Noodle sought sanctuary in Drew's studio and exchanged a knowing glance with Drew before he closed his eyes in an attempt to sleep. In the first stages of her frustration Beth chopped and changed pieces, not settling to playing any piece through to the end. Debussy's "Golliwog Cake-walk" went a good way to venting her frustration, even if the bell-like B flat octaves at the extremities of the piano were a bit heavy handed. As her mood calmed she tried some more tranquil music but this wasn't the time for Mozart. Quirky, dissonant Twentieth Century music was better suited to her mood and as her composure returned Messaien's "La Colombe" expressed her emotions perfectly. It had a calm tranquility that was just a little eerie and twisted. Eventually she'd played out all of her feelings and silence once again settled on the house. As evening came Drew carried a sleepy Noodle through from the studio into the lounge where he found Beth fast asleep on the sofa. She awoke as the dog nestled into her lap. Drew mixed a gin and tonic for Beth and a poured a whisky for himself. They spent the rest of the evening watching action movies and eating junk food. Benji came home later that evening. He didn't say anything at all about the events of the afternoon but just gave them an affirmative nod. He joined Beth and Drew in a drink and they all then made their way to bed for an early night.

Chapter Twenty

There was no need to prepare breakfast that morning as food was ordered and would be waiting for them at The Blue Willow tea rooms so Beth, Drew and Benji made a leisurely start to the day. They were just about up and dressed when it was time to meet as arranged. Eager for news everybody was prompt and the meeting was quickly underway. Eileen had allocated her staff to take charge in the café and she sat down to join the group. Understanding her need to know what had happened to Betty she was admitted as a member. Also, having the boss of the tea rooms sitting with them promised them first class service that morning. Without question everybody expected DCI James to take control of the meeting. As the group eagerly looked towards him he waved away his role as Chairman. 'This is Beth's territory, she's the boss here. Beth - you tell everybody what's been going on. Maddox and I will fill in the official jargon as you go along, if we need to. Stand by Maddox.' Maddox seemed surprised to be included at this early stage in the proceedings and was busy buttering crumpets for Toby who had attached himself to his lap.

'It's taken a long time for us to figure out what's been going on because, to begin with, nobody knew that anything actually was going on'. said Beth. 'Once we did realise that all wasn't above board matters were confused because we couldn't be sure if John had committed suicide or if the fatal substance was administered by a third party. In either case the question was "how?" The problem was that we were right, up to a point, on both counts.'

'Excuse me for interrupting, but surely it's not possible to commit suicide and be murdered at the same time. Or is it?' asked Kirsty.

'That's just it. In a sense that's exactly just what did happen. There's no doubt about the fact that John was nursing the intention to commit suicide. Emma found a stash of pain killers in John's wardrobe, yet we know for a fact that he never took such medication as a rule. Also, if they were there legitimately why were they hidden away? However, the fact that the tablets were still there means they weren't taken and the toxicology reports state that he didn't die from such an overdose. We'll never know if he'd ever really have resorted to taking them.' said Beth.

'Why would he think of such a thing? Were matters as bad as all that?' asked Eileen.

'No, not really, but a sense of financial hardship is relative. John had felt the property crash of recent years keenly and didn't like having to enforce economy at home. It also seems that he'd got wrapped up in some unsavoury business dealings abroad and was out of his depth.' said Beth.

'I didn't know about that. What sort of unsavoury business do you mean? I know Hyacinth mentioned a hint of something, but that's all.' said Mae.

'I've had Conrad brought into the station to "help us with our enquiries" and from what he says it would appear that John's vulnerability in the foreign property market laid him open to a known scaremongery racket.' said Benji. 'I don't think he entered into business with them willingly, or at least not at first, but neither was he strong enough to resist their lucrative propositions. Maybe he was just too plain scared to say "no." This made us wonder if he'd been quietly put out of the way, but there was no evidence of aggression or actual bodily harm. I asked Forbes to check carefully for puncture wounds but there was nothing, not even any bruising.'

'Which leads us right back to suicide, but evidence didn't support this theory either. John died after ingesting a fatal quantity of digitalis. John had made an appointment to see his optician despite having just had a new pair of glasses. Kirsty found that prolonged exposure to digitalis poisoning can cause visual disturbance and so that was further confirmation that my thoughts were likely to be correct. We presumed that the form would be consistent with Betty's missing heart tablets, it was the obvious conclusion. Betty's death would also seem to support that theory and conveniently link the two deaths together and Betty being the one to find John's body seemed to cement that theory nicely.' said Beth. 'We wondered if Betty had seen something on the day that John died or if her missing heart medication was responsible for John's death in some way.'

'I hate to think of such a kind, inoffensive person like Betty dying in a violent way. Was she murdered?' asked Eileen.

Beth placed a reassuring hand on Eileen's knee. 'I don't think so, I really don't think so. It just muddied the waters for a time, that's all.' said Beth.

'I asked Forbes to run the same tests on Betty and everything came back negative. It seems likely that she flushed her pills ad-hoc down the loo as old ladies will insist on doing and so died of a long standing heart condition in her old age.' said James.

'If it weren't for John's death I'd have had no questions about Betty's death and I'm reassured that it really was owing to natural causes. She was old and more frail than she'd have people believe. I think that you can rest easy, Eileen.' said Dr Wainwright.

'You can see how much confusion and overlapping coincidence has cluttered the trail.' said Beth. 'John didn't die as a result of taking heart medication but the mistake was a simple one because the basic ingredient of the pills in its natural form was used. Digitalis is the compound used to make digoxin and digitoxin which is widely used in the pharmaceutical industry. Foxgloves are common weeds and provide the natural form of digitalis, but we'd never have thought of this. This is where Kirsty provided us with an unexpected glimmer of hope.'

'It was sheer luck that made me notice that the foxglove plants had been cut. If the plants had just been pulled out, rather than cut, I'd never have thought twice about it.' said Kirsty.

'Even then the way forward wasn't clear. It's not easy to ingest enough of the poisonous material without being very sick. The leaves act as a natural emetic which usually makes you very ill but prevents you from dying.' said Beth.

'We'd said, right at the start, that it would be difficult because in whatever form, whether tablets or raw plant material, John would have had to have taken small amounts over a long period of time. He's hardly likely to commit suicide slowly, is he?' said Wainwright.

'And yet, in a sense, that's exactly what he did do.' said Beth.

'That's just weird.' said Henrietta.

'He did kill himself slowly.' said Beth. 'But not intentionally.'

'Of course Jean is the obvious suspect, but it's not easy to hide foxglove plant material in a meal. I read that it tastes disgusting and I gather that Jean never cooked.' said Kirsty.

'There have been only two people who have had regular access to John and could have induced him to swallow something that regularly. Jean, as we said, is the obvious choice. She stood to gain from a massive life insurance premium and she had daily access to his dietary intake. On the downside, the policy has been maturing for decades, so why now? Also, how did she administer the plant?' said James. 'The other person was Conrad Jefferson. John had turned to Jefferson in his time of crisis and had a dog-like trust in him. Also, you need to remember that Jefferson had just come out of prison. Very often you hear that people come out of prison deeper in crime and with better contacts that when they went in. It was highly likely that Jefferson had corrupt business contacts and his son was excellently placed at the centre of the web. If John was an embarrassment and needed removing Jefferson could have fed him anything as an exotic lunch during their business meetings. John would have been so eager to be seen to fit in with the big boys that he'd have made himself swallow anything. He'd presume that Jefferson had the same meal and would be desperate to appear cultured. It might have made him feel a bit queasy but he'd probably put it down to nerves or his diabetes.'

'But Hyacinth had never been to my garden. Conrad couldn't have known the foxgloves were there. I know that you can pick them from almost anywhere, they're on most of the roadsides around here - but it's my garden they were taken from.' said Kirsty.

'We were stuck until we knew that it was your garden the poison came from.' said Beth.

'James always said that he was sure that this crime had a local feel to it and Conrad Jefferson conveniently married the big business angle and the local nature of the crime.' said James. 'That reminds me. I've learned quite a lot from this little device.' He pushed an external hard drive across the table to Carlton. 'I've erased all of the files, thank you. Once I'd got access to the lap-top I was offically in the clear, but it gave me a helpful head start. I'd have been sitting on my hands for a good while and would have been stuck without it.'

'You know that news travels faster than fire in this village.' said Henrietta. 'I've heard that Maddox drove Jefferson to the station and then, with a lady officer, took Jean there too. It has to be one of them. Who is it?'

'Yes, Jean spoke to her neighbour and told them it looked like you'd finally made an arrest.

They were chatting together when the lady officer asked her to come to the station.' said Mae.

'I wasn't sure myself until I spoke to Beth yesterday.' said James. 'She'd already guessed and then used her devious skills to get the hard evidence that I needed. Forbes excelled himself and drove away back to his petri dishes, with the thrill of the chase in his heart. All he had to do was to match a sample to one taken from under John's fingernails, which he easily managed - with a little sanctioned overtime. You solved it Beth. You explain it.' Feeling that he'd done his bit, he sat back in his chair and munched away at a replenished plate of teacakes.

'We kept on getting stuck because we only ever looked as far back as the day of the Fête. I've always doubted that Conrad was guilty. He really is just a likeable gent who strayed over the edge of the law because he was a bit too good with numbers.' said Beth.

The full meaning of her words sank in as the group realised the implication of what she'd just said.

'So it really was Jean?' said Henrietta.

'Yes, I'm afraid so - and you were the one who exposed her. You provided the much needed evidence, Henrietta.' said Beth.

'Me! How?'

'Think back to all of the preparations for the Fête. Think about all of that silly nonsense about the jam competition. There was a long-standing debate about Emma's microwave method which meant that you could quite easily make just a jar or two at a

278

time. What sort of jam did Jean make as a treat for John and for her competition entry? said Beth.

'Rhubarb and rose petal jam!' exclaimed Eileen.

'What better thing to hide Foxglove leaves in? The sugar would hide most of the bitter taste and if you found a bit of a petal or leaf - what of it? 'said Beth. 'It would be quite easy to pretend it was all from the same batch. Instead there was a batch made by the traditional method and an extra jar or two just for John.'

'I said that it tasted horrid!' said Henrietta. 'Oh my goodness - I ate the poisoned jam!' The horror of what she'd inadvertently done struck her and her eyes pricked with tears. Without guarding her reaction she instinctively turned to Maddox and cried on his shoulder. It was difficult to choose which was his overriding emotion - concern and horror at the close call she'd had or joy at being singled out to comfort her in her time of need.

'A little taste wouldn't have harmed you.' said Dr Wainwright.

'But it does explain her reaction, doesn't it? No wonder she tipped it immediately down the sink.' said Emma.

'And this is where Beth's crafty nature comes into play. Without it we'd hardly have a case, but now it's signed and sealed.' said James.

'Jean made a great show of blaming herself for giving John the jam and causing his death. Maybe there was a shadow of remorse there but we dismissed it on the grounds of Jean over reacting.' said Beth. 'I'd a good idea that Jean was to blame and once I'd realised that the poison was in the jam I knew that I needed to get the jam jars in the hope that any evidence of containing poison wasn't completely washed away. I needed to act quickly because I knew that, if it matched the poisonous contents of John's stomach, we'd have the evidence we needed. It was just lucky that there was enough of a trace of the noxious jam left under the ridges where the lid screws onto the jar. The fact that John still had the remains of his breakfast under his fingernails proved the case still further.'

'I can't believe that she kept the jam' said Emma. 'She said she felt it was responsible for John's death and nobody believed her - and the evidence was still in her fridge!'

'It was effective too.' said Wainwright. 'In the presence of sugar digitoxin produces an insulin release. As well as resulting in the expected heart attack it may well have also induced a diabetic episode. By putting the poisonous plants in a jar of sugary jam Jean not only disguised the horrid taste of the foxglove leaves, she unwittingly made it twice as potent. It was probably only John's moderation that minimised the effects and made some delay in its success.'

'But why did she do it? I know you say that they'd had a rough patch, but they were still very rich.' said Eileen. The others joined her in her question.

'My dear ladies, you can never know the poison that entered her own soul.' said James. 'You've all contentedly worked alongside your husbands and family. You've willingly got up with ill children through the quiet of the night and you're willing to roll up your sleeves and rough it for the common good. In fact, the secret is that you're not only willing to do it, but you do so with joy and pride. You know the satisfaction of working side by side through whatever problems life throws at you. Although we can't excuse Jean we should pity her. When you've never had to work for something you can never know the joy of satisfaction. She'd had it so easy for so long that she couldn't appreciate the concept of digging in alongside John to work together through this. She couldn't see that there can be joy in lack as well as plenty.'

'And there I was worrying about her health and urging her to go out for lunch every day. That's disgusting!' said Henrietta. She'd composed herself now and was angry.

'So it really was as base as that. She killed him for the money! How boringly predictable.' said Mae.

'I'm afraid that most crime is.' said James.

'Hang on just one minute. You've been having your fun and playing with us, haven't you, Inspector James?' said Mae. 'You brought Conrad in for questioning just to throw us off the scent!'

Benedict had the decency to at least look a little sheepish. 'You must forgive my foibles. I did have a genuine reason, but I'll grant you that it was at the back of my mind. I didn't want to raise the alarm by bringing Jean in cuffed and under arrest until Forbes had clarified his results. Conrad was coming to help us with the business of these foreign heavies. All of that was real enough and the chaps at HQ wanted some extra details for their own reference. I also knew that Jean wouldn't be unduly worried if Conrad came in first. I included the female officer to add a hint of pathos. She'd think that she was coming to the station as the grieving widow and she willingly adopted that role.'

'You and Beth have alarmingly devious natures. I don't feel safe at all.' said Drew.

'We did think that some of the Greek undesirables had come to sort John out, and we considered it likely that Conrad was in collusion with them. As it happens the couple staying at The Raven were in England visiting their son. He's studying cello at the RNCM . They really were tourists and were genuinely thrilled to be experiencing British rural festivity at first hand. Once I knew that it was likely that Conrad really was honourable, despite his previous accounting tendencies, I called him in to ask if he could shed some light on these characters. That way I could at least update my colleagues back at HQ.' said James.

'So where is Jean now? What will happen to her?' asked Henrietta.

'She's being transferred to the cells in Whitchurch until her case is heard. There's little doubt that she'll be convicted, it's a strong case against her. There was enough of a trace of the stuff in the jar to match what John had under his fingernails from his breakfast and in the lining of his stomach.' said James.

'Right from the start everybody told me that she wasn't a particularly nice lady. She was pretty harsh when I first started cleaning for her. As time went on I thought a little better of her and people said that she wasn't so bad once you got to know her. When John died I saw a lot of her and I became genuinely fond of her. I guess she could be nice when it suited her and when things were going her way. That's no good at all though, is it? We were right in the first place - she really is a nasty piece of work.' said Henrietta.

The new school year was due to start and Primrose would be attending just three mornings a week. She was very proud of her new school uniform. Over the next few days Beth put her networking skills to a more wholesome cause. Toby's street credibility needed a little help and she knew just who to ask to deal with it. On the first morning of term Henrietta didn't walk Toby to school but accompanied Emma and Nathaniel who were taking Primrose to her first morning there. The usual group of boys were looking at Henrietta and wondering where Toby was when a police car, with sirens blazing, pulled up outside the school gates. Sergeant Maddox stepped out of the driver's door and made a great show of opening the rear passenger door and escorting Toby to the entrance. Maddox didn't hold Toby's hand as he normally would but kept a stern, manful stare directly ahead of him. The other boys were in awe as Toby made his way to the entrance. His kudos wasn't harmed by the fact that a little girl with curly blonde hair ran to greet him and gave him a hug as huge as her little arms could manage. It wasn't until Maddox, Henrietta, Emma and Nathaniel were safely out of sight that they all fell about laughing.

'Can I give you a lift home, Henrietta? I can leave the sirens off if you'd prefer it.'

Also Available by Sharon Bill
from Amazon in Paperback & eBook

They say that truth is stranger than fiction. Nearly 30 years of teaching at the piano keyboard has taught me that this is an undeniable fact. My dear Gran said that the world would be a boring place if we were all the same and teaching piano and flute in various cupboard like practice rooms, week in and week out over the years, reassures me that there is no threat of humanity becoming dull. If I present a wry viewpoint of various past pupils it is only fair to say that I also take an equally droll approach to myself.

Letters From the Broom Cupboard was the given title to an actual correspondence from my piano teacher during her own periods of incarceration in the privation of various school practice rooms which served to fill the looming periods of pupil absenteeism. This literary offering continues the legacy and I now write to you, dear reader, in my own hour of need.

Also Available by Sharon Bill
from Amazon in Paperback & eBook

Taking your ABRSM Music Theory exam can be nerve wracking and nerves can prevent you doing your best in any exam. Good preparation and planning is always the answer to this problem. In this exam guide I give you tried and tested technique, not only how to prepare before the exam but also the best procedure for actually in the exam room.

I've been entering pupils for ABRSM Music Theory exams for nearly thirty years and it is not unusual for them to pass with DISTINCTION, some even scoring 100%!

Follow these simple steps and improve *your* chances of gaining TOP MARKS.

Coming soon by Sharon Bill
from Amazon in Paperback & eBook

Check out **Sharon's YouTube channel** for a free accompanying series of music theory tutorials. You are guided, step by step, through the ABRSM Music Theory workbooks. Each video tutorial leads you through each exercise and free to download PDF information sheets give you everything you need to know.

There are lessons explaining all aspects of music theory and practical music topics which are simply explained so as to be easily understandable in 4k.

For everything you need to help you with your ABRSM Music theory visit....
http://www.bit.ly/SharonBillYT

& in the pipeline…

Artful Designs

The second

Beth Williams Mystery

For more information about Sharon Bill's

Writing, Blog and Music Tuition &

Free PDF Downloads

www.SharonBill.com

Facebook @SharonBillPage

Twitter @SharonEBill

Instagram @sharonbill_ig

YouTube Channel showing tuition videos in 4k

http://www.bit.ly/SharonBillYT

All video & social media page links are also

available at www.SharonBill.com

23174200R00170

Printed in Great Britain
by Amazon